COLD
STORAGE

COLD STORAGE

MICHAEL C. GRUMLEY

TOR PUBLISHING GROUP

NEW YORK

COLD STORAGE

Copyright © 2025 by Michael C. Grumley

A Forge Book
Published by Tom Doherty Associates / Tor Publishing Group
120 Broadway
New York, NY 10271

www.torpublishinggroup.com

Forge® is a registered trademark of Macmillan Publishing Group, LLC.

The Library of Congress Cataloging-in-Publication Data is available upon request.

ISBN 978-1-250-89875-3 (hardcover)
ISBN 978-1-250-89876-0 (ebook)

Our books may be purchased in bulk for promotional, educational, or business use. Please contact your local bookseller or the Macmillan Corporate and Premium Sales Department at 1-800-221-7945, extension 5442, or by email at MacmillanSpecialMarkets@macmillan.com.

First Edition: 2025

Printed in the United States of America

0 9 8 7 6 5 4 3 2 1

To all my wonderful fans

COLD
STORAGE

1

The slide of the Smith & Wesson was drawn back and released in one motion, allowing it to snap back, producing a subtle jerk inside the man's hand that firmly gripped the worn black polymer handle. The motion was smooth. Familiar. Natural. As though the weapon were part of him. An extension of his right hand and arm. A motion that had become so instinctive, and his senses so sensitive, that he could detect the shift in balance as the bullet was chambered within the stainless-steel barrel.

"I'm nervous."

He glanced briefly at the younger man in the truck's passenger seat before turning to gaze back outside. "We have the right place, don't we?"

The passenger nodded apprehensively. It didn't help his nervousness. If anything, it made it worse.

It had taken months to track down the location. A small A-frame cabin hidden within the tree-lined hills outside Ogden, Utah. A plot of several acres accessible by a shared gravel road winding up the west side of a small hillside like a gray meandering snake.

From inside the vehicle, both could see the dark outline of the cabin below. At least most of it. Peering down through dozens of pine trees parked on a largely forgotten side road.

After a long silence, he spoke again, attempting to allay the younger man's fears. "Don't worry. I'll take care of it."

His passenger gulped, attempting to slow his racing heartbeat. He was not a soldier or a mercenary, and he was afraid of violence. "We're not going to hurt anybody, right?"

There was no response from the older man. He remained gazing through the driver's side window into the blackness.

"Right?"

"Quiet," the older man shot back. Squinting further down the mountainside. Noting a distant pair of headlights. Slowly and methodically, winding their way up the numerous switchbacks. "This may be us."

Beside him, the younger man closed his eyes and swallowed.

The headlights slowed and turned into the cabin's driveway before traveling another fifty feet and stopping in front of the shadowed structure.

For a long time, the car remained in front of the A-frame, awash in the brilliant glow of the headlights. The vehicle sat motionless until the purring engine suddenly switched off.

With the low beams still on, the driver's door opened, producing a brief reflection as it swung out, then once again when the door was pushed shut.

From their position above, the older man noted the absence of the car's interior light and focused on the silhouette as the figure moved through the bright glare on their way toward the cabin's front door.

The driver tilted his head toward the other, who was also watching. "Well?"

"I'm not sure," he said. "I can't tell from here."

The older man grinned. "Close enough for me."

They waited until the automatic headlights went off, plunging the exterior back into night, replaced almost immediately by dimmer lights illuminating within the cabin before the older man reached for his door handle. Opening it slowly and stepping out, he carefully eased the door closed with a faint click.

He then watched as his passenger did the same, just as instructed. Slowly and softly.

He quietly motioned the younger man toward him and pointed down the hill.

"Why not take the road?"

"Dirt's quieter than gravel. Go slow. And step exactly where I step."

2

Now in front of the cabin, the older man remained stationary, examining its front porch in silence. He was shrouded within a shadow beneath the overhanging roof, just a step or two beyond the glow of the light from a nearby window.

His eyes then moved to the door. Solid with a standard knob and deadbolt, also attached to a standard wood frame and opening inward.

The two verified that no one else was in the car, which meant a single individual in the cabin.

The man in front of the porch estimated three steps to the top, skipping every other stair, and two long strides to the door. There were no signs of security, suggesting the door and frame were typical, and the doorknob and deadbolt were both secured by standard one-and-a-half-inch screws. Enough to pierce the thinner wood of the doorframe but not long enough to reach the stud behind it.

Of course, if he was wrong, his entry would be anything but a surprise.

The cabin's occupant was seated in a simple, somewhat dated living room. In a padded high-backed chair and deep in thought when there was a brief sound outside before the front door exploded in a sudden, violent crash, sending thin shards of wood flying across the room and across the floor as the door swung wide and slammed into the wall. Ricocheting and bouncing back before a large hand stopped it in midswing.

The woman in the chair screamed, her glass of wine crashing on the wooden floor. Panicked, she scrambled up and into the back of the chair's high back before tumbling over an arm and attempting to crawl away.

The intruder stepped through the open doorway into the small living room, smoothly drawing his Smith & Wesson. Then raised and leveled it before the woman.

She was utterly frozen. Unable to move. Staring into the dark circular opening of the gun's barrel. Unbreathing.

From his white-bearded face, the man's eyes scanned the remainder of the room and peered past the cabin's moderate kitchen, then down its short hallway.

With his gun still raised, he waited several moments for his cohort to appear, but there was nothing. Leaving him staring at the woman in his sights.

His gray-blue eyes were hard. Unblinking, with an even harder face. No expression. No emotion. Just cold and calculating.

Devin Waterman stared at her for half a minute, watching the hyperventilating woman before finally speaking. "What's your name?"

Her mouth struggled to move, let alone form words.

"Tell me your name," he repeated.

After several moments, the trembling woman finally regained control of her lips. "N-Nora Lagner."

Waterman stepped back, keeping the gun raised, and examined the hallway again. This time, more closely. "Anyone else here?"

The woman named Lagner shook her head.

"If there is," he said, "I shoot, *then* ask questions."

There was nothing. No sound. No movement. Only them and their breathing. Prompting Waterman to ease the grip ever so slightly on his gun. "Sit down," he commanded.

Lagner stared momentarily before stumbling forward, haphazardly making her way back to the chair as if she were blind.

Waterman watched as she lowered herself into it cautiously and carefully. "You know me?"

Again, she shook her head.

"Good," he said. "It's mutual, and that means I have absolutely zero compunction over shooting you. All I need . . . is a reason. Understand?"

Lagner nodded.

"Do you *believe* me?"

Another nod.

"Good. Then you're not entirely stupid."

The woman did not dare move. She remained steadfast in her chair, fearful and leaning forward, eager to comply.

Waterman then angled his head over his shoulder and called out loudly. "Get in here, kid."

A cursory look of confusion passed over the woman's face, and she glanced at the open door. Briefly noting where a large chunk of wood had been ripped away surrounding the now dangling deadbolt. Her eyes widened when Henry Yamada's face appeared from the darkness.

3

Yamada walked across the small room, stopping next to Waterman.

"Hey, Nora. Long time no see."

The woman's mouth dropped open. Her eyes moved back and forth between the two men. She was utterly shocked. "What the—"

"Shut up," interrupted Waterman.

Yamada watched Lagner for several moments, surprised to feel his nervousness gradually morph into anger. "It took a long time to find you," he said. "So, I guess you already know about your friend Duchik."

Lagner silently nodded.

"I wish I could say I was sorry," said Yamada, "but I'm not. Some people deserve what they get."

At that, the look of confusion in Lagner's large green eyes immediately turned to fear. God, they were going to kill her.

She watched as Waterman sat on the square coffee table in front of her, resting his gun on his knee but still pointing it at her, his right index finger still on the trigger. "Expecting anyone else tonight?"

"N-no."

Waterman glanced briefly over his shoulder. "Good. Because if someone comes in, guess who I'm shooting first." He didn't wait for an answer. "Now, do you know who I am?"

Nora Lagner nodded.

"Because?"

She hesitated. "Because I read your file."

"Then you have to know I'm not the bluffing type."

No answer.

"So . . . you're going to tell us everything," he said, "or this will be your last night on good ole planet Earth. Comprende?"

"Yes."

"Let's start with why you're still searching for us."

She swallowed and answered softly. "It's not my doing."

"Then whose is it?"

"People who were working with Duchik."

"Why, what do they want with us?"

"They don't want you," she said, "they want Reiff."

"What for?"

Her tone became almost matter-of-fact. "For verification."

Yamada stepped in. "Verification of what? You already have everything. All the files *and* his DNA. What else could you want?"

"There's a difference," she said, "between a DNA profile and the actual person, scientifically speaking."

Waterman and Yamada looked at each other before the older man frowned. "Who is this group? How big?"

"There were ten in total before he died. Now there are nine."

"Including you?"

Another nod.

"And they want what exactly?"

"Verification," Lagner repeated.

"I already asked you, verification of what?"

"That John Reiff is still stable," said Yamada.

When Lagner did not answer, Waterman studied her closely, squinting. "Why?"

Lagner blinked wordlessly at Waterman, reluctant to answer, until the older man gripped the gun and lifted it again from his knee.

It was effective. "To revive another," she quickly answered.

"Another person?"

"Yes."

"Who?" asked Yamada. "Duchik?"

Lagner shook her head. "Liam is dead. Reiff saw to that. The project was always about more than just John Reiff. It was intended to pave the way. Reiff was just the first one. But we can't continue without knowing he is free from any longer-term complications."

"You mean life-threatening complications."

"Correct."

Yamada, wearing a look of skepticism, was still studying her. "Who is it?"

"It doesn't matter," she answered.

"So, John is their medical 'canary in the coal mine.'" Waterman waited for confirmation from Lagner, but didn't get it, driving him to point the gun at her again.

"Killing me is not going to get you anything," she warned. "And finding *them* will be much harder than finding me. Which you were foolish to do."

"Why is that?"

She looked up and squinted at Yamada. "Even if you think you're being careful. All tracks can be traced." Lagner's voice began to turn aggressive. They were not going to kill her. At least not yet.

Waterman's reply was like ice. "Then letting you live will only help their effort."

Lagner's arrogance suddenly vanished.

"By your own words, you've acknowledged that we have to kill you."

Her eyes rewidened.

Waterman then stood up. "It's nothing personal."

Lagner suddenly panicked. "Wait! *Wait!*"

The older man calmly edged the slide back on his gun, verifying a bullet was chambered.

"*No!*" she cried. She looked at Yamada only to find him appearing just as shocked as she. "*Stop! Wait! I can help you!*"

Waterman gave a dubious frown. "By giving us away?"

"I'll tell you anything you want to know!" cried Lagner. "*Anything!*" She then blurted, "I'll tell you how to hide from them!"

"It's been almost a year, and they haven't found us yet."

She watched as Waterman once again raised the gun. "*Please don't! I swear I can help you!*"

He was unmoved but paused when Yamada placed a hand on his arm. "Devin, wait. We came here for a reason, remember?"

Nora Lagner latched on to the reference. "Of course you did! You want something. What is it? Just ask me!"

"She can't be trusted," said Waterman.

"I can!" cried Lagner. "You can trust me! Ask me anything, and I'll tell you, I swear!"

The gun remained lingering in midair, with Waterman's finger snaking through the trigger guard and resting lightly on the metal trigger. "Like what?"

"Anything!" she cried.

There was a long silence before Waterman spoke. "Where is it?"

Nora Lagner looked at him, confused. "Where's what?"

"Where is . . . *it.*"

Shaking her head, she looked nervously at Yamada. "*It* what?"

"The Machine," answered Yamada. "Where is the Machine?"

Lagner nodded eagerly. "I'll tell you, I'll tell you! Just lower the gun."

Watching it fall, she opened her mouth to continue until suddenly catching herself in midsentence, where she stopped and stared at them in bewilderment, thinking for several seconds. "Wait. Why do you want the . . . ?"

There was only one reason they would want the device, and it took Lagner only moments to realize it. When she did, her mouth dropped open in stunned silence.

4

As they barreled down the dark, winding road, Yamada dialed a number on the burner phone and handed it back to Waterman, who continued steering with one hand. The call was answered immediately.

"How'd it go?"

"Good and bad," answered Waterman.

"Did you get a location?"

"Yeah, we know where the Machine is. But we have a very short window."

"How short?"

Waterman put his other hand on the wheel while braking through a tight turn. When the road straightened again, he brought the phone back toward his mouth. "Two days, maybe three. Until they realize Lagner is missing."

On the other end, Wayne Coleman calmly placed his own burner phone on the table in front of him and enabled the speakerphone, allowing Rachel Souza to listen in.

"Where's it at?"

"Prescott."

Coleman mulled for a moment. "Four hours away. Five max."

"Ask her if we can be ready that quickly."

Rachel spoke up. "I'm right here. I'm thinking."

Studying the road in front of him, Waterman slowed for another turn before straightening the Explorer and punching the gas. "Well?"

Rachel bit her lip, still thinking. "We don't have a lot of choices."

"No, we don't. The kid and I should be back by oh seven hundred."

In the small, darkened room, Rachel hovered over an old Formica table as she replied, glancing at her watch and then at Coleman, "We'll be ready."

Minutes later, Rachel burst through the door of her makeshift lab. The term "lab" was a stretch. It was an old bedroom converted into a stopgap workshop, with nearly every square foot packed with medical and diagnostic equipment. Several computers with their adjoining monitors and keyboards occupied one corner, and two small, glass-doored refrigerators with petri dishes and test tubes were in the other. And to the right, dozens of cages stacked one on top of another, creating a veritable wall of wire and mesh filled with hundreds of mice.

She methodically scanned cage after cage, examining over a hundred tiny "house" mice, also known by scientists as C57BL/6. The most common strain used in biomedical research. And to her relief, all were still moving.

Rachel exhaled, followed by a deep inhalation as if trying to prepare herself for what came next.

It was the moment of truth. They had finally located Lagner and, more importantly, the Machine. The one thing that was absolutely integral to their plan. What she did not expect, however, was how little time they would have.

It meant everything she had done had better be right. The testing, the experiments, all of the trials. The slow, painstaking process of gene editing was unforgiving, and the chance for error heightened under such a compressed timeline. Meticulously recording every test, every result, every detail, regardless of the outcome. All carefully documented, then tested again and again to ensure her end results were not just accurate, but predictable. She had gone through thousands of tiny subjects whose DNA was as close to human as she could get under the circumstances. And given their limited resources while working in complete secrecy. Everything she had done . . . had better be right.

It was the medical equivalent of working in someone's garage for nine months with nothing but duct tape and an ice box. Okay, that was an exaggeration. But it sometimes didn't feel far off. Toiling away in a room with no windows, minimal ventilation, and illuminated by the sterile overhead glow of fluorescent lighting.

Trying to reason her apprehension away, she turned and glanced behind her right shoulder at their strange contraption, centered upon a medium-sized table and shaped like a giant porcelain egg. Slightly marred and nicked from constant use, with thin wires emerging from every direction of the device. Thin silvery strands resembling a mass of wild, unkempt electronic hair. Snaking together less than two feet away into organized and braided bundles, running down the nearby wall where they disappeared into a much larger computer casing.

It was extremely crude, but it worked. A miniature version of the same Machine they had been hunting down. This one small and compact and just large enough to house her tiny C57BL/6 subjects.

Its modest size and energy requirements allowed her to test the new genetic sequencing not just hundreds, but thousands of times. Endless attempts to apply the changes she had derived from the DNA of a capuchin monkey.

Dallas had proven difficult to find. Nightmarishly difficult. But find him they did. After turning over nearly every rock and twig within a quarter-mile radius of the habitat at what remained of the old Phoenix Zoo. Hampered not only by the environment and the monkey's small size but also by how clever Dallas ultimately proved to be. And not just impressively clever . . . almost *eerily* clever.

It was then that Rachel's attention was interrupted by a powerful truck engine roaring to life outside. *Wayne.*

5

Waterman and Yamada were late, but not by much, pulling into the driveway of a nondescript house in the middle of a sprawling Las Vegas suburb. Slightly rundown with a stucco facade and painted an all-too-familiar desert beige, it was like every other dwelling in the neighborhood. An unorthodox yet effective camouflage, allowing them to hide in plain sight and beneath the largest blanket of electromagnetic noise in a two-hundred-mile radius.

Once through the front door, the men navigated around several plastic crates of supplies waiting in the hallway to find Rachel Souza and Wayne Coleman waiting at the kitchen table.

Yamada wasted no time, withdrawing a laptop from his shoulder bag in midstride and dropping into a chair. He pushed the lid open and waited for the computer to resume before logging in with a short flurry of typing.

Already onscreen was a satellite map filling the window. "Here's the location."

Under a headful of frizzy gray hair, Wayne Coleman squinted at the screen. "I don't see anything."

"That's the idea," quipped Waterman. They watched as Yamada zoomed in from a wider image displaying a small city and surrounding desert to a tighter patch, the desert located northward. Appearing as little more than fifty square miles of barren hills, endless dirt, and scrub brush.

Coleman frowned. "Not helpful."

Yamada was not done. He dragged and zoomed again. This time, more detail appeared, revealing small trails and what looked to be remnants of old riverbeds and streams along with a distinct and dusty dirt road meandering southwest to northeast. Scrolling the zoomed image revealed where the road ended at a long rectangular object. It was slightly pixelated but immediately recognizable.

Coleman's frown deepened, and he glanced at Waterman. "A mobile home?"

The satellite view showed the mobile home in a clearing, roughly an acre in size, and encompassed by what looked to be a chain-link fence.

"Okay," said Coleman, straightening, "either I'm getting dense in my old age or—"

"Look closer," said Waterman. He pointed to a spot on the screen, revealing something else. Another, smaller square shape very close in color to the orange-tinted soil around it.

Coleman leaned in again. "What's that, an old foundation?"

"We think so," answered Yamada. One final zoom presented a closer, more pixelated image. The remainder of a large concrete foundation crumbling slightly around the edges, but the rest still very much intact. In the center was a large round rusted circle littered with dirt and small pieces of weeds and vegetation, and, perhaps fifty feet away, what resembled a short vertical section of concrete. "And we think that's the door."

Standing between Coleman and Waterman, Rachel had thus far remained quiet, merely observing. But she peered back and forth at them when their small kitchen suddenly fell silent. "Door to what?"

Yamada's eyes remained fixed on the screen. "If I'm right, it's an old Titan II missile site."

6

"*If* you're right?"

"A lot of records were destroyed, so I've been trying to cross-reference and piece things together. Not even Lagner knew the precise location."

"So how did you find it?"

Henry Yamada turned and grinned over his shoulder. "From an old real estate listing."

"Seriously?"

Yamada turned back. "A lot of these old missile sites were decommissioned decades ago. Long before the collapse. Many were dumped and sold on the open market."

Rachel turned to Waterman. "Who would buy an old missile site?"

"Depends on the condition."

Through all of the discussion, Coleman's face remained unimpressed. "So, this is what you got from her?"

"Yeah."

"*This?*"

"Yes."

"You're telling me your Machine is *here*?"

"We think so."

Coleman eased back and ran a hand over his worn and tanned face. "And what's in the trailer?"

"Security."

"That's what the Lagner woman told you?"

"Among other things."

Coleman stared at them for a long time before finally circling the table and grabbing a chair. He whirled it around and sat down, resting both arms on its wooden back.

"I thought this thing was supposed to be super valuable."

"It is," said Yamada.

"So valuable that they decide to hide it in an old, abandoned missile site, with some old fart looking after it?"

"No one else knows this thing even exists. Except them . . . and us."

He nodded. "And how do you know she told you the truth?"

Coleman noticed Yamada's gaze change to something vague and uncomfortable.

"Because," replied Waterman dryly, "she would have been willing to tell us everything to save herself."

"Well, I hope you're right. Otherwise, we just wasted nine months of reconnaissance work trying to find her."

Waterman then turned to Rachel. "Are we ready?"

"As ready as we'll ever be on such short notice."

"We knew that was a possibility," Waterman reminded her, then checked his watch. "Let's get moving. Plan Bravo."

7

The next twelve hours were hectic. The Machine's location was closer than they feared it might be, which was good. But their window for reaching it was much smaller than expected, and that was bad because the window was fixed. And that was assuming Nora Lagner had been honest with them.

The truth was, she couldn't be trusted, not after what she had done. If it had been up to her, they would all be dead, so they hoped that the reality of impending death forced her to disgorge the truth. Waterman was confident she did, but the others were not so sure.

They couldn't dismiss the possibility that Lagner remained defiant until the very end.

Rachel lowered the large binoculars for what felt like the hundredth time and tried to relax. Kneeling on a patch of dry dirt and waiting patiently. She looked at Yamada, who was still peering ahead through his own pair.

"See anything?" she whispered.

He shook his head.

They were too far away to see much beyond a tiny, single light in the distance.

Rachel turned and glanced around them. A 360-degree view of the dark horizon with the only other lights visible being a sliver of rising moon and below it a soft ambient glow from the nearby city of Prescott to the south.

She turned to the ground between them, checking the dark shadow of their handheld radio, and stared at it long enough to see the tiny green light flash again, verifying it was still on. Crickets could be heard from all directions against the rumbling backdrop of their idling vehicle less than a hundred feet behind them.

They had not heard anything for a long time. How did they even know

Waterman and Coleman were okay? What if something happened and they were too far away to hear it? What if it all happened suddenly, and they couldn't radio back?

"You think they're okay?" she finally asked.

"I'm sure they're fine."

She stared into the darkness and nodded before letting herself exhale. *Please let Henry be right.*

More than a mile in front of them, Waterman was not moving, his body motionless on the ground. Heavy and inert. Clothed in desert fatigues, boots, and boonie hat, lying in a prone position behind a large bush.

"What do you see?"

Waterman was propped on both elbows, looking through an infrared scope at the darkened mobile home a few hundred yards away. "One vehicle," he answered lowly. "The mobile looks new. Well maintained. No movement outside." He continued a slow scan, moving along the structure and pausing on some odds and ends near the ground. Some large buckets, what looked to be a roughly built wooden table, a hose, and a couple of fifty-five-gallon drums, *Trash cans.*

Waterman angled the sight of his scope upward and suddenly stopped. Without a word, he leaned on his right elbow and raised his left hand to make an adjustment.

"And a security camera up top."

"Great. Just one?"

Waterman continued scanning along the roofline until reaching the far end of the structure. "Two," he said, then traveled back to the house's other end. "Make that three."

From the end of the structure, he followed a slightly drooping power line up to the top of a nearby pole bathed in a bright yellow light. From there, the line traveled up an embankment to another darkened pole, and then another, and another, until eventually fading into the blackness beyond.

His scope traveled back to the house and moved along the roof, stopping this time on a square panel angled upward. "They're connected via satellite." Waterman focused on one of the mobile home's windows. The shades or drapes were closed but revealed an illuminated interior.

"Any movement inside?"

"Not that I can make out." He returned to the security camera near the midpoint of the roofline, which was facing him. "Cameras are probably wide angle and covering all directions."

Coleman remained quiet for several beats on the other end of the radio conversation. "Got any bright ideas?"

Waterman didn't answer. Instead, his scope's sight traveled back to the left side of the house and the power line. Where once again he followed it to the top of the nearby pole.

"There's a small transformer at the top of the power pole."

"Yeah."

"If we knock it out—"

"Then the power goes out, and they would immediately expect something."

Waterman nodded and continued with his scope. This time, peering at the dark power line running down to the house. After almost a full minute, he said, "What if we try severing the cable itself? Less noise."

Coleman's voice answered sarcastically. "Is one of us a sharpshooter that I don't know about?"

"With this silencer, I could take a few tries."

"They might still hear you."

"Maybe," replied Waterman. His eyes briefly left the scope. "But this place is also in the middle of the damn desert with no protection from the sun."

"So?"

"So, I bet it has insulated windows. Double, maybe triple." Waterman's scope spotted part of a square-shaped condenser just past the far corner of the building. "And air conditioning," he added. "That's a fair amount of sound suppression."

He was met with only silence.

"Well?"

"I'm thinking," said Coleman.

"If we can sever the line, they may not hear it at all. If they do, it probably wouldn't be more than a loud slap. Might even flush someone out to investigate."

"What about the light on top of the pole?"

"Not sure. I *think* it'll stay on."

"You think?"

"Are you an electrician?"

"No."

"Yeah, me neither." Waterman resumed scanning. Studying the four-wheel-drive Jeep. And beyond it, a shot of some of the missile site's original concrete foundation. "If you got a better plan, I'm all ears."

There was no reply from Coleman.

"Time's a wasting."

"Fine," he finally said. "But if we can't knock out the power—" Coleman's voice suddenly ceased in midsentence. There was no need to finish. Because the bright light on top of the pole as well as the glow within the house all went off on their own.

8

Rachel and Henry immediately noticed the sudden disappearance of light in the distance.

She glanced apprehensively at his silhouette. "What just happened?"

"Don't know."

"Is that good?"

He continued looking out into the darkness. "Probably."

A mile ahead of her, both men remained motionless. Laying in position and waiting.

Whoever was in the mobile home had turned off the lights. Both interior and exterior. And it probably wasn't to save on their electric bill.

"I think they know we're here," whispered Waterman into the tiny mike just inches from his cheek.

"I think you're right." Coleman moved slowly, reaching a hand forward and flipping his scope into night mode. Waterman was no doubt doing the same.

Several minutes passed with neither man making a sound. Instead, they waited, unmoving, to see what happened next.

Then Waterman saw a flash of bright green in the darkness. Quick and low to the ground. Gone as quickly as it appeared.

"Got a bogie. On the other side."

"On the move?"

"Not sure. Don't have visual anymore. But he's staying out of my line of sight."

"They probably spotted you with one of the cameras."

"Or we tripped something." Waterman's mind was racing. He looked around for cover. Nothing. Just a group of bushes at least twenty feet away. He looked to his left. There was a slight depression closer. Without waiting, he quickly rolled toward and into it, cutting off his view of the target but also making it harder for them to see him *and shoot him.*

He shimmied his body forward to where the dirt rose before him, trying to stay as flat as possible. All he could see was the top of the roof line.

"I got no visual of anything."

"I got ya," mumbled Coleman, carefully scanning with his scope. "Just stay where you're at."

There was no more movement from or around the home, which wasn't good. It meant they were up against more than one person. *A single person would not voluntarily leave safety and cover. Leaving meant someone was still inside to cover them. So where did they go?*

Coleman was a good two hundred paces from Waterman, with a broader field of view over the property. But even from his position, he couldn't see anything moving behind the mobile home.

The silence was deafening, with no sounds except the breeze filled with chirping crickets. It was now almost ten minutes since Waterman noticed the movement.

"Anything?"

"Nope." Coleman was still scanning dutifully. "You sure you saw something?"

"Positive."

He chewed on it for a long moment. "Well, I got nothing."

They both knew that didn't mean a damn thing. Their scopes had night vision, but scanning with it gave them a narrow field of view. If something *was* moving out there, it could have been easily missing while Coleman was looking elsewhere.

Waterman rolled onto his back and slowly exhaled, trying to slow his breathing, nestling his M16 down the length of his chest. He could see the small hill where Coleman was hiding. Silhouetted by the faint glow of city lights in the distance. He began to roll back over when he noticed something on the glowing horizon shift.

Slowly rotating his rifle and pointing it in Coleman's direction, Waterman aligned his right eye with the scope. Nothing. Just the shadowed outline of dozens of rocks and whistling brush. Not far away was a grouping of granite boulders—

There it was again! Movement. Sudden and brief. In the shape of a person's head and shoulders, crouched and approaching.

"Shit!" cursed Waterman as he fired. A clap sounded from his silencer. "Behind you!"

In a flash, Coleman rolled over, less than a second before the dirt exploded where he'd lain. Two shots from the silhouette behind before it disappeared, and the shots ceased. Rotating around in one motion, he stayed low and raising his rifle.

He struggled to control his breathing, which caught up to his violent exertion, pushing him to the brink of hyperventilating. But he managed to maintain, straining and eventually slowing his pounding heartbeat. His ears searched the breeze for the sound of movement, but there was nothing.

"You okay?" came Waterman's voice.

He nodded in the darkness and whispered between breaths. "Yeah. Quiet."

The crickets, which had ceased during the clash, began chirping again.

"You got me?"

Waterman was now on his stomach, watching through his scope. "Yep."

Coleman began moving, crawling forward several feet, and stopped. Again, he listened. Hearing nothing, he continued, crawling until reaching a decent-sized boulder. There, he removed his hat and placed it over his muzzle and silencer, gradually extending it out beyond the far edge of the large rock.

He let the breeze rotate the hat, ready to yank it back instantly. But again, there was nothing. He inched the side of his head out, followed by his left eye.

Not more than ten feet away, he could see the dark outline of boots. The soles were facing him and beyond . . . the shape of a body. He brought his rifle around the rock and aimed. It was clearly a person, face up, with no discernible movement from the chest.

"He's down." Coleman stayed low and continued on his stomach until reaching the body. There, he could see the glistening reflection of dark blood on the side of the head.

"Looks like you got him."

He could hear Waterman exhale through his headset. "Lucky shot."

"I'll take it." He relaxed the grip on his rifle and searched with his opposite hand for the man's wrist and pulse. After several seconds, he let go. "He's dead."

Coleman's right eye returned to his scope, scanning the far side of the embankment, trying to see how they got the drop on him, but he couldn't. There was nothing to be seen but endless rocks and scrub brush. "They saw us coming."

"Probably so," acknowledged Waterman. Rotating on his stomach to face the house again. "Which means they may have already sent word."

"You still have a line on that satellite dish?"

"Yep."

"Take it out, quick."

Waterman needed no prodding. He sighted the panel atop the roof and carefully squeezed off a round. Hitting and sending it flying with a loud clang.

Another bright green outline suddenly appeared from the top of the low-lying hill fifty yards to Waterman's left. It was met with immediate fire from Coleman and instantly dropped to the ground.

Silence returned, and both men focused again on the mobile home. It was then that their question was answered as to how many remained when the outside lights abruptly illuminated again, and a shadowed figure appeared from within. Both hands raised high over his head.

Rachel and Henry never heard the shots. They remained waiting, more frightened than nervous at the prospect that things had gone terribly wrong. They were both back inside the truck, doors locked and engine running, with Yamada's white knuckles gripping the steering wheel.

When Waterman's voice came over the radio, Rachel nearly threw up in uncontrolled relief and emotion.

"You guys there?"

She grasped the radio with both hands. "Yes. We're here!"

"Get over here. We don't have much time."

9

The old missile site was not what she was expecting. They already knew most of the above-ground complex was gone, allowing the remains to blend in with its desert surroundings. A foundation covered in a film of red-orange dust with only the lone, vertical concrete doorway remaining and allowing a narrow entry below ground. Which would present serious logistical challenges for them.

Once inside, the scene was startling. Thick floor-to-ceiling steel walls lined every visible hallway and room, with every square foot covered in a layer of rust and corrosion. As far as she could see, it was endless oxidation from a hundred years of abandonment and neglect.

Rachel didn't know what she was expecting, but it wasn't this. "Good God," she mumbled under her breath.

The place looked like a scene from an apocalyptic movie. Empty and hollow and completely rusted out.

She glanced at Coleman, but he said nothing. Instead, he was studying what was left of the complex with a curious look and taking turns looking down the numerous hallways.

"We were duped."

Waterman turned to look at her. "Maybe, maybe not."

She stared back with surprise. "What do you mean?"

"There's something down here," he said. "They wouldn't be guarding it otherwise."

Her expression slowly changed to confusion. "But . . ."

"Rach," said Yamada. "Notice anything?"

Her eyes moved from doorway to doorway as Yamada grinned deeply. "The *lights* are on."

It was true. The lights *were* on. The place was powered either by the electrical line outside or something else. What's more, part of the floor was swept clean. Not enough to remove the deep pockmarks of rust, but all the loose debris. The other rooms and hallways had been left alone. Only one had been tidied up.

With rifles against their shoulders, the four moved forward. Following the oversized passageway as it moved from illuminated room to illuminated room. All riddled with the familiar rust and corrosion but with the same cleanly swept floors.

They counted six rooms before reaching the last, where the doorway was covered in a giant, hanging clear plastic curtain. Where inside came the familiar hum of a cooling system.

Waterman reached the curtain and looked through it before reaching his free hand out and pulling one edge away from the wall.

Rachel gasped. There was no one inside, but the room was far from empty. In fact, unlike the rest of the site, it was spotless and packed, full of medical equipment. Various monitors, a ventilator, defibrillator, EKG, oxygen concentrator, everything. And in the middle of the room, resting upon an enormous metal table, was something that resembled a modern stainless-steel sarcophagus. *The Machine.*

10

There was something almost indescribable about a sunrise in the desert. The stillness of the air, the unending landscape, and the early morning glow off the orangish soil. All culminating in a strange feeling of expansive, insignificant, and joyous wonder.

The distant rocks and hills and a mirage wavering slightly upon the horizon prompted Douglas Kincaid to inhale deeply through his nostrils, savoring the morning aridness that felt so pure and enticing.

He held it for several seconds before letting the air back out and then repeated, closing his eyes and relishing the sensation through his senses.

A new day with endless possibilities.

Kincaid allowed his eyes to reopen, taking in the warm rays of the rising sun through a pair of tinted oval-framed sunglasses resting delicately upon the bridge of a wrinkled nose. Prominent upon the same face that had been around that magnificent sun almost ninety times.

A face weathered and wrinkled but not ancient. His body slender but not frail. And a mind still as alert as ever. He looked young for his age, much younger than others from his generation. And it was no accident. He knew how to take care of his body, which was one of the reasons he would not stay in this sunlight long. He preferred the outdoors but limited his exposure to mornings and evenings when there was more of the Earth's atmosphere between him and the sun, limiting ultraviolet damage.

Kincaid heard a noise behind him: the heavy door opening with its distinct click from the stainless-steel handle.

A man's voice spoke behind him. "Prescott is offline."

Kincaid continued to gaze at the morning sky but did not turn. "Why?"

"Not sure yet."

"How long has it been offline?"

"A little over four hours."

The old man exhaled and finally turned, facing the man, DeSilva, leaning out from the open door. "Is the satellite link down?"

"Yes. No weather issues, so probably a connection or mechanical issue. Just thought you'd want to know."

He nodded. Yes, he did want to know. He wanted to know about everything. Any and all details related to the project, no matter how mundane. He was not about to lose fifty years of his life's work. Every issue, every detail, mattered now.

Not everything was an emergency. In those fifty years, very few things had gone precisely to plan; quite the contrary. The world was unimaginably complex and dynamic, constantly moving and changing throughout a web of infinite variables, sometimes making the entire effort feel like a statistical impossibility. Every facet, every step, having to be constantly managed to keep things on track. But in the end, he had a secret weapon. The gift of humankind.

Humans, despite their incredible abilities and independent nature, were, in the end, creatures of habit, just like all species. Eventually seeking safety and familiarity above all else, and predictability. Both from the world around them and their place within. It was only natural. Repeated in all walks of life, in all areas of biology. Which also meant that humans were far more similar than they believed. And like sheep, they just needed prodding. Sheep, but complicated sheep.

Kincaid had experienced more than his share of adversity over the years in his pursuit and ultimate goal, and a satellite connection was not one of them. Yes, it was related to an essential piece of the puzzle, but a piece that only a handful of people even knew existed.

He replied to the man, saying, "If it's not up soon, send someone out."

"There's also some good news. Part of an unencrypted call, which might be *them*. We're running tests on it now."

The old man's eyes now widened with interest, and he turned around. "Is that so?"

He knew better than to get his hopes up. They'd had hits before, but their prey was very diligent. Always careful not to let their guard down. But just like all humans, they too were fallible, and he knew that eventually, they, like all sheep, would make a mistake, no matter how hard they tried. Kincaid and his team just had to be patient. John Reiff and his cohorts would eventually be found.

Kincaid returned inside with the younger man, down multiple flights of grated stairs leading underground and down a long concrete hallway until reaching a large computer lab. A long desk with multiple computer monitors awaited where DeSilva sat back down in his chair as Kincaid fell in behind him.

"A conversation," said DeSilva, typing on the keyboard. "Unencrypted."

The old man's expression grew disappointed. "*They* always encrypt."

"I don't think this one is their doing. I think the program faltered."

"Faltered?"

DeSilva turned. "Encryption happens between two endpoints, constantly encoding and decoding each data packet as it is sent. Back and forth for the duration of the call. But it's not perfect."

"Yes, I know. And it's unbreakable."

"It is," answered DeSilva, "algorithmically." Seeing the confused look on Kincaid's face, he then clarified, "Mathematically. Mathematically, the encryption is extremely difficult to break. But not if the endpoints themselves have a problem."

"Meaning what?"

"Meaning that most encryption on phones is software based. And software can be prone to problems, especially if a problem occurs on the underlying hardware."

"And you think that's what happened?"

"That's my guess," the man answered. "Either they turned off the encryption midsentence, which they wouldn't, or one of their phones glitched and caused the encryption to break. Leaving the last few seconds of conversation unencrypted, without them knowing it."

Kincaid quickly became more interested, leaning forward to see the computer screen. On it was an audio playback program of the conversation, currently paused.

DeSilva pointed to the upper right-hand corner, where a simultaneous transcript was scrolling vertically down the screen. At the top was a name attributed to one of the voices, also referred to as a "voice print." In large letters, the first name read UNKNOWN. The second read: DEVIN WATERMAN.

Kincaid felt his pulse increase. "Waterman!"

"Exactly."

"How sure are you?"

DeSilva clicked to expand a new window, displaying a swath of audio analytics and identification details. More commonly referred to as "speaker identification," it was based on a series of computer patterns and recognition technologies, things like frequency estimation, matrix representation, and a host of others. A powerful system that could match voice imprints from samples of a subject or target in mere minutes.

"The match has a ninety-three percent accuracy rating," he said, turning toward Kincaid. "Trust me, it's him."

The old man blinked and slowly straightened. "Do you have a location?"

"Yep." DeSilva nodded. "Las Vegas."

Las Vegas! Reiff and Waterman were closer than they thought. A lot closer. He peered forward again at the large screen. "What exactly did you capture in the call?"

DeSilva switched back to the audio recording and then hit a button to play the short exchange.

". . . need the vehicle gassed up and ready in thirty minutes."

"How far you headed?"

"Not far."

Kincaid continued staring at the screen, pursing his lips. "Is that it?"

"Yes."

Kincaid turned away, thinking. "So, they were headed somewhere and needed someone else's vehicle."

"And gassed up."

"Right." The old man nodded. "So, why would they need it gassed up if they weren't traveling far?"

"Poor gas mileage?"

"Or," thought Kincaid out loud, "he was being glib."

"Maybe both," said DeSilva.

"Yes," mumbled Kincaid, "or maybe both." He gradually began pacing. *Maybe both.*

His pacing abruptly stopped, and he turned his head to DeSilva. *Maybe both,* he said to himself, suddenly thinking of something else. "How far is Prescott from Las Vegas?"

The look on Kincaid's face immediately spread to DeSilva's. He knew exactly what the man was asking.

He returned to his computer, bringing up a new window on the screen with a giant map in real-time satellite view. He typed in a series of coordinates and watched the live map scroll in a blur, seconds later coming to a stop: northern Arizona. He began zooming. Nothing stood out from altitude. He continued, slower now, drilling down and watching as the details on the screen crystallized until stopping on a frame filled with rocks and outcroppings surrounded by thousands of dark green bushes of varying sizes.

In the center of the frame, the rectangular view of the mobile home's roof was clearly visible. The power pole was nearby, and farther away still, the outline of the site's old decaying foundation.

"Everything looks nor—" he began but cut himself short. There *was* something different. In the area between the remnants of the foundation and the trailer. Something . . . in the dirt.

Kincaid saw it, too. "What is that?"

He zoomed in further until the picture began to blur, then eased back out again, trying to find the sweet spot for detail since live feeds did not have the same resolution capabilities as a still picture.

"Does the ground look different to you?"

Kincaid slowly nodded behind him. "What are those shrubs?"

He squinted. "I'm not sure."

Then something moved. Not much, just a faint shift or a wavering, prompting his hand to move to the computer mouse and slowly drag. Zooming out by only a single magnification. Then another. And another. Pausing each time, searching, when the movement appeared again.

They still couldn't make it out. "Tilt," instructed Kincaid.

He nodded and typed a short command, instructing the map to cancel the satellite's auto orientation and allowing the same patch of dirt to be seen slightly from the side. That's when they saw it: the waver. This time more pronounced.

"Something is covering the ground," said DeSilva.

Kincaid had his phone out and was already dialing. "Yes. Like a camouflage net."

11

Camp Navajo, Arizona, was a shell of its former existence. Once the most extensive training facility in the entire state for all branches of military, its forty-four square miles of Army base was now largely unpopulated and unused. Long gone were its year-round interagency and intergovernmental training operations, now replaced by a much smaller area of active personnel and mission-critical maneuvers.

But it was still active. And situated just west of Flagstaff, Arizona, and less than sixty miles from the city of Prescott, allowing the UH-60 Black Hawk helicopter to reach the abandoned Titan missile site in precisely thirty-one minutes.

Neither Kincaid nor DeSilva could hear the powerful thumping of the Black Hawk's rotors tearing through the morning air or feel the shaking vibrations throughout the craft while it neared its destination and began to arc into a wide circle. They could only see it from overhead in their live satellite feed. And even then, the aircraft looked downright menacing.

It continued circling the site, searching, as one of two commandos, seated behind the pilot, spoke through his radio, patched directly through to Kincaid's phone.

"No signs of movement," the soldier noted, staring out through the helicopter's wide-open door.

The background noise was loud, making it difficult for Kincaid to hear him.

"What about the net?"

"Affirmative," came the commando's voice. "Approximately thirty by thirty and covering a large vehicle."

"What kind of vehicle?"

"Looks like a box truck. White. Can't see the make and model, but probably a class five or six."

Kincaid stared at DeSilva. *A large vehicle that would have to be gassed up to make it from Vegas to Prescott.*

"Is there anyone in it?"

"Negative."

Kincaid and DeSilva continued peering intently at the live video on-screen. "They're still underground."

The commando's reply was matter-of-fact. "Looks that way. Wait or go in?"

The was no hesitation in the old man's voice. "Go in!"

The chopper landed a few hundred feet from the mobile home, and both men jumped out. Hired killers, dressed in dark fatigues and moving effortlessly across the dusty terrain. They moved perfectly in step, one advancing while the other covered, then switching. M4 rifles raised, together they quickly reached the front corner of the trailer, where a cursory check through the window showed no movement, followed by a second more extended look for verification.

With no immediate movement around the truck or the short concrete pillar and its entrance underground, the commandos rounded the mobile home and moved briskly to its front door. It was unlocked.

With an unspoken nod, the leader pulled it open on a three-count and rushed in, sweeping both ends.

"Trailer's empty."

It was the first sensation of deep dread in Kincaid's veins. He had three men protecting that site. And none were there?

Moving back outside, the leader scanned the trailer's perimeter and spotted an object lying on the ground.

"Found your satellite dish," he reported. "Looks like someone shot it off the roof."

Kincaid closed his eyes and inhaled deeply.

Even if his own men were dead, Reiff and Waterman were still there. As was their camouflaged truck and means of escape. The two had clearly not expected to be discovered so quickly. The question was, what were they doing here? But Kincaid already knew the answer. They were trying to steal the Machine. To prevent him and the remaining "nine" from using it.

Reiff and Waterman had to know how difficult it would be to disassemble. Unless . . . they were here to destroy it, but if that was the case, they would already be long gone.

Kincaid almost laughed at them. All Reiff and Waterman would gain by stealing the device would be to buy time. Kincaid could simply build another. It would take time and resources, but it wouldn't stop him and the others. They were merely delaying the inevitable. Kincaid could not keep the smirk from spreading across his face. *After all this time, this is what they'd come up with?*

His worry quickly subsided as Kincaid realized how little the men actually knew. Liam Duchik was only a piece of the puzzle. A somewhat large piece but still just a piece. A calculated risk and obviously the only part of the plan Reiff and Waterman were aware of, which was reassuring news. And now . . . the two were trapped inside.

The door framed within the squat concrete pillar and leading below ground was locked, prompting the commandos to quickly destroy it. When they yanked it open, the men were met by a dark, descending stairwell.

From the sky, Douglas Kincaid and Daniel DeSilva watched in anticipation as their first man disappeared inside, followed immediately by the second.

12

There was no sound for several minutes as the commandos descended in silence. Moving slowly, step by step, down the winding metal staircase.

The stillness on the phone became longer and more intense with every passing second. Tension building with every echoing step of the soldiers' boots. Metal stair by metal stair. Until reaching the bottom.

There was ruffling followed by some light crackling. Boots carefully traveling across the ratty, deteriorating concrete floor.

Kincaid and DeSilva could hear the men breathing. An audible inhaling and exhaling as the soldiers continued, ready for anything.

The first words finally erupted over the phone's speaker in Kincaid's hand.

"We got nothing."

Confused, he lowered his mouth closer. "What?"

It took another minute, filled with breathing and scuffles on the other end. "We got nothing," the leader repeated.

"What do you mean 'nothing'?"

"Nothing. No one's down here."

"No one at all?"

Below ground, Kincaid's voice crackled over the leader's headset while he watched his comrade return back down the hall, methodically sweeping the area. When he cleared the rest of the empty rooms, he turned and looked back, lifting his night-vision goggles and shaking his head.

"Nope."

"What do you see?"

The man carefully walked back into the only clean, well-lit room. "Looks like a hospital room or something."

It took a few minutes to link up with the camera on the paratrooper's helmet. Finally coming through on Kincaid's phone as a miniature video feed. The picture was fuzzy, but he could make out the room and some of its contents. He instructed the soldier to walk around and slowly pan from side to side.

As far as he could tell, the equipment was all there. Including the Machine. Resting exactly where it had been.

The old man gazed at his screen, dumbfounded and reeling. Trying to understand, with eyes glazed until they widened again. *The truck!*

The rest of the missile site's lower levels had been sealed off, leaving the only other place unchecked the large white box truck outside. Resting motionlessly beneath the camouflage net, lightly billowing in the faint morning breeze. Soundless and unmoving, like a giant Trojan horse, just waiting for the two commandos to get close enough.

But they didn't. They took no chances, and instead, under Kincaid's orders, they raised both M4s and opened fire, plastering the truck's cargo area in an exploding barrage of bullet holes.

When their magazines were spent, each man quickly replaced them and raised his rifle again to his shoulder.

The sound of gunfire was quickly carried away by the desert breeze, prompting the leader to step forward cautiously. He listened intently through the door and, after still hearing nothing, inched forward and placed his hand on the elongated steel handle. And after another fast three-count, yanked it open.

Squinting, he peered inside at what appeared to be a large generator, over a dozen thick nylon straps, and a mound of thick and reflective sheets or strips resembling Mylar. All of which was sitting in a thin pool of clear water. Water that appeared to be quickly turning pink. From the corner, where the last of Kincaid's guards remained gagged and dead.

Over the phone, Kincaid and DeSilva listened to the commando's voice describe the scene from the ground. The old man gazing in complete silence, over the top of the monitor at the wall. Stunned and confused. Wondering what the hell had just happened.

13

Their second vehicle was a van. Painted white and covered in a mass of scrapes and scratches, bearing testament to its age and condition. Dirt-caked wheels that had long ago jettisoned their hubcaps, along with faint remnants of stenciled lettering on each side, discernable only under close examination. Letters that in a prior life had read A-M-B-U-L-A-N-C-E.

Outside, the van looked as though it was on its proverbial last leg, but inside, it was as modern as any ambulance could be.

"How is he?"

Rachel Souza shook her head, staring at the monitor on the opposite side of the vehicle's interior, commonly referred to by paramedics as "the box." "Alive," she breathed. "Barely."

Waterman stared down at the body between them, dabbing it occasionally with a towel to absorb extra moisture. The blue color in John Reiff's skin was finally changing, moving through a hue of light gray and gradually returning to something more pinkish and normal, indicating blood flow according to Rachel.

Reiff's body was wrapped in a thermal Mylar blanket, with only his face and chest visible. The rest covered to retain every bit of heat his system now had, the first of which came thanks to an IV infusion heated on the vehicle's dash as they drove. An old paramedic's trick. And on top of Rieff's head, a knit cap.

The last two hours had been touch and go, but Reiff's pulse, temperature, and blood pressure were finally reaching survivable levels, albeit slowly.

In the front seat, Wayne Coleman was driving as the morning sun slowly rose behind them, lighting up the left side of the cab. His mass of graying, frizzy hair, largely poking out from beneath a tattered baseball hat, glowed in the morning sunlight. Beside him, Henry Yamada sat glued to the laptop as they sped down the sparsely populated highway.

Waterman and Coleman knew the cover of darkness would only obscure them for so long before their pursuers would quickly work to identify all vehicles on the interstate once the sun came up and, one by one, systematically trace their routes backward.

They would also have detected the disturbance at their missile site and dispatched reinforcements, which Waterman estimated were probably there by now. Discovering not just the raid but what the small group's true goal really was.

The details extracted from Nora Lagner were critical. If her information was wrong about its location or it being operational, their night raid would have been an epic failure. They had one chance and one chance only.

The back of an old ambulance was the last place Rachel wanted to attempt reviving Reiff. What she needed was an actual medical facility, but they had no choice. Instead, they had to do it on the run. Leaving her feeling like a dentist in the 1800s, with only the limited tools and systems they could cram inside with them.

One bright spot was that there was decent equipment located below ground at the missile site alongside the Machine. But they didn't have time to use most of it. Once they had a detectable heartbeat, they had to get out as fast as they could. Three men clumsily carrying Reiff, with Rachel struggling to monitor his vitals as they ran. Back to and up the winding stairs during what was easily the most vulnerable two minutes of Reiff's life. His radial pulse was barely above sixty beats. The razor's edge of survivability. Repeatedly checking Reiff with a temperature gun showed his temperature also in the sixties causing them to make a beeline for the waiting van to get Reiff wrapped up before they lost him. Surviving that, it would take at least another hour to know whether his pressure, pulse, and temp would recover enough for his system to have a chance at surviving the ordeal.

If there was any silver lining at all, it was what Rachel had discovered in her months of testing the mice after they found the capuchin monkey and managed to isolate the all-important genetic sequencing. To protect Reiff from what happened to the other test animals. Because he was not far behind them. What appeared to be the body's mysterious, biological propensity to return to its previously frozen state.

Oddly, the monkey was the only one not to experience the same reaction, so the primate's unique DNA was captured and eventually replicated into hundreds of mice, who all underwent the freezing and reanimating process, using her small and more limited version of the Machine that Henry built. That's where the unexpected and hopeful silver lining occurred.

Rachel began reviving the mice not just once but twice, as would need to happen with Reiff. Surprisingly, she found the mice being revived for a second time actually recovered faster than they had after their first reanimation. Notably faster. Which over time suggested a possible biological "resilience" within the process itself. She did not understand it, but it was real, and it was repeatable over and over, which was the only thing that gave her a real hope of reviving Reiff. In a moving vehicle, with limited resources, while evading their pursuers.

The first time Reiff was revived, they nearly lost him, and that was with all critical medical systems present. This time was very different, and while mice were not humans, they were close enough genetically to provide the hope they needed.

The drawback, and it was significant, was the fact that there was no free lunch when it came to biology and medicine. Because the silver lining found in the testing of those mice also produced a second lining, with a color much closer to black.

14

If Douglas Kincaid had any sense that Rachel thought of him as her "pursuer," he would have laughed at the naivete. An almost juvenile reference in contrast to what was truly in motion and to the kind of person Kincaid really was.

Staring out the window, he now sat gazing silently down at the ground as it crawled steadily beneath him and his Eurocopter Mercedes-Benz EC145 luxury helicopter. The epitome of opulence in rotorcraft aviation, carrying up to nine passengers in complete luxury. With white leather seats and walnut trim, it felt more akin to the back of a Pullman Guard limousine than a chopper.

From several thousand feet up, the sprawling city of Provo appeared small and abstract. Discernible yet inconsequential. A feeling Kincaid knew well from the prism of wealth.

A prism in which the wealthy viewed the world. How they saw the masses and the classes. What many of them privately referred to as *the sheep*. The simple, the unintelligent, and the unambitious. Impressionable people living the same life day after day, content in trudging through existence with only the aspirations given to them by media and society. Content in accepting the mundane as meaningful. Pointless as relevant. Living, working their entire life, and then dying as uneventfully as the next. Swallowed up in the annals of history and promptly forgotten.

But not Kincaid. His life was different. It always had been, and he had spent the better part of that life ensuring it would stay that way.

He turned his head from the window and looked at the two men sitting nearby, the two mercenaries he had sent to the abandoned missile site, only to find Reiff and Waterman already gone. They were two of his best and part of his personal security detail. Strong, chiseled, and experienced in true combat during the Great Collapse. When modern society imploded under the weight of reckless unsustainability. When state turned against state, and then against the federal government itself. A complete collapse of the system and the American way of life. And not just at home but abroad. The Japanese system, the European system, the Chinese, the Russians, everyone. Every major country who had made the mistake of building their empires upon a foundation of printed paper money.

Countless died during those years, and a lot more would continue to do so. The Great Struggle that followed was still at its peak and would take decades to recover from if not centuries. Year after agonizing year of starvation, misery, and disease. At least for the masses. But not for people like Kincaid. He was beyond the suffering of the sheep. Even beyond the men sitting next to him in silence, although they did not know it.

In truth, they didn't know who they were ultimately protecting or what. To them, it was simply about the money. The means to an end. A better end. Working for "the Nine," a secret group who was involved in something much bigger, bigger than two commoners could even imagine. And that was the way it should be because so few were capable or deserved to reap what they were sowing for years.

The Eurocopter began to descend, then eventually slowed, heading toward a moderate-sized mountain range covered with tall trees that stretched for miles from the south to the north. Disappearing below a midday sun that illuminated the earth below as far as Douglas Kincaid could see from his window, leaving him to look upon a flat, open area near the summit of a smaller peak.

Nora Lagner was AWOL. Her last cell signal traced to a tower a few miles from her cabin. Satellite images showed no movement around the dwelling in the previous twenty-four hours. Of course, Kincaid could have called the sheriff instead of flying out, but he had learned long ago the importance of keeping things confidential, including the people he was forced to rely on.

The hike down did not take long, as the three made their way to a graveled road visible from the air and then downhill to the location of Lagner's mountain home.

Cautiously, they approached the driveway and stopped within sight of the front door. Standing behind his men, Kincaid noticed a section of plank missing from the porch railing.

His senior detail, named Wicks, removed his sidearm from the holster and moved forward. Keeping his weapon at waist level, he stepped methodically, easing forward until reaching the short flight of steps and continuing up onto the porch. He remained still, listening before moving to the front door.

He could see the doorframe was damaged, with splinters littering the porch and door. He glanced backward at Kincaid and waited for the old man to nod his consent. Wicks then placed his left hand in the middle of the door and gently pushed inward.

He could hear something inside. But the sound, whatever it was, quickly disappeared.

He extended a boot while simultaneously bringing the gun to the edge of the doorframe. Checking to the right then stepping inside and quickly sweeping to the left. In one fluid motion, he moved through the empty living room to a nearby wall. Aiming into and past the large kitchen before stopping on the hallway next to it while his eyes continued scanning the rest of the front area.

The furniture was out of place, and a smattering of larger splinters and chunks of wood littered the open floor. Several feet away on the kitchen counter lay a variety of tools along with a large butcher knife.

Something sounded from the hallway again. Listening for a full minute, Wicks began moving again, traversing down the hallway along one wall.

He moved silently past some framed photos without looking at them. His attention focused on an estimation of where the sound had originated from. From a closed door at the end of the hall.

He eased next to it and listened again, remaining perfectly still. Gun raised in front of him with his finger on the trigger, breathing slowly.

After a long pause . . . he moved. Turning and taking one step back and driving a powerful foot into the door near the knob, sending it open in an explosion that was immediately accompanied by a high-pitched scream.

On the floor was Nora Lagner. Terror in her eyes and wearing only her underwear. Her left arm was raised over her head and bound at the wrist, and from there, chained to a large plank of wood that had been firmly affixed to one wall of the bathroom. On the floor in front of her was a scattering of miscellaneous food items and two large empty pitchers, all seemingly within reach of her legs and free hand.

15

Nora Lagner's relief was fleeting. Especially when she saw the face of Douglas Kincaid appear in the hallway behind Wicks.

She'd run through dozens of scenarios in her mind and knew immediately which one was occurring. Kincaid would not have come looking for her for simply being offline. That meant something must have happened, and she could guess what it was.

An expressionless Wicks disappeared while Kincaid's second mercenary stood over her. She couldn't remember his name. Wicks returned with a drill and released the plank from the wall, and then the chain wrapped around it, allowing Lagner's arm to fall like a heavy weight to the floor with an audible groan from Lagner.

Still in the hallway, Kincaid cleared his throat and motioned for both men to leave, which they did. He then stepped inside the moderately sized bathroom and closed the door behind him, gazing down at her. At least she was able to reach the toilet.

The old man turned and removed a hanging towel from the bar and tossed it onto Lagner's lap, allowing her to cover herself. As she did so, he reached down to drop the toilet seat lid and sat.

His intense blue eyes stared at her for a long time, looking her over before stopping and examining the marks on her arms. "How much did you tell them?"

Nervously, she shook her head. "Very little."

Kincaid nodded, almost humorously, and glanced around the simple bathroom. At the green-and-white marble counter, single sink, soap, and a small jar of fake decorative roses positioned beneath a large oval mirror.

"Who was it?"

"Waterman," Lagner croaked, "and Yamada."

Kincaid appeared moderately surprised.

She wanted to speak but couldn't. She was paralyzed with fear. She knew Kincaid. She knew that the calmness on his face was merely a facade. A deceptively calm expression hiding a stream of shrewd and calculating thoughts in his mind. Taking everything in.

She opened her mouth and fumbled her words in desperation. "I—I can explain."

A smile formed on the man's face, sending a shiver down her spine.

"It . . . wasn't my fault," she began pleading. "I don't know how they found me—"

Kincaid raised an eyebrow. "Yes, that is curious, isn't it?"

"I didn't do anything wrong. I swear it."

The piercing blue eyes continued peering down at her, unblinking.

Lagner adjusted her position on the floor and then asked apprehensively, "What . . . happened?"

Kincaid's eerie smile returned. "Take a guess."

She swallowed. "I only told them about the missile site."

"Is that so?"

"Yes! Douglas, I swear to God!"

"Just the site? Nothing more."

"I swear," she pleaded. "They didn't ask me about anything else."

"Nothing?"

"Nothing important," she quickly corrected. "They didn't *know* to ask about anything else." She then added, "But I wouldn't have told them anything anyway. Not about that."

His voice remained low and calm. "Nothing else other than the site."

She shook her head emphatically. "That's all. I swear. I swear! They only wanted to know where the Machine was."

"That's all?"

"It's all they asked about. The only thing they wanted to know." Lagner suddenly leaned forward. "And I know why!"

Kincaid stared at her for a long moment before tilting his head. "What do you mean?"

The fear in Nora Lagner's voice was replaced by something else. "I've been going over it in my head," she replied. "There's only one logical answer why they wanted the Machine."

To thwart our plans, thought Kincaid. But he remained quiet, waiting for her answer.

"Because . . ." she said, "Reiff is frozen!"

"Pardon?"

Lagner repeated herself with even more conviction. "Reiff is frozen. Again. It's the only explanation! Why else would they want the Machine?"

From his perch, Kincaid simply blinked at her.

The old man's eyes rose as he contemplated. "Then they failed."

Lagner's voice dropped to a whisper. "What?"

"They failed," he said again.

"What do you mean?"

"They came," explained Kincaid, "but they didn't get it. They killed two of my men, but they didn't take the Machine."

Of course. The truck that was left behind. The room below ground. It wasn't just the lights that were on; some of the equipment was on, too. Systems that would not typically be left on.

Kincaid eased back and closed his eyes, letting the threads connect and letting his head shake from side to side as another grin expanded across his lips. "That's what it was."

"What *what* was?"

He opened his eyes as the revelation unfolded before him. "They didn't come to steal the Machine," he finally said. "They only needed to borrow it."

Unfortunately, the revelation proved short and unsatisfying. It was immediately followed by another and even more significant problem. A mystery, more worrying, and one that had the potential to be a significant wrench in the rest of their plan. One huge and very substantial wrench. One that could bring their entire effort to an absolute and utter standstill.

Why exactly had Reiff been frozen again?

16

The Nine, as they now referred to themselves after losing Duchik, needed Reiff, and they needed him badly. Even more now than before. Their plan could not move forward until they had him. Until they could be sure that their human guinea pig was healthy and the process of revival worked without any dangerous long-term side effects. That he had survived his reanimation from cryonic suspension permanently. Until then, The Nine could not commence without being sure they could survive it themselves.

But now, the plan was in peril. If Nora Lagner was right and Reiff *had* been refrozen, it could only mean one thing. That there were complications.

It would also explain why the group had gone dormant for the last nine months. They were not merely hiding as Kincaid and his colleagues had assumed. They were waiting.

It all made sense. And while the revelation was not good, there was still a possible upside. If Kincaid was correct, if Waterman and the rest were, in fact, biding their time, waiting until they had a cure for Reiff *and* an opportunity to revive him, then breaking in and using the Machine to revive him meant they must have achieved it. And locating Reiff also meant learning how they succeeded.

Perhaps The Nine's plan had not been torpedoed after all. Perhaps this long delay was not only beneficial but necessary. Even essential to their ultimate plan. Perhaps Rachel Souza had just solved a problem they didn't even know they had. That together, she and Reiff had just paved the way for them all.

Kincaid was now outside, standing at the end of Lagner's extended driveway, listening as his phone rang another number. The voice that picked up was DeSilva's.

"I'm here."

"What have you found?"

"I've traced Waterman's unencrypted call to a cell tower in Las Vegas. With some triangulation, I should be able to narrow it down to a neighborhood."

"How long will that take?"

"Not much longer. Maybe another thirty minutes. The process isn't what it used to be. You find Nora?"

"Yes. It appears our friends paid her a visit a few nights ago."

"Is she alive?"

"Yes." The old man nodded. *For the time being.* "I need you to search for a vehicle recently traveling from here to the area you've identified."

"Okay. Ogden to Vegas," confirmed DeSilva. "I'm guessing they left before daylight, but if they were still on the road at dawn, I should be able to find them."

It took just over an hour and a half for DeSilva to isolate them. From overhead, his best guess at the make of the vehicle was a dark green Ford Explorer, appearing on satellite a little past 5:00 A.M., crossing the Nevada state line and passing through the small town of Riverside. Stopping for gas shortly after, in Jackman, the two people could be seen standing outside the vehicle for several minutes. The resolution of the images was not sharp enough to make out their faces, but judging from size and stature, the occupants who emerged from the vehicle appeared to be Waterman and Yamada.

"You're sure?" asked Kincaid.

Facing the computer, DeSilva nodded. "This is the only vehicle traveling back from Ogden's direction, continuing to the area I triangulated Waterman's previous phone call to. And both figures at the gas station match the descriptions. So no, not sure, but it's highly likely this is them." He continued, "The truck returned to a small housing tract just outside of Vegas."

"Do you have an address?"

"Of course I do."

Hiding in plain sight, mused Kincaid. "Send me the address. I'll arrange the welcoming party."

17

"He's twitching."

Rachel Souza nodded while watching the tranquility monitor and his vital signs. "It's normal," she said. "His nerves and muscles are reawaking." She raised the temperature gun and took a reading. "Getting close, but we're not out of the woods yet."

She and Waterman both turned to look out the front windshield as the old ambulance began its ascent up a short ramp and into the concrete parking structure.

It was a third full at best, with most parked cars congregating near brightly painted orange elevators. They continued until they found the large blue-gray Chevy Suburban waiting for them. Parked alone several spaces from the nearest car.

Coleman backed into the adjacent spot until both vehicles were back-to-back. He and Yamada jumped out and moved briskly, opening both of the old ambulance's rear doors, then turned and did the same for the Suburban.

Waterman helped in collapsing Reiff's stretcher down to its base before the three carefully rolled it out, along with his IV bag and stand, which Rachel handed to Yamada. Together, they lifted and moved him between vehicles, and into the empty rear of the Chevy. Next came the devices and two large boxes of supplies, all transferred in less than two minutes. Then Coleman pulled the ambulance forward to park it alongside other cars.

The back of the suburban was smaller and tighter, providing only enough room for Rachel. For his part, Waterman threw two heavy duffle bags in ahead of himself and climbed into the truck's second row of seats, where he could reach back to assist if needed. Coleman and Yamada were back in front, and the giant SUV roared to life.

Cautiously backing up, Coleman dropped the truck into drive and slowly accelerated, following the signs toward the exit. Once outside and back down the ramp, they reached the main street and turned right. Setting a course for the highway and back the same way they came.

Waterman looked at Rachel. "Okay, doctor. Walk us through the next couple days."

Positioned in a half squat, she tried to relax by leaning against the truck's rear window. "Once we get him home, I'll take blood samples and run some tests. If his numbers look good, we'll need to let him rest for a while. It's a slow process; the body needs time to recover and begin operating again. But at the moment, he's in a survivable state."

"A survivable state," repeated Waterman. "That's some bedside manner you got there."

Rachel shrugged. "He can't hear me. At least not yet."

"Well, when he can, be sure to congratulate him on his new condition."

"Sorry," she mocked, "I forgot to dumb it down. I meant to say he's no longer a popsicle."

Waterman grinned at her sarcasm and turned back around. "Was that so hard?"

It took one brief pit stop and two more hours until they arrived. Backing into the familiar driveway and easing closer until coming to a stop about ten feet from the front door. Once again, the three men exited and opened the vehicle's rear doors, sliding Reiff's flattened stretcher out carefully. This time without the IV.

Rachel jumped down and rushed forward ahead of them, opening the door. Led them down a long hallway and into the open living room where more systems and supplies were waiting, including several waist-high tanks of oxygen, a concentrator, and rolls of thick, heavy plastic resting on the light brown carpeted floor.

Rachel supervised as the men lowered Reiff's stretcher to the ground then gently popped it up. It was a miracle, she thought to herself, feeling a huge load of anxiety fall from her shoulders. They'd actually managed to pull it off. The fight wasn't over, but at least they could take a moment to breathe.

18

The two SUVs rounding the nearby corner were unmarked. Black and featureless, they moved together in concert down the residential street. Slowing and coming to a muted stop one house early where both remained out of sight of their intended target.

Six doors opened simultaneously, and six men stepped out. All dressed in fatigues with assault rifles in hand.

After a brief perusal of the quiet street and a nod from Wicks, the six quickly broke into a run.

Two moved around the nearer side of the house, and two more sprinted across the driveway to the opposite side yard, with the last two rushing directly at the front door.

There was no knock, no pounding on the door, or even a ram to bash it open. Instead, the man in front fired rounds while in a full sprinting before throwing himself against the door, crashing through and barely losing stride.

The other four outside swept both sides of the property, peering through each window as they moved past before meeting up in the backyard. Without a word, the first man to reach it smashed the sliding glass door with the butt of his rifle, then flipped it around and used the barrel to clear the remaining shards of glass. All four rushed in.

The six men converged in the house's open living room. And found it empty. There was a sofa, a coffee table, a television, and a larger dining room table in the adjoining room, and beyond it, in the far corner, a small desk and computer.

While two of his men disappeared down the nearby hallway, Wicks scanned the entirety of both open rooms before noting something affixed to the living room wall. Higher up in the corner, near the beige-colored ceiling.

Henry Yamada stared at his phone, watching through a video feed the living room of the Las Vegas house. In the video, four of the intruders stood in silence, all staring up at his digital camera.

Yamada turned his head to Waterman, who was watching over his shoulder. He raised his eyebrows questioningly at Waterman, who, after a long moment, finally nodded.

With that, Yamada swiped to another application.

In the living room, Wicks lowered his weapon and reached for his pocket to retrieve his phone. He began dialing but stopped when his peripheral vision detected something in the corner. In the dining room, atop the small desk, the computer monitor suddenly came to life, displaying a picture.

Centered and filling the entire screen was a picture of a giant hand. A human hand, with its middle finger extended.

19

From the back of a moving town car, Douglas Kincaid listened to Wicks's voice. His blue eyes bored into the back of his driver's seat like daggers.

He was beyond angry. Beyond incensed. What he was feeling was complete and utter fury. When Wicks finished, Kincaid finally lost it, yelling and hurling the phone at the floorboard.

The whole goddamn thing was a setup. A diversion. They knew Kincaid would backtrack them from Lagner's cabin. And they knew Kincaid would come after them. And instead of avoiding it, the bastards actually helped him. There was no error with Waterman's phone. No glitch in that call's encryption. Waterman knew Kincaid was searching for him and purposely turned off the encryption in mid-call to make it sound like a malfunction, allowing Kincaid's team to pick up his voice and track the cellular signal to Las Vegas, where Kincaid would then use satellite imagery to pinpoint the exact house.

It also meant that when Waterman and the others fled the missile site after defrosting Reiff, they didn't head back to Vegas at all because they had already cleared it out!

Kincaid's eyes were like ice. *That son of a bitch.* They were all going to pay. Every single one.

They were screwing everything up, and they had no idea who they were dealing with. No idea what Kincaid was capable of when he found them. This had gone beyond just a need to find Reiff. This was now a matter of pride.

The old man could feel the rage coursing through his veins like fire. A physical manifestation of the violence he was going to unleash on them all. Waterman, Souza, Yamada, Coleman, and anyone else involved. They were ruining everything he had worked the better part of his life for. And they were on the brink of wrecking far more than they could ever imagine.

Reiff was originally just a piece in an immense puzzle. An important piece, but still just a piece. But now, he had become much more than that. He was no longer just important; he was critical.

After the collapse, many of their previous restrictions no longer applied. As a result, The Nine had now repeated the experiment dozens of times with other subjects. Some voluntarily, some not. It had become clear that suspending the human body before the final moment of death was crucial. But they needed more time. The regenerative bacteria moved slowly between cells in a near-frozen state. So, the progress in those subjects was still far behind Reiff's. And time was running out.

Now that they'd learned that something had forced him to be refrozen until a cure could be found, he'd become all the more critical to their plans. But the question in Kincaid's mind . . . was whether the cure worked.

What if the solution to whatever ailed Reiff had failed? What if he succumbed again, or had further unknown issues?

Once again, they were being forced to wait. They had to know if Reiff could survive not just his prior illness, but also this second reanimation. Both of which would take time. Possibly more time than Kincaid and the rest of The Nine had.

Because it wasn't simply about them; there was something else they had to do before they could undergo their own freeze on the path to immortality.

20

It was a ranch-style house. Single story and long, nestled and hidden within a small canyon along the eastern edge of Sitgreaves National Forest in eastern Arizona.

The owner's name was Nick. The old rancher who had helped them before when Reiff was awake and mobile. Unlike his current condition, now lying immobile and unconscious on a worn queen-size bed.

His respiratory numbers had finally reached normal levels, a little faster than last time. Rachel did not have all the systems she wanted, but she did have the essentials, including an ECG monitor also confirming normal heart and pulmonary functions.

"How's he doin'?"

Rachel turned from the monitor to find Nick in the doorway, dressed in his familiar checkered flannel shirt, jeans, and boots. She placed him in his late sixties or perhaps seventies. Still solid and rugged with a tan, weathered face beneath a dark gray cowboy hat. "As good as can be expected, I guess."

The older man glanced at Reiff's figure and gave a friendly wink. "Not at all like I remember him."

It caused Rachel to chuckle. "He's probably the only one who hasn't changed."

Nick strolled forward into the room, stopping near the end of the bed. "He's a good man."

"Yes, he is."

He then turned to her. "Was he really frozen for twenty years?"

She nodded. "The first time."

Nick angled his head and then shook it. "Don't reckon I'll ever understand how that's possible."

"It's not as unnatural as you might think."

"How do you figure?"

Rachel gave a mild shrug. "There are a lot of different species on the planet that can freeze and revive. Many in extreme climates do it every year."

"That may be, but we ain't one of 'em."

"No, but we do have some common genes. Adding some others allows us to do the same thing."

"And why in the world would we want to do that?"

"To live longer?"

Nick's face frowned. "Why are so many people obsessed with living longer than they should?"

Rachel grinned but said nothing.

"Besides, wouldn't you just wake up the same age?"

"Normally. But there's been some advancements to help reverse our body's aging process. Therapies."

Nick looked down at himself. "They'd have to be some awful powerful therapies to reverse *this*."

Rachel laughed. "Maybe you can get frozen next."

"No, thank you. I like myself just the way I am. Old and cantankerous. I earned it."

She gave a broad grin. "Boy, I can't wait."

"Keep hanging around with Waterman, and you'll get there."

"So that's why I've been getting more argumentative."

He grinned. "I'm sure it's helping."

Rachel turned to him with a sincere expression. "Thank you for taking us in again."

"My pleasure. Don't get a lot of company these days."

"How long have you known Devin?"

"A long time. Before the collapse. Now we're both part of the Network."

"I've heard of the Network."

He shrugged. "No one's come up with a better name, so that's what everyone calls it. Just a network of people across the state and across the country looking out for one another. And keeping under the radar. Just a lot of good people, careful not to attract attention from the higher-ups."

"Like the new government?"

"Something like that."

"So you're anti-government?" she asked.

"Not at all. Government, at least minimally so, is necessary for any well-functioning society. But I *am* anti-corruption. And pro-freedom," he added with another wink.

Peering down at Reiff, Rachel's eyes appeared almost trancelike for a few moments. "It's funny. I used to be pretty naive with all that stuff. Until this happened with John. Now I get it."

"Yeah, once you get a look behind the curtain, you can't exactly unsee it again."

"The corruption?"

Nick shook his head. "Corruption is everywhere. Even in our day-to-day lives, in small bits. And truth be told, there's a fine line between corruption and plain old human nature. And self-interest ain't always a bad thing. No, what I'm talking about is getting a look at the vastness of it all. What's really happening behind those curtains. The sheer scale of it all."

Rachel studied him before winking back. "You seem pretty smart for a cowboy."

The older man grinned again and turned for the door. "Even cowboys think from time to time." He stopped at the doorway and looked back at her. "You need anything, just let me know."

Rachel smiled and watched him leave, staring at the open door. He reminded her of the old adage about not judging a book by its cover.

Something told her this "Network" was made up of a lot of people like Nick.

21

It felt like emptiness. Long before the images came.

Vast emptiness. Stretching over boundless fields and endless rolling brown hills.

Wind strewn and silent. The only sound coming from a warm, whirling breeze.

A modest town began to materialize. In the middle of nowhere. In meager contrast to the vast surrounding emptiness. And in it, perhaps a hundred small, scattered structures.

The structures drew near, and most appeared closed or empty. Only a handful of people were out in public. Unspeaking and worn, going about their business. The business of surviving.

And on their faces, the same trace expression. Anguish.

22

Rachel was in the room when the next movements came. An uncontrolled twitching in Reiff's right index finger. Then his left, where the pulse ox sensor was clamped and nearly shaken loose.

And then nothing.

She was immediately on her feet, securing the sensor and placing her hands lightly over his. She could feel more trembling, subtler, and continuous.

The blanket over his right foot abruptly jumped before gradually settling back down into place. Reiff's nerves were reawakening and beginning to recommunicate with one another, just like the first time.

Rachel remained still, hovering over him, watching as different parts of his body moved or jerked before going dormant again. The only reliable motion was his chest and diaphragm, as he breathed in and out. Weak but consistent.

Eventually came the fluttering in his eyes. Reflexively at first, before gradually growing more consistent. Purposeful. As if reacting to something.

The pain was excruciating. His body felt like it was aflame, as though billions of cells were screaming in protest or anger. Muscles in his arms and legs, even his fingers, felt like they had been stabbed. Or worse, like the fibers had been ripped apart and then pushed back together again.

Then came his chest. An ungodly pain that felt like his lungs were breathing in fire and his heart pumping lava. His entire system tried to scream in response, to release the agony, but his mouth would not allow it. It remained defiantly shut, either unresponsive or inoperable, trapping the screams inside. Until his body and mind simply could not take it.

Darkness.

23

The second awakening was better. More movement and less contorting. Primarily because she got there early this time, injecting a dose of morphine as soon as the first twitching began. Keeping his system active longer through the pain, until it began to display more normal and complete movements. First, in the hands, where it progressed from trembling to a gradual curling of fingers into a half-closed fist. His feet were shifting back and forth independently. And on his face, his recently shaven jaw was attempting to open.

This time, everyone was in the room. Surrounding the bed and ready to help secure him through any sudden convulsions. Maintaining comforting hands on each arm and leg while Rachel calmly stroked his glistening forehead.

24

The emptiness returned through the pain until the sprawling vastness was all he could see. Another town in the distance. Larger this time. A small city.

More people could be seen outside, under the bright sun. Silent but with purpose in their plodding.

More storefronts were open, while others appeared abandoned and vandalized. On one corner was a small grocery store where people came and went in silence.

There was no sound. No noise at all. Nothing from the glass doors opening and closing. Nothing from the occasional cars that passed. As though a mute button had been pushed. Leaving no noise . . . anywhere.

A few moments later, a dark-haired woman exited the store with two small children in tow. Unaware of how shabbily they were dressed.

The woman stopped on the sidewalk, several feet away from the door. She looked across the empty street. Staring silently and curiously. As if seeing him.

She tilted her head but seemed to remain transfixed. Until her lips finally moved. There was still no sound, but she appeared unaffected as if he could hear her. Receiving no response, her lips moved again; this time, she was suddenly closer. The words she was forming looked familiar.

Over and over, the woman's mouth seemed to be speaking the same words. Until finally, a trace of sound emerged. Faint and muffled at first but gradually growing louder every time she repeated herself until the words became recognizable.

Can . . . you . . . hear . . . me?

Rachel hovered close to Reiff's ears, waiting for a response. Any response. Before repeating herself in a gentle voice.

"Can . . . you . . . hear . . . me?"

Still nothing.

"Can you hear me, John?"

After several tries, something happened. Emanating from Reiff as a brief guttural tone in his throat.

She glanced up at the others around the bed.

The sound repeated, fleeting but intentional, while she reached down and placed a hand on top of his and squeezed. "It's Rachel, John. Can you hear me?"

This time, the sound was significantly louder. Prompting her to step back in relief, covering her face with her hands. He was in there.

25

It took almost seven hours for his eyes to squint and an hour more for his mouth to move.

He couldn't speak. All he could manage was to blink while his gray-blue eyes struggled to identify anything. At first, it was only shadows, which gradually began to develop form. Then shapes, and eventually patterns.

Even though he could not make out her face, Reiff could hear her voice and her words. Some garbled, often clear enough to discern.

There was still a lot to assess, but mental acuity was far down the list. First, Rachel had to determine whether there were any severe, short-term effects to deal with. Things like organ or vascular unavailability, followed by more moderate-term effects in overall functionality, especially between systems.

Having him conscious did not mean they were out of the woods. Not by a long shot. But *communicative* meant he could help her.

But even if things ultimately looked to be survivable, she was still worried that Reiff might soon display the same frightening symptoms of most of the mice who had also been reanimated a second time.

26

"We need to terminate."

The statement fell like a hammer.

"Explain."

The first voice, male, with an Eastern European accent, belonged to a man named Sorontine. Large and round-faced with deep wrinkles. "We have to assume the worst," he replied.

Sitting in front of his computer screen, Kincaid nodded. "I agree."

The next voice was a slightly younger woman, looking into her camera beneath a head of dyed dark hair. "How much did she reveal?"

"We don't know yet," answered Kincaid. "She claims very little. Only enough for them to access the Machine."

The rest of the faces onscreen all appeared equally dubious. Nora Lagner had changed from an asset to a liability. No one argued that. The question now was how *much* of a liability?

"How critical is she at this point?"

DeSilva, the youngest of all of them, contemplated. "She's the expert on the Machine. Losing her may still present problems later. Replacing her is not impossible, but it would change a lot of variables."

Another woman, this one with Asian features, was the first to reply. "Keeping her could be far worse."

DeSilva agreed. "It could."

Kincaid remained stoic. They needed to know precisely how much Nora Lagner revealed to Waterman during her interrogation. The truth, not just what she claimed.

Lagner was one of them. One of The Nine. The remaining members from the original ten following the demise of Liam Duchik. Only nine individuals on the entire planet who knew everything.

But now, one of them had been compromised. Even if Lagner was telling the truth, it was still potentially enough for someone on the outside to sabotage the plan. But if she had revealed more . . . it would be catastrophic.

After Lagner had been found, her condition did not suggest any mental or physical abuse, so her version of the story was possible. Especially since she also knew the risks. All of them did.

"Magnanimity only goes so far," Sorontine snorted as if reading Kincaid's thoughts. "We have to know."

He nodded again. There was really only one way, and they all knew it. Chemical interrogation. But it was a line not crossed lightly.

"If we do it, we could break her even further," replied Kincaid thoughtfully. "Even permanently."

"If she revealed too much," said the dark-haired woman, "we must terminate her. Regardless of the consequences."

"We'd have to find another with her skillset," offered DeSilva. "Which means vetting. And that will take time." One by one, other faces on the screen became visibly dismayed at the thought. Two of the remaining Nine were not present on the screen. They were already frozen. Arthur and Donna Huston, a powerful duo in the new government, both of whom were succumbing to their illnesses too quickly and could not wait any longer.

It wasn't Nora Lagner's skillset per se that concerned Kincaid or what concerned any of them. It was the ticking clock. To find and vet someone they could trust. Integrity and loyalty were far more crucial than any skillset. And someone single to avoid contradicting priorities. The Hustons were the only couple and brought significant resources and influence to the table. In their case, the benefits far outweighed the risks. But if they had to replace Lagner, they would not absorb those risks again. Not this close to the end.

The plan only worked as long as the secret could be kept, and that meant The Nine had to be able to trust each other more than life itself. Because, in the end, that's precisely what the project was about.

A deep voice sounded from the screen. "Unless there is another way." The face belonged to a man named Cannon. Broad and indomitable. A man whose very presence exuded strength and power.

"You mean Waterman."

Cannon's reply was concise. "I mean all of them. Kill the four, and Lagner is no longer a liability. Regardless of what she revealed. We can then terminate her later when her part is complete."

"It's a good point," agreed Sorontine. "We need to capture Reiff anyway, and Rachel Souza. If we capture all of them together or in close proximity, we can eliminate the risk all at once."

"*If* we find them."

DeSilva's face became smug, staring into his own camera. "Oh, I'll find them."

27

The compound was located on a hundred square acres outside of Phoenix. Obscured and deep within the Tonto National Forest basin and an ideal location. Remote and largely invisible, even from the air. Nestled within deeply carved multicolored walls comprised of dozens of layers of ancient strata. Dry and arid, and in an area of the state that few would ever go looking.

The compound was fully functional and fully equipped. With multiple wells, a small nuclear generator isolated in solid rock, backup battery arrays, two hydroponic farms, enough freeze-dried food to last another thirty years or more, along with air purification systems piped through numerous venting shafts embedded invisibly within the sedimentary rock walls.

It was the perfect camouflage. The perfect concealment that had already served them well for almost three decades. Through the pandemics, through the cyberwars, and the societal collapse. It was blast-proof, gas-proof, and able to provide extended protection from radiation and toxic chemicals. And yet, it was not unique. Many citizens around the globe had built similar underground structures and bunkers to protect themselves. The Nine's compound just happened to be vastly superior.

It was sometime later when Nora Lagner appeared, rested and released from medical examination. Thankful that she had been allowed to wake up at all.

She found Daniel DeSilva in their main comms room. Considerable and filled with an entire wall of video screens, with most monitoring different areas and angles of the compound, even some from live overhead satellite feeds.

DeSilva glanced over his shoulder when she took a seat behind him.

"Feeling better?"

"Yes. Thank you."

He nodded and continued studying the oversized monitor in front of him.

After several minutes of silence, he finally lifted his hands from the keyboard and leaned back heavily in his chair. Onscreen were overhead satellite shots of five separate vehicles from different locations. Two appeared to be cars, one a truck or SUV of some kind, and two vans.

"You're looking for them?" she asked.

"They're in one of these," he said. "The only five vehicles that were close enough at the time to have originated from our missile site prior to sunrise. All traveling in different directions."

"You're tracking them."

DeSilva folded his arms and nodded again.

"Any idea which one?"

"Not sure." After another long silence, he finally swiveled in his chair and faced Lagner. "Tell me more about this revival process."

"What do you mean?"

"I mean specifics involved in bringing someone back. How much time would it take? What kind of conditions would be involved? What kind of equipment necessary?"

"You mean if someone was mobile."

"Correct."

Lagner thought for a long moment. "The things they would be focused on first," she said, "would be temperature and respiration. Keeping him as warm as possible to ensure functional respiration, both air and liquids. When we brought Reiff back the first time, we went through numerous scenarios. Temperature and respiration were priorities one and two. Similar practices to treating someone with severe hypothermia. For example, falling into or being trapped in a frozen lake, so things like thermal blankets and heaters to thaw them and warm the entire body as quickly as possible.

"As for respiration, I'm not entirely sure. Once Reiff's heart had restarted, there wasn't a lot of equipment necessary for the first several hours. As long as his heart was pumping and his lungs were working, it was more about monitoring and keeping them going." She stopped to think. "It's conceivable they could get away with minimal systems for the first few hours, something to measure his vitals, probably an IV, and maybe a defibrillator if they had to restart his heart in an emergency. But

I'm not a doctor; I'm only guessing based on their procedures the first time around."

DeSilva mulled her words. They were both helpful and unhelpful. Helpful in knowing that if she was right, the equipment Waterman and the others would probably have with them. And unhelpful in the likelihood that all of the vehicles he had identified could probably accommodate said systems.

"Anything else?"

Lagner thought again. "Reiff would, of course, be unconscious and therefore lying flat."

"Horizontal."

She nodded. "Exactly."

Satisfied, DeSilva turned back to the screen and typed on his keyboard, eliminating the two smaller cars. "Now we're down to three."

28

"Is he sleeping?"

"For now." Rachel exhaled and dropped into a chair at the kitchen table with the others. *But for how long?* "He seems to be coming out of it faster this time, so we should be able to begin with the testing sooner. Then we'll know what we're dealing with."

Waterman frowned. "Sounds like you're expecting problems."

"There are always problems. The only question is, how bad are they going to be?"

Coleman gave a puzzled look from the end of the wooden table. "But you already did all that testing."

"On mice," she replied. "Mice aren't humans. They're similar enough to provide some semblance of what to expect, but it's not foolproof. Mice DNA is a ninety-seven percent match to ours, but a lot of surprises can still come out of that last three percent."

Coleman nodded at her answer before returning to Nick and Waterman.

"We can't stay here forever."

"No, we can't," agreed Waterman, turning to his other side to face Yamada. "How long do you think it'll take them to track us?"

The younger Yamada shrugged. "Hard to say. If I were them, I'd be looking at how many cars were within range of their missile site at dawn and begin tracing their routes. With satellite feeds, it's probably just a matter of time before they single us out and track us to that parking garage. Which I'm sure is what they did after they found out we were at Nora's cabin. My guess is they then start tracking all the vehicles that left the garage during the next hour or so. That will be a lot more cars to follow, but eventually . . ." Yamada trailed off and shrugged. "That's what I would do."

"Then a matter of days," said Coleman, "if that."

Nick and Waterman both nodded in agreement. They hit the missile site and revived Reiff at night to avoid detection. But night did not last forever. And they could only drive so fast without attracting more attention before the sun finally made them visible to satellite cameras, leaving the rest of their escape taking place in broad daylight.

The parking garage provided some cover and a brief diversion, but not enough to permanently throw someone off their trail. And they sure as hell couldn't just sit waiting around in that garage. So, they were forced to keep moving in broad daylight.

"At least with Reiff stable now, it expands our options." Coleman looked at Rachel. "How long until he's mobile?"

"How mobile?"

"How long until he can *walk*?"

"I see." She nodded, replying under her breath as she stared at the table. "Ambulatory."

"Whatever. How long until he can walk and sit in a car."

There was no response from Rachel.

"It changes what kind of transportation we need. If he—"

She cut him off by shaking her head and turned to Waterman.

"We have a bigger problem."

"With Reiff?"

"Yes."

"What is it?"

"What . . . is . . . the . . . problem?" growled Coleman.

Rachel ignored him and continued talking to Waterman. "John is showing signs similar to the mice I tested." She stopped and thought about how best to explain and decided to back up. "The mice I tested showed that the genetic changes worked. Their bodies wouldn't try to revert back to a freezing state like the test animals before and like Reiff did. But it also showed that the longer the twice-frozen mice *remained frozen*, the more difficult it was to revive them. It didn't take long for the mice to become permanently unrecoverable a second time. Of course, rodent lifespans are much shorter, so it's proportional."

"And that means what?"

She continued. "The ability to revive the mice who had been frozen and then refrozen decreased by approximately five percent per week. This was why we had to not just find the Machine but revive Reiff as quickly as possible. Thank God we were able to bring him back while we could."

Coleman frowned. "This would have been nice to know."

"I explained this to Devin," she replied. "But I wasn't as worried then as I am now. I assumed the effect would be slower in John. But I don't think it is."

"Okay. Well, mission complete then. It worked. We got him in time."

Rachel shook her head. "That's not what worries me. What worries me are some of the effects those mice displayed after being brought back a second time. One issue specifically," she explained, "was that all rodents showed problems with their sleep."

"What kind of problems?" asked Waterman.

"They began sleeping less and less until finally, they wouldn't sleep at all."

"That's not good."

"It's more than just not good. Short-term sleep deprivation is not particularly severe for, say, two to three days. Resulting in small problems like reflexes, immune response, and behavioral changes. But if it goes longer, into five or six days, things get worse, fast. As in real cognitive issues and problems with the brain being able to process information correctly. Not just externally but internally, too. As in the management of vital internal systems. If lack of sleep becomes extreme, it can lead to organ failure and even death."

Waterman exhaled and slowly pushed himself back into his chair. "Great. As though we didn't have enough to worry about."

Coleman dropped his hands onto the table. "Wonderful. So, our choices were to wake him up and risk him not being able to sleep or wait too long and not wake him up at all."

"Something like that."

"And you think this deprivation is already happening?" asked Yamada.

"Just the beginning signs, but yes. He is sleeping for the moment with the help of a sedative. But how long that lasts, I don't know. The mice took longer to show signs so there *is* a chance it doesn't progress as quickly."

Waterman let out a loud sigh. "Well, that certainly changes things, doesn't it? What exactly do you suggest we do?"

"If it keeps getting worse," explained Rachel, "we'll have to find a hospital. Before he slips into full-blown psychosis."

"And how long do you think that will take?"

"It's too early to tell. The drugs should continue to work for a while. But I don't know how quickly they will wear off as his body develops a tolerance. We can increase the dosage, but eventually, that becomes a dangerous road."

Still leaning back, Waterman crossed his arm. "I guess there's no free lunch, is there?"

"No. Especially in medicine."

The room remained silent for a long time. Each person contemplated what they had just been told until Waterman cleared his throat.

"Do you think he's going to have them again?"

Rachel raised her eyebrows. "Have what?"

"The visions."

Her head slowly nodded beneath her long, dark hair. "Yes."

"How can you be sure?"

She looked away, this time peering through the window behind Yamada. At a sprawling hillside of native velvet mesquite trees. "Because of the mice."

29

"Care to expand on that?"

Rachel thought over the question and shook her head. "I think it would be better to show you."

She rose from the table and walked the ten or so feet to the living room's sliding glass door and pulled it open. She motioned to the men, who all stood and slid their chairs back, following her through the door and onto a wooden deck outside.

They followed Rachel, who traversed the deck and continued down a set of stairs, walking across a large backyard section of neatly mowed grass. Nick kept his half-acre yard surprisingly well-groomed.

They continued past a long, waist-high hedge, then a small rose garden, and across another large patch of grass toward an outdoor storage shed. At ten by twelve feet, the shed had previously served as Nick's workshop. But inside, his shelves of tools had been replaced by dozens of small cages and hundreds of active, squirming mice. Large boxes took up the remainder of the shed's floor space, the rest of Rachel's research and testing equipment.

She moved two of the boxes until reaching the one she was searching for, proceeding to yank the flaps open one at a time. She pulled out a tablet computer and powered it on. A few moments later, holding a tablet with one hand, she began swiping repeatedly over its screen.

"This is a lot of my research data," she said, still searching until finally finding what she was looking for.

She then navigated to the shed's only counter and laid the device down for everyone to see.

"Many of the mice also showed signs of visions like John experienced. Which became even more acute for several of the mice who were frozen and revived a second time."

"How can you tell?"

She motioned for Waterman to watch the screen and then tapped the picture to begin playing a video.

On the screen was a large wooden maze, instantly recognized by Yamada, who had helped construct it. The mazes were designed with walls that could be changed and reconfigured.

As the video played, a light gray mouse appeared at the edge and began trying to navigate through the various turns. Gradually learning its way to a tiny brown glob of something.

"What is that?"

"Peanut butter," she answered. "Works better than cheese."

Waterman continued watching. In the video, a timer positioned next to the maze displayed, in large numbers, the seconds it took for the mouse to find its way through and finally locate the peanut butter.

"Forty-nine seconds," said Rachel.

When the video ended, Coleman looked up and shrugged. "Okay."

"That was a mouse *before* it was frozen," replied Rachel. She then reached down and swiped past more videos with different names and timestamps until stopping on another. "Here is the same mouse after it was frozen and revived."

The next video began playing, showing the mouse entering the maze. This time, the glob of peanut butter was located in a different corner, and the maze had a different configuration. To their surprise, the mouse made a beeline for the treat, wriggling its way through the tiny corridors and directly to its reward, making no mistakes or wrong turns.

"Wow." The men glanced at one another and then Rachel.

"Notice anything different? And no," she said before they could ask, "it had never been through this particular maze before."

Coleman wrinkled his eyebrows. "So . . . freezing it allowed it to know where the peanut butter was?"

"You tell me."

"How would I know?"

She grinned. "How would I?"

"Aren't you the doctor?"

"Vascular surgeon," corrected Rachel, "not a neurosurgeon. And certainly not a research scientist."

"So, what are you saying? You don't know why this happened?"

"Precisely. And yet, this same phenomenon also happened with a lot of other mice who had gone through the cryonic process. And John."

"You have no idea how this is possible?" asked Waterman.

"None whatsoever. At least not *how*. But I may know *why*."

They all stared at her expectantly, with raised eyebrows, including Nick, who was peering over their shoulders from the shed's open doorway.

"John's accident took place about twenty-three years ago," she began, "when he was initially frozen. By then, many people had already frozen themselves cryonically in hopes of being reawakened in the future and cured of whatever condition or disease they had. But back then, the law prevented a person from having themselves frozen while they were still alive. It was essentially viewed as assisted suicide. So that meant everyone who had until then been cryonically preserved had to have it done *after* death and as quickly as possible.

"This meant," continued Rachel, "that every patient until that point had officially died. Clinically. And that meant future doctors would not only be tasked with curing their disease but also reviving them from a state of death, assuming they were frozen quickly enough after the fact. This," she said, looking directly at Waterman, "is where John is different. As you know, the accident he was in trapped him inside the bus in a freezing river, which may have resulted in him being the first cryonic patient to actually be frozen while he was still alive. Before his body and his brain where considered clinically dead."

Her eyes moved from Waterman to Yamada. "What we tried to replicate with John the second time, on the bridge."

They both remembered.

She turned her attention to Nick and Wayne Coleman. "The question is, when John was frozen, was he still alive . . . or dead? I don't know the answer, but I have my suspicions."

"You don't know?"

Rachel shook her head. "I can only speculate."

"And what is your speculation?"

"My guess . . . is that John was not killed in the freezing process but rather had reached a state of cryonic suspension *before* death could occur. As did his brain. If that's true, then his brain may have been frozen in a state of being 'on' rather than 'off,' as would be the case in death." She glanced at Yamada and Waterman, who found themselves quietly nodding. "It's the only thing that makes sense to me."

Coleman tilted his head. "But how does that allow him to have the kind of visions you described?"

"Not visions," said Rachel. "Memories. John was convinced that what he was seeing were actual memories. Of things that happened while he was frozen. As for *how*, that's the part I can't even begin to explain."

"Then speculate," mused Coleman.

"I can't. The *why* is as far as I've gotten. But I'll tell you this: Even as a vascular specialist, I've seen a lot of strange things. So, while I can't explain it, I'm not entirely shocked by it either. And I'm becoming more certain that I'm right every day, especially after experimenting with the mice. Because most of those I froze while they were still alive also showed subtle symptoms. But none of the mice I froze *after death* had already occurred showed the same signs."

Yamada gazed back down at the tablet on the counter. "Which explains how that mouse knew where the peanut butter was in a maze he'd never seen before."

Rachel gave a slight smile and winked. "She."

"What?"

"A maze *she'd* never seen before."

Yamada grinned. "Right."

"And yes," she added, "that's my theory, too. But wait . . . there's more."

"Great"—Waterman frowned—"we're in an infomercial."

The younger Yamada turned to him. "What's an infomercial?"

"Forget it."

Rachel went on. "Like I said, a lot of mice showed signs of 'knowing things' after being revived. The first time. But almost half of those were then frozen and reawakened a second time as part of my testing, and that's where things got even stranger. And to be honest, I don't think I would have ever noticed . . . except by accident."

Rachel retrieved her tablet from the counter and began searching again, this time taking less time to find the videos she was looking for, after which she briefly held the device against her chest and looked at the men in front of her. "Like I said, this was by accident."

She placed it down again and pressed play. The video began, showing a darker mouse traversing another maze. Quickly zigzagging through, but this time, instead of finishing in the corner, it reached a different endpoint inside the labyrinth and stopped. Unlike the first video she had shown when the mouse would reach a dead end and promptly turn around, this one did not. Instead, it remained still for several long seconds before almost reluctantly turning back.

This time, there was no commentary from Rachel. When it was finished, she merely swiped and played another. Of a different mouse with the same result. Where it quickly reached the same end point and sat quietly before it, too, eventually turned back. Rachel played another and then another. All different mice displayed the same behavior and odd results.

"This was almost a month ago," she finally said, noting the time stamp on the last video. "By then, I had already revived enough mice for a second time that I was confident we could revive John—*if* we could get to the Machine. I was running a lot of these second-survivor mice through the mazes without paying as close attention as I had before. And I completely missed their repeated stops at that particular dead end. In fact, I didn't notice it for several more days until I was changing a maze and was about to delete some of those videos."

"What's so significant about where all those mice paused?" asked Waterman.

"It's significant because later, when I had changed the layout of the maze again and moved the peanut butter, that dead end is where I just happened to put it. When I accidentally dropped the peanut butter as I was reaching over the new maze and decided just to leave it where it fell, three hours *later*."

"And that means what?"

Rachel did not answer. Instead, she remained quiet, waiting for one of them to catch on.

Henry was the first. "Whoa."

"The twice-revived mice," replied Rachel, "didn't just go where they thought the peanut butter was. They went to the location where the peanut butter was *going* to be."

30

The men looked at Rachel as if they hadn't quite heard her correctly.

"It's not a coincidence," she said.

"How can you be sure?"

"Because it happened with multiple mice the same way, all of whom were two-timers. The mice who had only been revived once did not do the same thing. Statistically, that's very significant."

Waterman raised his hand to scratch the whiskers on his chin. "Huh."

Coleman was dubious. "So, what exactly are we saying here?"

Rachellowered her head, taking on a look of disappointment. "I'm not saying anything. I was not able to do any more testing after that. The mice began showing the signs I just explained. They began sleeping less and less and becoming more erratic and eventually showed signs of significant mental stress and anxiety. Even if I did test them again, I couldn't be confident of the results. Not long after that, many of them died."

"Died?! How many?"

"Over half of the test subjects," she replied in a low voice. "Which are not good odds. Which brings us back to John."

Again, the small room fell silent, this time for much longer, as everyone remembered Rachel's worries about Reiff's sleep deprivation. It was then that Yamada decided to change the subject.

"So now, whoever Nora's friends are, they're after us."

"Looks that way," affirmed Waterman.

Yamada turned and faced him until the older man peered back with a curious look.

"Yes?"

"Is it just me, or does it feel like there's something else?"

"Like what?"

"Am I the only one beginning to feel like there's something we're missing?"

"What kind of something?" asked Coleman.

Henry was still facing Waterman. "Do you remember anything odd in Nora's demeanor when we were at her cabin?"

Waterman glowered sarcastically. "You mean other than her pleading for her life?"

"Do you think she really believed we were going to kill her?"

Waterman didn't answer. He would have if necessary.

Yamada's eyes moved to Rachel.

"What is it, Henry?"

He seemed reticent. "I worked with her, Rach. For three years. Day in and day out. I know her pretty well."

"And?"

"Something's not adding up," he said. "Why exactly do they want to find us so badly?"

Coleman rolled his eyes. "Jesus, take your pick. We have Reiff. We broke into their secret site and used their machine. We killed two of their men. And we're the only ones that know what they're up to. Any of those is more than enough."

Yamada nodded. "Do we though?"

"Do we what?"

"Do we *really* know what they're up to?" asked Yamada.

"Where the hell have you been for the last year? I thought that was the whole damn point of all this."

Yamada ignored Coleman's scowl and turned his attention back to Waterman, who had his arms folded and was quietly studying their young technical expert.

"What are you getting at?"

"What I mean is . . . why the urgency?"

"Because it's the best way to capture someone," snorted Coleman.

Waterman, however, was still listening.

"Look at how quickly they descended on the house in Vegas," said Yamada. "They did that in mere hours."

"Yeah."

"Why so fast?"

"That's kind of the way it's done, kid."

"Maybe. But what if there's something else? What if there's another aspect of this we're not aware of?"

"Like?"

"I'm not sure," he replied, "but before you and I got to Nora Lagner, something tells me *they* were not aware John had been frozen again. She was clearly surprised to find out we were after the Machine. And if that's true, why were they trying to find us the entire time? I don't think it was just because we escaped. They have all of the data, and they had the Machine. They covered up the whole lab incident, made it completely disappear as if nothing had ever happened."

Both Waterman, Coleman, and Rachel were now listening carefully.

"So why," asked Yamada, "are they still so desperate to find us?" One at a time, he looked at the others. "Is it just me, or does it feel like there's something bigger going on here?"

31

His panting was constant now. At this altitude, his lungs were taking in fifty percent less oxygen, causing his carotid chemoreceptors to rapidly increase the rate and depth of his breathing. In addition, his heart was contracting more tightly to pump more oxygenated blood through his struggling body.

He stopped atop the ice pack to rest, leaning forward onto his poles for temporary support, gripped tightly in each of his heavily mitted hands.

As he continued his rapid and icy inhalations, he was reminded of the words of Everest climber Rob Hall. *"Human beings simply aren't built to function at the cruising altitude of a 747."*

Standing and sucking in air, he could not have agreed more. Of course, he wasn't on Everest or nearly as high, but the stress on his system was just as real.

He raised his head to find the front guide walking back toward him.

"You okay?"

The man straightened and nodded. Passing on having to holler over the frigid wind.

"We're almost to camp," the guide yelled and motioned farther up what felt like a never-ending slope of ice and snow.

In his fifties, the man nodded in response and instinctively looked behind him. His second guide was not more than twenty feet behind him, unfazed and waiting patiently to continue.

There was a danger in them going up alone. He knew that. And they were not out to set any records or reach any peaks. But his body clearly did not know that. They were in no hurry. It was a private trip and a private climb.

As he gave his lungs and heart a chance to recover, the guides watched their client peer down at the snow before raising his boot and resetting his footing by driving the steel points of his crampons back into the hardened snowpack.

He resumed trudging. One step at a time, as his breathing quickly returned to its previous rapid pace.

Ironically, he wasn't cold. Just exhausted. His down suit was more than adequate, along with his double-insulated hands and feet, plus insulated helmet and mask. Overkill for his younger guides, but not for him. They insisted it was for his own comfort, which was, of course, true, but it was also clear the last thing they wanted was him dropping dead on them.

He had not been able to train as long as he should have. Just enough to ensure he wouldn't have to be carried back down as a corpse. There wasn't enough time for anything more.

It took another ninety minutes with several more stops to reach their destination. A small nook tucked into the base of a modest cliff wall. Not quite a cave, but enough to provide protection from the freezing wind and noise.

Upon reaching it, he dropped his poles and unclipped his heavy pack, letting it fall onto the snow and then himself following suit, collapsing onto his knees. Where he continued to suck in air as he rolled over onto his back to rest his exhausted legs.

The still-covered face of his guide, named Stoltz, appeared above him. Staring down to make sure he was still conscious. Unwrapping the cloth from around his mouth, the younger man grinned through a set of perfect teeth and a tanned jawline. "You made it."

"Thank . . . God."

The guide disappeared from view, and he began walking back downhill, meeting his partner to discuss details for their encampment.

It was the end of the final climb, putting them within just a few hundred feet of the final coordinates. The last drive, which they would do tomorrow. On rested legs and a full stomach.

The camp consisted of little more than their three multicolored tents, designed for high-altitude conditions and made of high denier ripstop nylon; they remained sturdy against the wind until it began to fade a little after midnight, down to a light breeze. And then just a few miles per hour by morning, allowing them to get a reasonable but cold night's rest and waking to a nearly cloudless sky. Its color was an impossibly deep blue. It was explained to him with less atmosphere in the way the sky became much bluer at higher altitudes. He didn't know whether it was true or not; it seemed like it.

After two cups of instant decaf coffee and a bag of reconstituted biscuits and gravy heated by a portable white gas burner, he felt like a new man. Sore but strong. Tired, but more than capable of finishing.

Without the need for his mask, the air felt warmer. Fresher. Leaving him a sensation that his lungs were filling faster and easier. Whether real or just a psychological response to being so close to the end, it didn't matter. Either reason allowed him to vigorously stomp through the icy tundra at record speed, throwing up chucks of ice as he moved until reaching a white and utterly featureless plateau.

Stoltz in front came to a stop and promptly turned around, waiting while his client closed the gap. Behind them, Williams, the second guide, once again brought up the rear. Removing his thick knit cap with a smile while plodding forward with little effort to meet them.

"This . . . is . . . it?" their client asked, still panting.

Stoltz nodded and clapped him on the shoulder with a broad grin. "Yep. You made it!"

It *was* an accomplishment. There was no doubt. But one quickly supplanted by eager anticipation. Excitement at the thought of finally laying eyes on what he had come for.

"Where?" he asked between breaths.

"This way." Stoltz motioned over his shoulder and continued walking, ice crunching loudly under every step. Withdrawing his handheld GPS as he tromped forward, Stoltz weaved slightly as he followed the directions on his device, up and over gentle, meandering mounds of undisturbed snow.

He finally stopped on top of one and double-checked his coordinates before peering down at his boots. "Looks like the last storm covered it back up."

Good.

Behind them, Williams closed in and, without a word, reached behind his head to retrieve a collapsible shovel. The other two men did the same, and together, they all began digging through the snowpack.

32

It did not take long. Perhaps thirty minutes of labored digging before one of the shovels glanced off something with a loud pang. They fell onto their knees and began clearing around it, repeatedly picking up their shovels to dig and clear away more, over and over, until creating a deep enough depression to reveal a portion of the object.

After another hour, much of the mound had been cleared away, allowing their client a clear and unobstructed view. Whatever it was, it didn't look like much.

The object, perhaps two feet high and three feet long where it disappeared back under the snow, appeared to be made of metal. Painted gray or a light charcoal. Protruding now from the white surface like an edged piece of something much more significant. With a texture resembling some kind of ribbed-like surface.

The two guides watched as the older man grabbed his pack and retrieved something from a side pocket. A handheld device whose large screen looked more like a phone than a laser spectrometer.

He took several readings from multiple angles and studied the results. He then began taking digital pictures. Again, from every angle and just about every conceivable distance from the object. Close up, then back a foot, then back another foot, over and over. When he was finished, he stood up over the object and did the same thing from the top.

The guides waited patiently and silently. So long that Stoltz was beginning to wonder if it would ever end, when their client finally stepped back against the short wall of ice behind him and just stared. Mesmerized for a long time before he finally turned to his guides. "How many people know about this?"

He'd asked the question of them many times, like some test, prompting Stoltz to sigh. "No one. Just us and Libby."

Robert Libby was their go-between. Their middleman. A broker of sorts who had put them in touch with one another. Two young explorers looking to capitalize on a discovery that someone else might just be willing to pay a pretty penny for.

And a pretty penny indeed. Neither Stoltz nor Williams would ever have to work again after this. No more dead-end jobs to fund their love of climbing. No more scrimping and saving just to buy a new piece of gear. Or a ticket aboard a cattle car to the next country on their list. Eating and sleeping in dingy hostels and motels to save a buck, hoping they wouldn't get sick in the process and ruin the next climb.

It was a dream come true. Both men could now see it. Here, on a nondescript mountain in the middle of the Himalayan range, separating the vast India subcontinent and the Tibetan Plateau. Where the two discovered the strange object by pure chance, following an unexpected light snowfall and the two of them becoming lost a year earlier.

Now, everything was about to change forever. All they had to do was get their client back down in one piece and keep their mouths shut for the rest of their days.

The trek down was easier, at least moderately so, allowing gravity to do most of the work while maintaining careful footing with their heavy boots and crampon spikes. One cautious step at a time.

There were several hazards they would have to traverse again. Crevasses to cross and steep inclines, they would now have to descend carefully. This was a little-known secret to most nonclimbers: just how many actually died on the way down as opposed to on the way up.

Gravity had its advantages and its disadvantages. Yes, it was easier on the muscles, but the physics of it all was an entirely different animal. An entirely different predator.

Each step down the mountain came with more weight and more force. In other words, more impact. Especially the more tired a climber was, traipsing downhill on a layer of ice that lay glistening in a warm sun the entire day. Ice that was just waiting to give way and slide out from under you when you least expected it.

Hiking down was easier on the body, but one still had to remain diligent. Every step of the way.

There was little talking as the three men moved slowly but carefully, absorbed in their thoughts. Stoltz and Williams eager at the prospect of their newfound fortune. And one with little risk. Even if their client backed out, Libby could easily find another interested party through his same political connections. Maybe even someone who would pay more.

All they had to do was get him safely down from their covert climb.

Covert was the operative word. Their client had to be assured that no one else knew about the find. And likewise, that no one would know about their climb so he could both verify its location and authenticity.

His two young guides were not experts, but their instincts were correct. What they had found was indeed something incredibly unique. Extraordinarily so. Something he was able to corroborate firsthand with his instrumentation. The readings were not only clear but downright startling, which meant that not only the boys would have to keep quiet, but Libby as well. Forever.

As he continued trudging downhill one step at a time, he wondered if his young guides had considered all of the ramifications. All the possibilities. They were smart, yes, but they were also young. And that meant inexperienced. Even naive.

33

It happened at the first crevasse. The largest of the two and the deepest. Filled with the most ice and snow.

Only fifteen feet across but nearly a hundred feet down, requiring them to traverse the metal-rung ladder slowly and carefully. One at a time.

Stoltz was first with his safety line tied to both men behind him and Williams kneeling to secure the horizontal ladder. With impressive balance, Stoltz crossed one rung at a time, producing a loud clank with every heavy step. Slowly and methodically. Foot by foot until reaching the opposite side and turning around to take up the slack in the safety line.

Next came their client. Less stable and more careful, kneeling and traversing on his hands and knees. Tightly gripping and shuffling across the thick aluminum ladder one movement at a time.

With Stoltz now kneeling and securing the other end, Williams appeared more relaxed. Calmly tightening the slack out of his safety line before stepping carelessly onto the ladder with the same loud clanking from his spikes.

Clank.

Clank.

Clank.

What neither of the preoccupied climbers noticed, however, was what their client was doing behind Stoltz.

In one smooth motion, he had dropped his pack, unzipped it, and removed the glove from his right hand. By the time the small Smith & Wesson M&P Shield was withdrawn, Williams was halfway across the crevasse. And upon spotting the gun, he suddenly froze in place.

Hearing Williams stop, Stoltz glanced up at his friend on the ladder, who was no longer moving, waiting for him to either say something or continue. But he didn't.

Stoltz stared at his still partner for a long second before shrugging. "What's wrong?"

There was no reply from Williams.

"Matt!" called Stoltz, unaware of what had unfolded directly behind him. Until he briefly glanced over his left shoulder.

Stoltz also froze. From several feet away, the older man was pointing the dark barrel of a gun directly at him.

"What the f—"

"Sorry, fellas."

They were the last words Williams heard before the gun was raised and two loud claps sounded from its barrel. The guide, still motionless on the ladder, suddenly grasped his chest and collapsed forward, hitting the metal ladder like a rag doll before tumbling and disappearing out of sight.

There was no time for Stoltz. Barely turning in time to see his friend vanish in horror, he never had time to turn back. Two bullets tore into his back and sent a spot of blood up and out of his mouth. He keeled forward instinctively reaching out for the ladder, and lazily slumped forward onto it.

Without a word, their client, a man named Kincaid, stepped forward and shoved Stoltz with his boot. Causing him to roll sideways, away from the ladder, and disappear like Williams into the mouth of the crevasse.

Kincaid calmly peered over the edge. Both bodies were at the bottom, partially covered with snow. Neither appeared to be moving. He then looked up and around, scanning the snowpack they had descended, and found nothing but cold white silence.

They wouldn't be found for a while. Maybe a few years if he was lucky. But even if it were sooner, Kincaid would be nowhere to be found. And their friend Libby would also be long dead.

He returned to his pack and briefly examined the gun before stuffing it back inside, pleased that he still had three of the seven rounds left. He then zipped the top closed and rummaged through another pocket. He withdrew a satellite phone, flipped the thick antenna up, and began dialing.

34

The thick and sweltering heat of Key West, Florida, was the polar opposite of the freezing Himalayas. Instead, baking beneath a bright afternoon sun and high humidity. And yet, it did not stop the crowds from descending upon the tiny island city en masse.

Throngs of people dressed in a multitude of bright colors meandering through the hot afternoon streets, shopping, eating, and enjoying every tourist attraction the island could possibly offer. Two of the most popular being the museum of renowned author Ernest Hemingway's home and, just a short distance away, the famed Key West Lighthouse.

From there, both attractions and their flocks of tourists were less than a quarter mile from a nondescript and run-down two-story office building. A modestly dilapidated structure in visible need of maintenance, housing several local business fronts. Many of which were already closed for the day.

One business, however, still appeared open. With sizeable black lettering stenciled upon its glass door: KEY WEST EXPLORATIONS.

The inside consisted of a midsized, badly carpeted room, two ancient metal desks and chairs, an empty water cooler in the corner, and several world maps adorning the dingy wall behind them.

Thankfully, the struggling air conditioner had not failed yet and managed to stave off the worst of the humidity. The room itself was not cool, but it was, in every sense of the word, better than nothing.

The office's only occupant was a large, rotund man in his mid-sixties, wearing a red-and-yellow tropical shirt barely covering his ample belly. His skin was aged but tanned, including his legs below a pair of dark dress shorts.

He was the only person in the room and the only person to look up when the front door swung open, and a much younger man stepped inside.

The owner looked up and paused his conversation, holding his phone while he nodded and briefly studied the young man before him. He politely ended his call and set his cell phone down on the desk.

"Hi, there," he said, smiling. "What can I do for you?"

The younger man, tall and perhaps in his mid-twenties, glanced around the room without comment. Leaning to peer past an open corner at the small doorway near the back. Perhaps a hallway or bathroom.

The man at the desk momentarily followed his gaze before turning back. "Sorry, the bathroom's not open to the public. Is there something I can help you with?"

"This is Key West Explorations?"

"Yep. Sure is. You looking for a trip of some kind?"

"What kind of trips do you have?"

"Nothing but the best in high adventure." The man smiled. "Locally, we have a number of wreck and treasure dives, plus some caves and other interesting excursions. What are you in the mood for?"

The young man, with Eastern European features and dressed neatly in summer garb, studied the giant maps on the wall. "Are you the owner?"

"Yep. Robert Libby. At your service." The older man pushed himself from his seat and extended a hand. "Whatever you're looking for, if I can't make it happen, I know someone who can."

His visitor displayed a friendly, disarming grin and reached forward to shake. He then glanced again toward the back. "No one else?"

"Nope. Just me. Getting ready to close up here in another half hour, so you have great timing."

"I'll say." The man in front twisted around and casually glanced back at the front door. When he turned back, his hand was holding a handgun with a suppressor barrel, better known as a silencer.

"Hey, what the—"

Three slugs tore into the man's midsection following three successive *thwap* sounds.

Instantly, Libby fell back into his chair, bouncing heavily off the seat before rolling over and onto the floor with a sickening thud.

The younger man, Liam Duchik, watched him fall with little expression. Waiting to see if there was any additional movement. Satisfied, he leaned out once again to triple-check the back area before returning his gun to a concealed holster and turning for the door.

35

Douglas Kincaid was now several more levels below ground in a giant frigid cavern. Wearing a thick jacket and standing on a metal catwalk, staring through the glass at the massive object in front of him. The lights behind the thick transparent wall were not on, leaving it shrouded in partial darkness but still visible.

The object was roughly cone shaped. Nearly a hundred feet long and thirty feet high. A light gray metal, unblemished and featureless, except the tail end, which was circled in a unique ribbed-like texture. At the front, the bottom half of the nose opened into a large cavity that reminded Kincaid of a mouth. An "intake" of some kind.

Had it really been over thirty years? Thirty long years since finding it on that mountain. It was hard to believe. So much time had passed. So many years . . . but some things were still burned into his brain as clearly as the day they occurred, including its discovery.

Kincaid remained standing in the near darkness. Entranced, even to this day, with the find that started it all.

36

There was only silence and blackness.

And then . . . something else. A feeling. Not of a person but a sensation.

Of restriction, or containment.

Within the darkness, images flashed and faded. Some too quickly to make out, while others appeared slower, but still random and meaningless. While throughout, the feeling of containment remained. A sensation that felt oddly just out of sight and out of reach. But a feeling strong and familiar.

The darkness began to fade and gradually revealed . . . a room. Large, white, featureless. Bright walls that could not be discerned as hard or soft, nor their distance away from him. With a sensation that slowly changed from containment to one of security. Safety. So long as he remained inside.

The white floor at his feet began to change, darkening in color and then moving. Displaying patterns swirling around in unpredictable movements before turning a dark shade of green.

The green swirling continued while shapes became long and thin. Like snakes slithering around and around, closing in on him until reaching his feet. Where they suddenly sprang up from the two-dimensional floor. Now swirling and waving vertically like vines in a strong wind. Touching him and quickly wrapping themselves around his legs. Growing, stretching, all the way up past his abdomen. Twisting and wrapping themselves around him.

They were plants.

Then, all at once, the blackness returned. Everything disappeared. Leaving him wondering, unsure of whether he had seen anything at all. Or was it just a hallucination?

He could not tell who was present when his eyes opened, but someone was quietly sitting past the end of his bed against the wall. Blurry and shadowed in the room's soft ambient light.

Everything was blurry, but he could make out general shapes. A large, framed picture on the wall. A glowing window to his left. And what he guessed was a chest-high bookshelf near the corner.

There was something else. Something obtrusive and in his way as he looked around. Something . . . on his face. Heavy and over the bridge of his nose and mouth. An oxygen mask.

"Who is it?" he mumbled, but his words sounded garbled in the plastic mask.

"I got to tell you," said a familiar voice, "every time they thaw you out, you look even worse than before."

Within the mask, Reiff's lips spread into a weak grin.

Waterman stood up and approached along the left side of the bed. He stopped and peered down at his friend before bending to gently remove the mask. "Doctor says this will need to be on for a couple hours a day." He patted his friend's shoulder. "How you feeling?"

"Okay," John replied slowly.

"If this is what you consider okay, then I should be a hell of a lot more grateful."

Reiff made a concerted effort to respond intelligibly. "I think . . . that goes . . . without saying." He watched as Waterman chuckled and turned back around, picking up the chair and bringing it forward.

"Well, John," he said with a sigh, falling into it, "I guess you don't do anything half-assed. Even coming back from the dead."

"I like . . . the drama."

This time, Waterman laughed.

Reiff rolled his head and paused on the partially open door, blinking. "How long?"

"About nine months."

He gave a slight raise of his eyebrows.

"You tired?"

He had to think for a moment but nodded.

"Rachel can help you with that."

Reiff shook his head. "I don't . . . want . . . any drugs."

"It's kind of necessary at the moment, but don't worry, we'll wean you off as soon as we can."

Reiff didn't reply. Instead, he changed the subject. "Where . . . am I?"

"At Nick's." Waterman then added, "We're kind of on the lam again."

"What a surprise."

"The good news is that you're doing well. Rachel says you're coming out of it faster this time."

Another nod.

"The bad news," said Waterman, "is that you're not allowed to eat for a while. Something about your organs needing to talk to each other again."

From the doorway, Rachel smirked. "It's a cellular thing, not an organ thing."

Waterman shrugged. "Potato potahto."

She strolled in, stopping on the opposite side of Reiff's bed. "How are you feeling?"

"Terrific."

Waterman shook his head. "For me, it's 'okay'; for her, it's 'terrific.'"

Reiff managed a smile. "She's prettier than you."

"That's not exactly a high bar."

Reiff suddenly coughed, violent but brief.

"Was that a laugh?" Rachel teased.

Reiff's words were still slow. "Why . . . did he say something funny?"

She chuckled and reached out to gently rub his arm. "Are you in pain?"

"A little."

Rachel reached out of view to retrieve a stethoscope from a nearby corner table. "Let's have a listen," she said and fit them into her ears. She pulled his sheets back several inches and placed the round diaphragm against his bare chest. "Try to give me some deep breaths."

They went through a series of initial tests, ranging from breathing to eye movements and dilation, through mobility in his arms, legs, and then individual digits.

When finished, Rachel nodded approvingly. "Not too bad."

"Don't get too confident," teased Waterman. "That's the line my doctor uses, too."

Rachel gave him a playful glare and reached above Reiff's head to grab the oxygen mask, laying it carefully on her side of the bed and turning off the machine. "We need to use this for a couple hours a day for the next few weeks," she explained. "Not just for your lungs but for all those cells we're trying to reenergize. Unfortunately, you can't eat for a while again."

"I heard."

She eased down onto the side of Reiff's bed while holding his wrist and checking his pulse. It felt strong. "What else are you feeling?"

Reiff took some time to think. "Feels like nerve pain, pretty much everywhere. But not quite as bad as before."

"Good. How about mentally?"

"Well, I still know my name."

"What I meant is, have you had any visions?"

"No," he lied.

At this point, he didn't know what he was seeing. What was real, and what was hallucination, or a dream. The last time they'd gone through this, Rachel and her colleague Perry Williams went to great pains to explain how much was jumbled up inside his head, in trillions of cells that were trying to reestablish pathways of communication. And that it was too early to worry about. So, there was no point yet in trying to decipher things again right now.

Reiff lowered his eyes and glanced at his left hand, gradually raising it and trying to make a fist. Then again and again. Repeatedly opening and clenching.

In response, Rachel held up his right hand, keeping her palm against his. "Try and squeeze my hand."

He tried, as firmly as he could before letting his hand relax again.

"Good. You're definitely coming along quicker." She reached down and gently patted his chest. "Who knows, maybe we'll get some food into you sooner, too." With that, she stood and began to pull away when Reiff's right hand grasped hers.

"How?" he said.

She stared at him and tilted her head. "How what?"

"How . . . did you bring me back?"

She smiled. "We can talk about that later."

"I'm awake," he replied. "Tell me now."

She glanced past him at Waterman, who merely shrugged. "Okay," she sighed. "If you really want to know."

"I really want to know."

She stared down at him with an expression of amused resignation. "We found the monkey," she finally said. "The capuchin."

"So he survived," murmured Reiff.

"Yes. He was still inside the zoo, hiding. It took us a while to find him. When we did, we took some DNA samples."

"And?"

She peered at him quizzically. "How much do you remember?"

"A lot."

Rachel nodded and continued. "Then you may remember that the other test animals died. Why, I still don't know. But there was something in the capuchin's genes that allowed him to avoid what happened to them. Some kind of bio-temperature breakdown in their bodies. Dallas's cells weren't doing that, or if they were, something was preventing it. I didn't know what I was looking for at first, but over time, I eventually found some biomarkers connected with cellular behavior that I'd never seen before. They seemed to act as a kind of stabilizer to his cells' nuclei, like an extra layer of protection. As far as I could tell, it was this stabilizing factor that appeared to keep the cells from regressing."

"So how did you give it to me?" asked Reiff.

"I haven't," she replied. "Not yet."

He raised an eyebrow, and she explained. "The DNA changes that were made to you the first time you were frozen took a long time to take effect. At that temperature, biological activity is essentially stopped, but they found a way to allow absorption of their DNA changes. This time, we don't have that luxury. We couldn't keep you asleep for another twenty years. We had to do it the old-fashioned way, which is to affect your sequencing *after* you were revived and normal again. The upside is that the absorption will be much faster now."

"So I don't have the cure yet."

She shook her head. "I had to make sure you were stable first."

"And if I couldn't be revived again, there would be no point giving it to me anyway."

At that, Rachel frowned in reluctant acknowledgment. "Luckily, that was not a factor."

"And when were you going to inject me?"

"As soon as I thought your system was ready."

"And?"

"You're ready."

"But you were going to tell me first, right?"

"If possible. Fortunately, you came around sooner than I was expecting."

He looked between her and Waterman. "Sounds like everything is already set."

"We've had nine months to plan," replied Waterman. "We just needed you to survive another defrosting."

"It's nice to know you were worried."

Waterman smiled. "Well, you know what happens to food when you freeze it too many times."

37

The concrete parking structure was located in downtown Phoenix, just a few blocks from Interstate 17, up a short ramp and into the first parking level, where the patrol car slowed to a crawl.

Much of the first level was empty, with only a dozen or so cars grouped in the middle near a set of orange-painted elevators. A couple hundred feet beyond them sat a white van parked alone in a row of empty spots.

The patrolman continued slowing and finally eased to a stop a full car length behind the lone vehicle. He grabbed his radio and called in the license plate, studying the van while he waited for a response. He was unsurprised when the plates came back stolen.

The patrolman pushed his door open and stepped out. Faint etchings of letters could be seen along the vehicle's left side, and the two square windows in the back appeared blotted out or painted over from the inside.

He kept his distance and slowly circled, studying the left side, the rear, right side, and then finally the front, where he tried to peer in through the windshield and the cab behind it, but he couldn't make much out.

He saw no movement of any kind, and stepping forward to extend his hand revealed the short metal hood to be cold. No sign of a recently running engine.

He circled back to the rear double doors and windows, and checked the handles to find both locked. With no sound from inside, he then pulled his baton from its holder and firmly tapped against one of the windows.

Nothing.

He tapped again harder. Not to elicit a response this time but to get an idea of the window's thickness.

Satisfied, he stepped closer and, firmly grasping the baton in both hands, he forcefully drove one end into the pane, shattering it.

The second impact created a hole, and the third and final strike knocked a considerable chunk of glass from the frame. Using the baton to clear the rest of the shards, he carefully pulled himself up onto the rear bumper and looked inside.

Several minutes later, DeSilva ended the call and tossed his phone onto the workspace in front of him.

"What did he find?"

"Just some supplies and dangling wires. Instruments are gone, but the rest looked like a normal ambulance inside."

Nora Lagner pursed her lips. "Well, we found our getaway vehicle."

"Guess so." DeSilva leaned forward and returned to his keyboard. "Now we just need to figure out where they went."

Overhead surveillance showed eighteen cars leaving the garage over the next hour. Their guess was that Waterman and the others left sooner than that, but they could not be certain. That left them eighteen new targets to track. Twenty years ago, before so much was destroyed in the cyber wars, they could have tracked all eighteen vehicles in a matter of minutes. Now, the process was much more tedious and manual. But it could still be done.

While DeSilva worked in silence, advancing frame by frame through satellite images, Nora Lagner remained behind him quietly thinking.

There had to be other ways to find them, faster ways. They just had to figure out what they were.

Waterman, Yamada, Souza, and Coleman disappeared without a trace for over nine months. Found only recently from what they thought was an encryption error from Waterman's phone. But it was clear now that it was no error. It was intentional. A diversion while escaping with Reiff's newly thawed body.

Waterman was clever, unfortunately. He knew it was easier to hide in a highly populated area than in some remote or backwoods location. In addition, they all looked like normal everyday people, and as far as she and DeSilva could tell from the recent footage he had gleaned, the four also made it a point to dress as plainly as possible. All of this to prevent standing out in public, in a place with few operating public security cameras.

And they were using cash, as many people now were. They had to be. No records of electronic transactions could be detected anywhere for any of them. The warfare had also knocked out much of the financial network, but even with the system that was available, there were no financial traces of any kind that they could connect to Waterman or the others. DeSilva suspected the group had stashes of cash in different locations, allowing them to transact invisibly. And most likely they still were.

They were also using untraceable devices like burner phones. That much was obvious. The phone they recently detected Waterman's voice on was traced to a small independent vendor in Kingman, Arizona, and most assuredly purchased over the counter with cash. They even assigned an area code of 212: New York City.

There were other hints, too, none of which ever revealed where the group was. Would DeSilva be able to find them? Probably. But how long would it take? And by the time he did narrow down a location, would they still be there?

There had to be something else. Another way to find them. If not where they were, then what they were doing. And the most pressing question for Nora Lagner was still the same: Exactly why had Reiff been refrozen, and *what* did Rachel Souza know or figure out to help him? And how?

Lagner slowly shook her head in frustration and tried to reflect. On the project and all the progress they'd made in the last six years, hidden away in their covert lab. Secreted away in that old building where they first managed to build the Machine.

So much progress and so many breakthroughs. All of that was now at a standstill. Virtually irrelevant without the final product, Reiff, and their ability to move forward.

All that work, all the experiments, all the data . . .

Nora Lagner suddenly stopped.

Still behind DeSilva, she blinked, carefully retracing her thoughts.

All that work . . . all the experiments . . . all the data . . .

All the experiments.

They had run hundreds of experiments before reviving Reiff. Hundreds of experiments . . . on hundreds of animals.

Most of them did not survive. But some of them did. *The survivors.*

Rachel Souza and Henry Yamada carried out the experiments while refining the science behind the Machine. Well over two years of testing.

The survivors.

Once the Machine was perfected, the testing then turned to larger and more complex biological subjects. First rats, then guinea pigs, then rabbits, then pigs, dogs, until they eventually successfully tested apes, the closest genetic cousins to humans.

It finally hit Nora Lagner like a tsunami. *Whatever problem occurred with Reiff must have also happened with the surviving animals!*

Her breathing briefly stopped, excited at the possibility. *The animals,* she thought again. *'Where' were the animals?*

She began rolling back through events in her mind. The project. The lab. The team members Rachel, Henry, Dr. Williams, and Robert Masten, the director of the project. Over and over, she rewound and fast-forwarded the details in her brain.

She then thought of Duchik, one of the original "Ten." A high-ranking member of the NIH who was the mastermind behind the project's secret funding. Behind the research to bring back the first cryonic patient, John Reiff.

But after their miraculous success, Williams, Yamada, and even Rachel Souza began to develop suspicions. That Reiff was somehow more than just a random patient. And then everything went off the rails.

But what happened to their surviving animal test subjects?

Once Reiff was deemed healthy, the animals were no longer needed, and she now remembered Rachel was arranging to have them relocated and cared for. *But where?*

Still unmoving in the chair, Lagner was racking her brain, trying desperately to remember. *Who? Who had Souza arranged to send them to?*

It was someplace local. But how local? Phoenix? Arizona? A nearby state? She didn't know.

Lagner closed her eyes and tried to relax. The answer would come to her in time. She was sure of it.

Then, a thought occurred. Wherever the animals were being transferred to, there had to be some remnant of documentation on it. An email, a phone call, something.

Her first movement was in the form of a faint smile, creeping across her lips from one side to the other. It had to be documented somewhere. She was sure of it. And *she* was the one still holding a copy of *all* of the project's data.

38

The amount of data was immense. Terabytes upon terabytes of data. Over six years' worth of technical tests, medical analysis, video footage, and DNA tests. Leaving Nora Lagner pondering where exactly to start.

She was now in her office. Large, uncluttered, with a giant monitor in front of her.

Robert Masten had been the project's director, and she was the chief information officer, which meant technical and administrative access to everything. Hence her trying to decide where to start. In other words, where the information she sought was likely to be found.

Rachel had not only been the project's vascular specialist but also their de facto zoologist, not by training but because animals had more in common at the vascular level than at the organ or visceral level. Reheating a body had to be done extremely carefully, and as Rachel herself had said many times, if the blood wasn't liquid enough for a body to pump, nothing else mattered. No matter what type of animal. Therefore, the ongoing care and study of the surviving animals ultimately fell under her purview, and ultimately was why she had been the one to arrange homes for them.

Whatever Lagner was looking for would be found in Rachel's records.

She leaned forward and began typing, bringing up a window and logging into a central computer console. She then proceeded to boot up several virtual computers that housed all the project's archived email data. It took another thirty minutes for all systems to boot up and all databases to reconnect. When all systems were verified, she logged into the old email console itself and brought up several administrator tools, including the system's search function. Selecting the correct database and then Rachel Souza as the user, she began searching for any references to the words "transfer of animals."

Thousands of email results appeared with the word "animals" highlighted. But nothing with that exact phrase.

Lagner tried again, searching for the words "zoo or sanctuary."

This time, nothing came up at all.

She tried a third time with the text "animal long term care."

Again, thousands of results highlighting individual words from her search, but nothing with the entire sequence.

Staring silently at the screen, Lagner eased back into her chair and folded her arms. This was going to take time.

It did take time. Over three long hours until she finally found what she was looking for. And it was not in Rachel's emails or her computer's browsing history. It was in the phone system's database. In the form of digital records and voicemails exchanged between Rachel and a woman named Samantha Reed at the Association of Zoos and Aquariums, who just happened to work at the Phoenix Zoo. There would no doubt be accompanying documentation somewhere as well.

After locating and carefully listening to the voicemails, Lagner picked up her phone and dialed Samantha Reed's number. After a few rings, the call was answered.

"Hello, this is Samantha."

Lagner's voice was calm and friendly. "Hi, is this Dr. Samantha Reed?"

"Yes, it is. How can I help you?"

"Hello, Dr. Reed, my name is Peggy Denton. I'm a colleague of Dr. Rachel Souza."

There was a momentary pause as the woman on the other end tried to place the name. "Oh yes, of course. What can I do for you?"

"Dr. Souza is currently on assignment and asked me to call and follow up with you." Lagner had no idea how much information the two women had shared or when, but her guess was that Rachel would not have revealed the full extent of the project or their testing on the animals.

"Oh, I see. Sure, no problem. What sort of information were you looking for?"

Lagner gambled again. She had no idea how many of the animals had been transferred or what condition they were in. Or what condition they were *still* in. If John Reiff's condition was enough to put him through the agony of refreezing, it must have been dire, even terminal. If the animals were also terminal . . .

Lagner cleared her throat, maintaining a friendly demeanor. "We were just checking to see if there were any . . . updates."

There was a pause on the other end. One that felt long, possibly too long, before Reed's voice responded. "You mean the capuchin?"

Lagner quickly acknowledged, "Yes! The capuchin."

"As far as I know, he's doing fine. Let me ask one of our keepers. Would you like to hold on a minute?"

"Of course, thank you." Lagner couldn't help but grin with relief. Why had Reed not mentioned any of the other animals? Surely, the zoo would have taken more than one. But if Reiff was sick, it stood to reason that some of the animals could have been sick as well. Perhaps even more since they had been revived before Reiff. Some long before. Lagner's logic then reversed direction. If some of the animals *were* sick, it may have proven a warning sign to Rachel. Who would have, in turn, warned Reiff. And if the animals actually died, it would explain why John Reiff would be quickly refrozen in an attempt to avoid the same fate until they could find an explanation. And a cure.

That had to be it. It made perfect sense, and it checked all the boxes. It must have been the *animals* that would have tipped them off and potentially saved Reiff's life. Or at least bought him some time.

Lagner gradually began nodding to herself. Now, in retrospect, assuming it was all true, the idea to refreeze Reiff was a stroke of genius. And Lagner's guess was that that idea came from Rachel.

It sounded like the zoo only had one of their test animals. Did they only take one, or had the others died? And if they had, was it in Rachel's care or theirs?

Nora Lagner couldn't believe her luck. Or was it her intuition? It didn't matter. What mattered was that the pieces had finally fallen into place, along with the explanation of why Rachel Souza and the others had gone completely silent and disappeared. It wasn't just for their survival; it was part of a plan. To figure out how to save John Reiff. Why on earth hadn't she pieced it together before?

Samantha Reed's voice returned. "Hi, are you still there?"

"Yes, I am."

"We're happy to report that Dallas remains healthy. Still no signs of the terminal issues we saw in the other animals. Would you like me to send you a copy of his latest examination?"

"That would be wonderful, thank you," replied Lagner. She suddenly had a thought. "Actually, I'm in the area for the next few days. Would you mind if I stopped by and had a quick look at him?"

"I'm sure that would be fine. We're open Thursday through Sunday from ten to six, but I'm here by eight if you need to come earlier. Just give me an idea when, and I'll arrange one of us to meet you."

"Wonderful. Thank you very much, Dr. Reed. We really appreciate it. I will call you back as soon as I know."

Nora Lagner ended the call and remained in her chair, staring forward with her hand still wrapped around her phone. *Unbelievable,* she thought. *Simply unbelievable.*

39

Kincaid was still underground but now only a couple of levels deep. In another area of the compound, about fifty feet above their artifact, where it remained deep below and insulated within the rock's natural strata, maintained at the same frozen temperature it was found in.

A few levels above the object and still below the rest of the compound were a myriad of systems and the technological heart of the group's underground compound: power, water pump and purification, air filtration, and disposal systems. Systems running around the clock to make the compound's self-sustainability possible.

It was also where they had relocated their cryo units after being discovered in their previous location. In one of several hidden caves nearly a hundred miles to the south, directly after Duchik's death, which reduced the group's number from ten to nine. A brutal reminder of just how quickly long-term plans could change and just how mortal they all still were.

No matter how much planning, how much power, or how much money they had, it could all be snuffed out in an instant from any number of causes. Like Duchik's death at the hands of John Reiff.

Along the wall of the sizable subterranean room were ten cryo chambers in all. Individual pods for each of them, except Duchik, of course. Where the remaining nine would be individually frozen for decades. While their bodies slowly absorbed the genetic changes into their semi-frozen cells. Ever so slowly, reversing the aging process by repairing their genes' biomarkers and re-lengthening trillions of telomeres.

Truth be told, Kincaid did not like having the cryo units located within the compound. He was not a believer in keeping one's eggs in a single basket. It provided little in the way of safety through diversification. Convenient, yes, but redundant, no. However, after John Reiff managed to find their previous location, the group had little choice but to move them again, and the compound was the fastest and easiest option. Because time was almost up, biologically speaking.

Kincaid was sitting on a lone chair positioned before the cryo chambers, running the length of the machine-bored sandstone room. At the end closest to him, two of the chambers were sealed and active, where inside, behind small green-tinted windows, rested the frozen figures of Arthur and Donna Huston. The first two members to be preserved.

For the Hustons, the biological clock had already run out. It was a figurative reference; the clock running down was not on a wall; it was inside their bodies, with very little of their natural lives remaining.

There were, of course, many, many cases in which people were frozen in some accident or sudden state and later revived. Kids skating on a frozen lake, car accidents, being lost in a snowstorm, where time and time again, the victims were brought back. But in those cases, the circumstances were different. Those victims had not been pronounced clinically dead *prior* to the freezing. Instead, they were still technically alive *as* the freezing took place. And that appeared to be the key. And why John Reiff turned out to be the perfect guinea pig. His was a bus accident in a frozen river in the dead of winter in which he was the only person trapped inside. Not just a lone victim but one with no family aware of his sudden demise. Allowing Reiff to be swept into a secret research program leaving no trace of his presence on the ill-fated bus. The first person frozen in just the right circumstances whom Kincaid could successfully make disappear.

And that was where the biological clock came in.

Kincaid and the other members of The Nine knew being frozen alive was key. They'd known it for decades, and the key to being successfully reanimated, which presented a significant conundrum in the form of an ultimate question: When exactly were they to freeze themselves?

It was the ultimate question because the longer they waited, the longer they risked some form of accidental or unexpected death. A car accident, a stroke, a heart attack, a random act of violence, or just old age.

The world was a dangerous place, especially in its current state. And there was no way to know when or how death would come. No way to know when that fateful moment would take place, when death would suddenly and unexpectedly appear. And with several of the group being in their eighties and nineties, the odds only increased each day that they might die before they had the opportunity to freeze themselves.

Kincaid stared at the capsules holding the preserved bodies of the Hustons. The only married couple of the original ten, Arthur and Donna, both suffering from years of disease and failing health. Finally choosing to proactively enter hibernation before it was too late.

The question now shifted to how much longer the rest of the group had. Duchik's opportunity was snuffed out in seconds. So, what if the Grim Reaper came for them as well?

John Reiff was not the Grim Reaper, but he was nevertheless a symbol of it. A man who turned out to be nothing like they thought, with a past they had completely underestimated. Perhaps it wasn't just symbolism.

If Reiff were to find out just how much of a test subject he really was, would he then come for the rest of them like he had for Duchik?

Even if he didn't, Kincaid and the rest still couldn't risk biological clocks reaching zero before they hibernated. But they couldn't hibernate *yet*. There were still crucial questions that had to be answered before it was safe. Questions that were absolutely imperative if they were to have any chance of being reawakened successfully.

40

Reiff was upright, hunched slightly but steady, while Rachel Souza administered a clear solution into his new IV tube. She then stepped back and smiled as he gazed quietly over the glistening green grass in front of them.

Individual droplets clung to the tiny blades and reflected a glint of sunlight that made the short-cut lawn glisten and glow in the crisp morning air. Beyond the grass, several dark green cypress trees towered above, and beyond those, a soft blue, cloudless sky.

They both turned as Waterman and the owner, Nick, approached. For the life of her, she couldn't remember the man's last name.

"How are we doing?"

Rachel glanced down at Reiff. "Good. Just taking our morning dose of autophagy therapy."

"Autopha-what?"

"It's part of the body's natural cleansing processes, replacing bad cells with strong new cells. This chemically stimulates it by manipulating a protein called Beclin 1, in essence turbocharging the process."

"Is that the special antifreeze you developed for him?"

She frowned. "No, he gets that in another hour. And it's not antifreeze."

The two men looked at Reiff, focusing on the clear oxygen mask covering his nose and mouth.

"You know, with that mask on, you look a little like a fighter pilot."

Reiff glanced up at his friend with a grimace. "I'll take it."

"Well, you're looking better," offered Waterman.

"Yeah?"

Waterman then shook his head. "Not really. Just trying to make you feel better."

A muted laugh emanated from inside Reiff's mask.

"I will never understand you two," stated Rachel, bending down to once again wrap the blood pressure cuff around Reiff's left arm.

"It's a veteran thing," Waterman replied. "And an old man thing."

She chided while inflating the cuff. "He's not as old as you."

"Sure he is. Just better preserved."

"Much better," added Nick.

Waterman laughed and knelt next to Reiff and patted his friend's knee. "She's still okay," he said in a serious tone. "Elizabeth. The whole family is fine."

Reiff's eyes softened.

"Whoever Duchik's friends are, they seemed to have gotten the hint and left her alone. I knew you'd want to know."

"Does *she* know?" he asked through the mask.

"Yes." Waterman glanced up at Rachel. "We told her the best thing she could do is just focus on her family and let us work on trying to bring you back."

Reiff's body seemed to relax, and he eased back into the wheelchair.

"We'll take you to see her," said Rachel, "when you're stronger. Right now, you're still too weak." She studied the blood pressure results. His vitals were still improving.

Content for the moment, Reiff looked away, observing Nick as he walked to his nearby shed and retrieved two more foldable chairs from inside. He returned and set them down for him and Waterman.

Reiff raised a hand and pointed weakly to another area of the yard, perhaps fifty feet from the cypress trees to a huge mound. "What's that?" he asked their host.

Nick turned and followed his gaze. The mound was enormous, almost eight feet tall, with straight, sculpted sides, resembling a mammoth earthen cake. Reiff guessed it to be about fifteen feet across its flattened top.

"That's a Pain pile."

He gave Nick a questioning look.

"Named after Jean Pain, a French innovator back in the 1970s. He came up with novel ways to get energy from Mother Nature."

"What do you mean?"

"It's a compost pile," he explained, "made of wood chips. Slowly breaking down through a natural composting process."

Reiff turned back, looking curiously at the old man.

"Most people don't know that a compost pile can reach internal temperatures of up to one hundred forty degrees and maintain it for a long time. A very long time. Jean Pain was one of the first to show people how to tap into that." Nick nodded at the mound as he spoke. "That pile right there started out at nine feet tall, comprised entirely of organic woodchips. Soaked and packed, and layered with a few hundred feet of half-inch plastic irrigation hose as we built it up. While composting, the pile maintains an internal temperature of between one hundred thirty and one hundred forty degrees day in and day out for the better part of a year. It creates over three hundred and sixty-five days of constant hot water for the house by pumping fresh water through the hoses wound around inside it."

Reiff raised his eyebrows in surprise.

"The world has had to learn to live a lot more efficiently over the past twenty years," commented Waterman.

"That's not all the pile does," the old man continued. "It creates all my cooking gas, too."

"You're kidding."

"Nope. That guy Pain also showed how you can put a barrel in the middle of it filled with organic matter and capture the biogas created from it."

"For an entire year?"

"Yep. I run the biogas through a small pipe right into the kitchen where I have a burner."

Reiff stopped to think. "I don't remember seeing this when we were here before."

"As I recall, you didn't stay very long. And it was at night." Nick returned to the pile. "At the end of the year, when it's time to tear it down, I have a couple tons of perfect black compost." He then added with a chuckle, "You should see my garden."

"A lot of people do this now," said Waterman. "A lot were doing it before the collapse, primarily in third world countries. Especially the biogas bit. Now damn near everyone's doing it."

Nick nodded. "And the heat from composting is pretty darn reliable. Day in and day out, no matter what the weather. Rain, snow, you name it."

"Snow?"

"Yup. A lot of people use them up north. Even covered in snow, these babies pump out a heck of a lot of heat. Lots of people even run air vent tubing through 'em to heat their houses. And it's all free, except for a few days of labor now and then to tear down or build the pile."

"Sounds fascinating."

"It is. In a lot of ways. Though not a lot of people enjoy the labor involved, but when it comes to heating your house or growing food, a lot of people get over it and adapt real quick."

"I bet." Reiff took one more look at the giant heap before dropping both hands to the oversized wheels of his chair. "I'd like to see your garden."

41

Waterman and Rachel were both surprised at Reiff's request as he tried to push the wheels of his chair forward until Waterman stepped behind to assist.

The garden was more extensive than they were expecting, perhaps seventy by fifty feet, and ringed by a square, waist-high wooden fence. Two different gates led in or out, with the four of them entering through the closest. Nick leading the way and holding it open for Reiff's wheelchair. An apprehensive Rachel followed them in and pulled it closed behind her.

Reiff looked around, quiet and amazed. It wasn't the size of the garden that fascinated him; it was the plants within it. Lining both sides of a narrow gravel path and filling almost every foot of available space was a plethora of plants and vegetables. In a variety of different shapes and colors, but what truly stood out, even from a distance, was their size.

Swiss chard, collard greens, and kale that appeared to be *two or three times* their normal size. Waist-high, at least. Past them were rows of green carrot tops nearly two feet in height, and beyond, he could see squash and cucumber plants that were absolutely enormous, with leaves larger than he'd ever seen.

Even Waterman was shocked. "Holy crap, Nick. What are you feeding these things, radiation?"

The old man grinned. "Don't feed them anything. It's the woodchips."

"From your compost pile?"

"Yep. What's left of them at the end of the year." Nick motioned to the ground where the base of all the plants was covered in a deep layer of partially composted woodchips on top of rich, dark black soil. "Ever hear of Paul Gautschi?"

"No."

"Another innovator. Everything you see here is free, renewable, and nontoxic."

Reiff continued forward on his own, pushing his giant wheels forward, fascinated at the scene around him. When the others followed, he finally removed his mask and peered up at the old man. "How?"

"You'd be surprised at what's possible when you just get out of the way." He then looked around his garden and shrugged. "It's the same principle as the Pain pile, but Gautschi used it differently. By again concentrating Mother Nature's natural process of organic decomposition." When Nick saw the others were not following, he explained. "It doesn't matter what you use, woodchips, mulch, leaves, whatever. Pain may have pointed it out, but Gautschi took it to a whole new level and showed that by creating very thick beds of mulch around your plants and trees, everything becomes supercharged. I never fashioned myself a farmer, but the collapse of the world changed things. Like everyone else, I started researching for ways to become more efficient and self-sustaining." He then smiled. "I may have gone a little overboard."

"You're saying *mulch* did this?"

Nick laughed. "Common everyday mulch. Turns out it's not just what you use but how you use it. Gautschi showed that over time, the natural breakdown of organic matter becomes damn powerful. Super concentrated, over the years, creating an extreme, nutrient-dense compost tea that slowly soaks into the ground. And after several years, that soil becomes so nutrient-dense that the plants grow like they're on steroids. But they're not." Nick shrugged. "My garden produces so much now that I have to give most of it away."

"To whom?"

"Anyone who will take it. I've shown other people how to do this, and it's catching on. We're all giving food away now."

"Wow," was all Rachel could say.

"The only tools I use are a shovel and a rake to move the woodchips and composted soil around. Well, and a wheelbarrow. Just have to have the tree guy drop off a few loads of chips every winter."

Reiff had never seen anything like it, and he continued to roll himself forward, fascinated. Wheels rolled over the packed gravel with a soft crunch until he came to a stop in front of a number of taller plants. Beans and peas, growing up and around giant stalks of corn for support. Swirling around and around like dark green snakes slithering up from the dense garden floor. Just like he had seen in his hallucination.

42

Douglas Kincaid's face was still and unmoving as a piece of stone. His eyes open and unblinking as he looked at Nora Lagner.

She had found him in his quarters, an expansive, luxurious apartment taking up a large portion of the complex's second floor below ground. A level of luxury and extravagance that predated the collapse, making the word "luxurious" the mother of all understatements. A level of excess that frankly could be seen throughout the entire complex, designed specifically to house The Nine in decadent comfort for decades, even if they were not all currently living there. But they would be eventually.

With Calacatta marble flooring, Kurdish and Persian rugs, a kitchen with every dish and utensil made of Waterford crystal, Lagner often wondered how many such items still existed in the world outside. Even the small table between them was fashioned entirely from extravagant Waterford.

She quietly waited for him to answer the question she'd asked. Wondering to herself if he even noticed the excessive opulence anymore. Perhaps after leaving and returning to the complex? Like his trip to her cabin, where he and his goons found her tied up. Did he notice then?

He traveled less often these days. She hadn't noticed how much less until recently, having been busy running the research lab. But now she noticed. And she thought she knew why; why he traveled less and less often. *He's afraid.*

He was getting closer. Nearing the upper limit of his body's livable age, even with all of his preventable treatments and medications, she could still see it behind the cold, intense eyes staring back at her.

Kincaid wasn't sure what to make of Lagner's new information. About the monkey she claimed to have tracked down, as well as the fate of the other test animals.

She was an intelligent woman and no doubt knew she had already been the subject of more than one discussion among the remaining members. Not only did she know the rest of the group personally, she also knew what kind of people they were. How ruthless and unwavering they could be at seeing the project through. Because, in the end, it came down to their *own* lives. Surely, she knew the others would sacrifice her without the slightest hesitation.

His eyes continued staring across the crystal table between them. There was little doubt she was trying to save her own skin by showing she was still a valuable member of the group. What Kincaid needed to know was just how much of her story was actually true.

"How sure are you?" he finally asked.

Lagner was eager in her response. "Pretty sure."

"*Pretty* sure?"

"This Reed woman had no reason to lie to me," she said, "or doubt who I claimed to be."

Kincaid did not reply, prompting Lagner to lean forward.

"Trust me, there was nothing in her voice to suggest she was hiding anything. She believed me."

Kincaid continued mulling it over. "And you think by having this monkey, it will give us the cure to what was ailing Reiff?"

"I do."

"We don't even know what Reiff's affliction was."

"Not yet." Lagner nodded. "But I think this Dr. Reed does. She saw at least *some* of the other animals before they died. So, she must also be aware of what killed them. And she would have certainly documented it, including the symptoms they witnessed. Possibly even taking samples. And that should be more than enough for us to learn what happened to John Reiff and find a solution. Just as Rachel Souza did."

"So, what do you propose?"

"I've already spoken to two of the remote experts we used at the lab. They were only involved in the specific research we were doing there. They don't know about the rest of our plan."

Kincaid continued mulling. It certainly seemed more an opportunity than a risk, especially with time running out. If they could not locate Reiff and Souza in time, they might still get what they needed.

"Even if we obtain the monkey *and* samples from the other animals, there would still be testing involved. Which takes time."

"True." Lagner nodded. "But remember, Rachel Souza figured it out

119

and developed an antidote in just nine months while in hiding and with minimal resources. We have far more resources available to us. What she did in nine months we may likely be able to do in just one."

Kincaid nodded. *One month,* he thought to himself, *one month is little risk indeed. Perhaps Lagner is worth keeping around after all.*

Nora breathed a silent sigh of relief when she saw Kincaid nod. She was getting through.

There was a sudden knock on the door outside. She raised her eyebrows questioningly, and Kincaid flicked a finger, motioning her to answer.

Obediently, she rose and moved to the door, well aware of who was on the other side.

When she opened it, DeSilva was wearing a cheeky grin and immediately entered without invitation.

From his chair, Kincaid watched the younger man approach. He was just forty-nine, strong, intelligent, and trustworthy, reminding Kincaid in many ways of his younger self, except for all the murders.

DeSilva and Lagner were considered "Tier Two." Two of The Nine who were decades younger than the oldest members, who were Tier One. After all, someone had to be alive to thaw and revive the first group. Once the Tier Ones were revived, they would, in turn, freeze and later revive the Tier Twos.

DeSilva stopped several feet in front of Kincaid and stated, "We have them."

The old man raised an eyebrow.

"Reiff and Waterman, and the others."

"Where?"

"At a small ranch near the eastern border. Owned by a man named Nick Bailey. He's part of the Network."

"Are you sure?"

DeSilva nodded. "Pretty sure."

Kincaid frowned and looked at Lagner sarcastically, who had used the same phrase, before finally turning back.

They were well aware of "the Network," as it was called. A nationwide underground of individuals calling themselves "patriots," covertly working to undermine the country's new government. A supposed dangerous and menacing group who, in reality, was little more than a hodgepodge of veterans and other ex-military. All involved in some watered-down version of nationalized guerilla warfare.

The Network did not frighten anyone, and certainly not Kincaid, which is why he found himself smirking at DeSilva's announcement. "Anyone else with them and this Bailey person?"

"I don't believe so."

"Good," acknowledged the old man, pulling out his cell phone. After a moment of searching, he pressed a button on his screen and dialed.

The call was answered by a deep-timbre voice. The same voice previously on Kincaid's video group call. The strong and ruthless man named Cannon was also a Tier Two. *Colonel* Lawrence Cannon.

"Yes?"

"We have them."

"Where?"

"Eastern Arizona," announced DeSilva. "I'll send you the coordinates."

"How many?"

"My guess about six. Reiff, Waterman, Souza, Yamada, Coleman, and the place's owner named Bailey."

"Any armaments?" asked Cannon.

DeSilva shook his head. "Not that I can see."

"I have two Black Hawks available. Send me the coordinates, and I'll get them in the air."

"Perfect." Kincaid ended the call and thought for a moment, peering back up at DeSilva. "Once you send him the location, you and Nora have a new assignment."

Surprised, DeSilva turned and looked at Lagner. "What assignment?"

"A visit to the zoo."

After they left, Kincaid remained in his chair. In less than thirty minutes, his fortune had changed entirely. Not only did they now have a location for Reiff but they also had a potential backup plan. He found himself musing at the sudden irony. Lagner may have just saved her own life while making Reiff and the others completely expendable.

43

Within minutes, two UH-60 Black Hawk helicopters were spinning up at Camp Navajo, with two four-man ranger teams sprinting across the open tarmac. Dressed in full gear and climbing up through the open doors of each chopper.

The rotors continued spinning, increasing in speed and whipping the air until each craft reached their necessary lift and rose into the air. Springing from the pavement like massive beasts of war. Climbing quickly and immediately angling toward the east while dozens of soldiers and airmen watched from the ground.

44

Back inside the house, Devin Waterman and Nick Bailey helped ease Reiff into an upholstered chair. Old and worn but comfortable, allowing his weary body to lean back with an audible groan.

Directly in front of him, Rachel lowered her medical bag onto the coffee table and withdrew the blood pressure cuff.

"Again?"

"Again," she retorted. "You might recall that you were a popsicle just a few days ago."

"I'm feeling better."

"Better than a *popsicle*?"

Reiff and Waterman glanced at each other, and the older of the two shrugged. "Kind of a low bar, I guess."

Reiff didn't respond, he instead sighed as Rachel wrapped the thick nylon strap around his arm. She waited for it to inflate and studied the readings once again. While she waited, she pulled out a small pulse ox sensor and slipped it onto the opposite index finger, plugging the other end of the tiny cord into the monitor.

"Now," she finally said, "you were saying?"

"Never mind."

She pulled the coffee table forward over the shaggy rug and sat facing him. "How else are you feeling?"

"Okay."

"What about pain?"

"Manageable."

"Good." She nodded. "Let me see you raise your legs."

With some effort, he raised his right foot and then slowly lowered it again. He did the same with his left, not reaching quite as high but close.

"How about your arms? Can you raise them above your shoulder?"

Reiff struggled, one at a time, lifting both hands almost straight above his head. "Can't keep it there very long."

"That's okay. Regaining strength will take time. For now, I'm more interested in how well your motor neurons are firing and their resulting contractions. Show me your hands and fingers."

Reiff opened and closed each hand. Then bent each finger one at a time.

Satisfied, Rachel straightened and relaxed, resting her hands upon her knees. "How are you feeling mentally? Are you tired?"

"Yeah."

"How's your concentration?"

"A little difficult."

"Did you sleep last night?"

"I think so."

Rachel turned to Waterman, standing a few feet away, but spoke to both of them. "At some point, we're going to need to get to a medical facility. If not a hospital, someplace we can get access to some specialists. There's only so much I can do myself. In the meantime," she said, looking at Reiff, "there's something you need to know. About being revived again."

"Okay."

She wore a cheerless expression when she spoke. "We should expect some . . . complications."

"Like what?"

"Like some neurological issues. Your difficulty concentrating could be a red flag."

"I'm just tired. I just need sleep."

Rachel seemed to deflate slightly. "That's kind of the problem."

"What do you mean?"

She sighed and thought for a moment. "The only test subjects I had to use were mice, and before you say anything, understand that mice *are* a lot more similar to us than you might think. Anyway, the reason we had to bring you back quickly was because of what I was seeing in the mice. The longer they remained frozen for a second time, the harder it was to revive them."

"Okay."

"They were also demonstrating some neurological irregularities and had trouble sleeping. Which may not sound serious, but over time it is."

"Fine," replied Reiff. "Just give me a sleeping pill."

Rachel nodded at that. "I can do that, but it will only work for so long.

Eventually, we'll need to get some neuroimaging to see if we're dealing with something more serious."

"Like what?"

She hesitated. "Like possible brain damage."

Waterman spoke up. "How much time do we have until we need to find a facility?"

"Ideally, as soon as possible."

Reiff tilted his head and stared back at her quizzically. "What did you do for the mice?"

Rachel hesitated, unsure of how to answer, when she was suddenly interrupted by Wayne Coleman bursting into the living room, followed immediately by Henry Yamada. "We have to go," he announced loudly. "Right now."

"What's wrong?" asked Waterman.

"I just got a tip. Two Black Hawks just left Camp Navajo a few minutes ago. And they're headed this way."

"Shit."

Coleman continued across the room toward Reiff. "Time's up. We're out of here in ten minutes!"

45

"They're moving!" exclaimed DeSilva, watching the monitor on his lap, connected via satellite, while Nora Lagner drove. Their F-150 truck crested the top of the canyon, and she pulled over in a giant cloud of billowing orange dust.

DeSilva retrieved his phone and dialed, reaching Cannon directly. "They're mobile," he said, putting the call on speaker and placing the phone on the truck's dashboard. Both hands returned to his keyboard, and he began typing.

Cannon's deep voice was unfazed. "When?"

"A few minutes ago. A Suburban just left the property. Headed northeast toward Springerville."

"How long until they get there?"

DeSilva shook his head as he scrolled the satellite map. "Not sure. Maybe twenty to thirty minutes. How far away are you?"

"Stand by."

Cannon's voice disappeared, leaving them in silence. When he returned, he said. "Choppers should intercept in less than ten minutes."

46

The road out was long and winding, snaking back and forth as it made its way toward civilization. Several elevation changes and accompanying switchbacks forced the Suburban to suddenly slow through each sharp turn before accelerating again.

It slowed to navigate a tight turn and, once again, immediately reaccelerated with a roar of its engine, blanketed by the loud rumbling of the dirt road beneath the spinning tires.

Even the relatively dense canopy of overhead tree branches could not conceal it, thanks to the long tail of reddish-brown dust billowing out like a beacon.

From the air, the long, meandering path of the dirt road was easy to see, including where it intersected an older paved road a mile or so ahead. But the truck would never reach it.

The helicopters split from their formation and separated. One slowed while the other accelerated, flying above the speeding Suburban as the vehicle desperately wound back and forth, slowing and accelerating, over and over, in a futile attempt to escape.

Less than a minute later, the Suburban came roaring up over a modest incline to find one of the Black Hawks settling onto the ground in front of it. Both wheels kissing the earthen surface on each side of the road's double tire paths. Behind the Suburban, the second chopper was doing the same, severing any possible escape route.

No sooner had they touched down than both ranger squads jumped from their respective aircraft and rushed forward. All M4 rifles poised and ready to unleash hellfire upon the now idling truck.

There was nowhere to go. The right side of the worn road was strewn with rocks and boulders, along with large trees and mounds of scrub brush. And on the left, a precipitous descent down a steep embankment.

There were no options but to wait and watch as the commandos approached in a wave of dark green. Step by step until surrounding the truck at a hundred feet out, where they waited for several long minutes for the dust to settle.

The dry dirt road left the windows caked with a thin film, making it difficult to see inside. Leaving no choice but for the team's leader to eventually step out of the line and close in.

Their orders were to capture the woman and one of the men—middle-aged with dark hair and most likely weak from a recent medical procedure. All other occupants were to be subdued and kept on-site until further instructions. And in the event of an armed fight, to kill them all.

The team leader stopped approximately ten feet from the truck with his rifle high on his shoulder and aimed directly at the driver's dust-covered window.

"Everyone exit the vehicle!" he shouted. "Now!"

There was no response.

"*I said exit the vehicle. Now!*"

The truck's engine abruptly turned off.

The soldiers all waited in silence, with weapons covering all four doors of the vehicle.

Still no movement.

The lead, a staff sergeant, pressed the M4 against his cheek and took aim when the driver's window began to roll down in one smooth motion, revealing a man sitting in the driver's seat.

"*Out of the vehicle!*"

The man inside the Suburban remained still. As motionless as a statue. Neither turning to look at the soldier or his weapon.

The sergeant eased a step closer, stopping and nearly firing when the rest of the windows began rolling down.

The remaining three windows disappeared below their sills together, revealing nothing but open emptiness behind the driver.

The others could be lying down, in wait. "I said, *get out.*"

The man in front, wearing a plaid shirt and cowboy hat, finally turned and looked at the soldier. "Why?"

The question briefly took the team leader by surprise. "Just get out!"

"What for?"

"Did you hear me?" the soldier replied, almost screaming. "*Get out.*"

The driver of the Suburban was older, perhaps in his seventies, and unfazed by the rifle pointed at him, almost as if he didn't see it. "What exactly do you fellas want?"

Again, the leader appeared momentarily perplexed. It was not what they were told to expect. "Just get out," he repeated. "Or I'll shoot."

"Shoot me for what?"

This time, the soldier did not respond. Instead, he took another step forward. "Who's with you?"

"No one."

"Bullshit! They're lying down."

"No one is lying down."

"Don't play games with me. Where's the woman and her patient?"

Unperturbed, the driver shook his head and pointed forward through his windshield. "I don't know what you're talking about. But you're in my way."

The sergeant glanced to his right at four rangers positioned behind the vehicle. He gave a slight nod, and two men rushed forward. Guns still high until reaching the vehicle and taking a cautious look through both back windows.

They shook their heads at the sergeant.

The sergeant eased closer. "Let me see your hands."

The old man complied, raising his hands and resting them both on the steering wheel. "Now let me see yours."

The younger man grinned. "You can already see them."

"Not really."

The sergeant's eyes moved back to his men, who were now taking a longer look inside the vehicle before relaxing their weapons.

The sergeant then lowered his own. "Who are you?"

"Who are *you*?"

"Don't screw with me, old man."

"I don't have to tell you anything."

The sergeant reached the driver's door and peered inside, past the driver at the empty passenger seat, then the empty rear seats. "Show me some ID."

"Who sent you?" asked the old man.

"Not your concern."

"No? Didn't you swear an oath, son?"

The sergeant's eyes returned to the driver.

"Well?"

The younger man then nodded. "I did."

"And to whom did you swear it?"

There was no response.

"Your oath was to the Constitution, was it not?"

"So what."

"I took the same oath," said the driver. "A long time ago. And the law is still the law."

The commando looked around. "The law doesn't matter out here. And this is the last time I'm going to ask, *Who are you?*"

"Of course, it matters," retorted the old man. "You swore your life to protect it. And that Constitution says we all have rights. One of those is the Fourth Amendment, and now even Arizona says I don't have to identify myself unless you can articulate a crime you think I have committed." He gave a hard stare at the soldier. "So go ahead, articulate. Otherwise . . . move your goddamn helicopter."

The team leader looked back at the man, looking him up and down before noting something stitched into the brim of his cowboy hat. Small letters that read A-R-M-Y.

A tiny, almost imperceptible grin began to spread across the soldier's lips.

47

What Nick Bailey and Devin Waterman knew, and even Coleman for that matter, was that there was a big difference between professional soldiers and highly paid mercenary thugs. Something called patriotism, which included, among other things, an extreme apprehension against firing upon one's own countrymen and fellow citizens.

An ethical line in the sand that had been drawn during the Great Collapse. When the secessions began, and states ultimately began turning against one another. But unlike the first Civil War, the second time around, the states did not resort to violence because, for all its mistakes, the nation seemed to have learned a valuable lesson. One that was put on display for the entire country to witness when the armies of Massachusetts and New Hampshire faced off in armed threat at their shared border. And where a captain by the name of Tierney refused to follow orders and attack his fellow countrymen. Establishing a military stance and precedent that would later sweep across the other states like a conflagration. As a reminder that it was the corrupt politicians and oligarchs who had set the stage for the world collapse. Who had not just put the proverbial kindling in place, but also lit the match. It was not the people. A reminder that it was the politicians who started the wars, but the people who had to fight them. Words from Tierney's own lips that would echo for years after the confrontation. Remembered by many, but not all.

Unfortunately, DeSilva was not one of them. Now staring down at his laptop in bewilderment. Trying to understand what was happening from the satellite feed on his screen.

From overhead, he could see the tiny figures of the ranger teams surrounding the suburban, with a few of them now at the side of the vehicle, still and unmoving. Until eventually, one appeared to step back and turn, moving past his men and continuing toward one of the helicopters, whose rotor blades were still spinning.

"What the hell?" he mumbled before looking at Lagner sitting behind the steering wheel.

"What's happening?"

He shook his head. "I don't know."

DeSilva began typing, switching to a slightly angled satellite view, but still could not understand.

"What are they doing?"

He shrugged. "Just standing around."

Lagner leaned over to have a look, and DeSilva began to say something when his phone rang, still on the dashboard. He snapped it up and looked at the number, then answered, "Yeah?"

From her seat, Lagner could hear the deep timbre of Colonel Cannon's voice. She watched as DeSilva stared forward, listening. The look on his face was one of genuine surprise.

"They're not there?"

The realization of his mistake was instant, as was the reaction. Prompting DeSilva to quickly put the call back on speaker and return to his keyboard.

Rapidly, he scrolled his satellite feed back to Bailey's ranch house and studied it. Nothing stood out. Everything appeared the same. No movement around the house at all.

But DeSilva wasn't fooled. He zoomed out and reexamined. Then zoomed again, and that's when he saw it. *Another dust trail.*

This one was fainter, obscured below a broader canopy of trees as the unseen vehicle fled deeper into the heart of Sitgreaves National Forest. Providing only glimpses of its outline as it briefly appeared through open patches of forest.

"It was a distraction," said DeSilva. "They're headed northwest, about five or six miles out. Get your birds back in the air!"

"What are they driving?"

DeSilva squinted but couldn't discern the make from the brief glimpses. "Not sure." He zoomed in, lost too much resolution, and quickly zoomed back out again. "Something light colored. I'm guessing an open-bed truck."

"Okay," replied Cannon's voice. "Stand by."

Onscreen, the target disappeared completely again under a long stretch of forest.

"Shit. I'm losing them," announced DeSilva. He scrolled up, searching ahead for more open patches of road where the vehicle might appear again.

Cannon returned. "They're on their way. Don't lose the truck."

DeSilva was gritting his teeth in frustration, scrolling back and forth in an attempt to locate them again. "Easier said than done. They're not on a main road where I can get a good bead on them."

"How fast are they traveling?"

"Not sure. Maybe twenty or thirty miles an hour." He shook his head. "Or forty."

"Jesus, which is it?"

"I'm doing the best I can!" shouted DeSilva, frantically searching.

Cannon was no longer listening. He had blinked off the line and returned once again after a long silence. "They're in the air. ETA, ten minutes."

"You better hurry. I don't see them at all now."

48

DeSilva was right. It was a truck. And it was white.

Old but in great condition, with Coleman at the wheel. In the passenger seat was Reiff with Rachel Souza sandwiched in between them. Trying with both arms to protect Reiff's frame from jostling too much while his own hands were trying to do the same, with one propped against the cracked and aging dash and the other tightly gripping the door handle.

Coleman was trying to keep the shaking to a minimum, not just for Reiff but for Waterman and Yamada, who were both behind them in the truck's open bed with little to hold on to. At times, bouncing uncontrollably and struggling to keep themselves from flying out.

When Coleman finally slowed to a stop under a thick section of canopy, the thumping of helicopters could be heard approaching.

Coleman peered through the dirty windshield as he gradually pressed on the gas again. Studying the GPS coordinates on the tiny screen, he repeatedly checked both sides of the gravel road. Left, then right, then left again. Continuing to search until Waterman banged on the top of the cab. Coleman abruptly stopped again and looked past Rachel and Reiff through the right-hand window.

Waterman was already up and over the side of the truck by the time Coleman threw it into park and flung his own door open, jumping out and quickly circling the hood.

He came to a stop next to Waterman and studied the side of the empty road with him. The easement was completely obscured by tall trees and thick green brush.

Next to a tree trunk stood a person. And next to him, another appeared. Two strangers dressed in camouflage fatigues and holding rifles across their chests.

One of the men stepped out from the bush. "You Waterman?"

Devin Waterman nodded. "Yep. You Ramirez?"

The camouflaged man in front nodded and studied the truck behind them. Noting first Yamada in the bed, and then the figures inside the cab.

The helicopters were getting closer.

"We don't have a lot of time. Let's get this done." Both men lowered their rifles and made a beeline for the passenger door as Waterman pulled it open to reveal John and Rachel.

The two men in fatigues were younger, and they moved efficiently. Carefully extracting Reiff before lifting each of his arms up and over their broad shoulders. Rachel followed while Henry Yamada jumped down behind them.

"Hussle!" growled one of the men, and they took off in a rapid walk back the way they came, into the thick brush while supporting Reiff, whose legs were struggling to keep up.

Waterman motioned Rachel and Henry ahead and then turned to face Coleman. "You okay?"

His friend nodded. "Yup."

Waterman slapped him on the shoulder and moved to the bed of the truck, where he retrieved his two duffle bags. He swung them over each shoulder and headed into the brush after the others.

Without another word, Coleman returned to the driver's side of the truck and climbed in. Closing his door with a bang and dropping it into drive.

49

The old truck was moving faster now and leaving a much larger dust trail behind it. Billowing up and out until reaching the tops of the trees and beyond. A veritable smoke signal.

Together, the Black Hawk pilots slowed and maintained their course over the rising cloud, waiting for a visual on the target, and after a few miles, were rewarded with an open glade in the trees.

But the vehicle did not appear.

Both helicopters reduced their altitude and circled the clearing, searching. Seeing nothing until they continued lower, below the tree line and less than a hundred feet above the open patch of grass and dirt.

They could see the truck. Facing them as though waiting for something.

Both aircraft continued their descent until easing onto the ground, where the rangers jumped out again from the choppers. This time, collapsing onto the ground and coming up on their stomachs and elbows. Guns up and aimed at the waiting truck.

They scanned through their scopes, across the ground, up the truck's dingy hood, and through the front windshield.

It was empty.

A few miles away, the two men carrying Reiff continued through heavy foliage, trailed by Rachel Souza, Henry Yamada, and then Devin Waterman. All carefully winding in and out of the trees.

After several minutes, they came upon a heavily shaded area where another 4 × 4 truck was waiting. Large and powerful, and painted entirely in camouflage.

They loaded Reiff into the King Cab's back seat, flanked by Rachel and Henry, while Waterman and one of the other two men climbed into the truck's bed. Both armed and searching the tree line.

The driver slid behind the wheel and slammed the door shut behind him. He did not turn on the engine. Instead, they remained quiet and still, listening to the sounds and directions of the helicopters.

50

Kincaid was absolutely beside himself. Incensed at hearing they'd lost Reiff. Not just Reiff, *all* of them! *Are Cannon's rangers completely incompetent? How in the hell could they lose them all, with helicopters?* He paced back and forth, fuming. *Or was it DeSilva who had screwed up? Good God, I am surrounded by imbeciles!*

His anger was so intense he could barely speak. Struggling to even communicate with Lagner over the phone. *Christ, am I the only competent one?*

Kincaid tried to calm himself, taking several deep breaths and attempting to focus on Nora Lagner's words. Something about the zoo. And the monkey.

He needed to get himself under control. To reassess. And found himself nodding reflexively. "Fine," he managed. "Whatever. Just go."

His hands were shaking in frustration when he hung up and dropped the phone onto the table with a loud clatter. He could not lose control. Not now.

The drive to Phoenix took almost two hours, and they arrived a little before sunset as the distant horizon readied itself for another glowing evening sky. Reminding Nora Lagner of the planet's silent ambivalence of what went on across its billion-year-old surface.

The new zoo, or better described as "what was left of the original zoo," maintained its old facade and entrance: a brown earthen tone with a slatted overhead planked roof. Below which, Dr. Samantha Reed stood waiting for them, sporting short brown hair and dressed in the staff's familiar zebra-striped vest.

Lagner parked the truck at the empty curb and exited with DeSilva. Both smiling and graciously shaking the doctor's hand, when Lagner quickly reassumed her fake identity of Peggy Denton.

"Thank you so much for meeting with us," she said. "Especially on such short notice."

Their host smiled and welcomed them through the entrance. "You're very welcome. I'm sorry Rachel couldn't join you."

"So are we." Lagner nodded. "She should be back in a couple months."

"What is she working on?" Reed asked.

"She's trying to get some funding together for a new research center on the East Coast." It was as safe an explanation as Lagner could contrive. All researchers needed funding, and a "new" research center was something any philanthropic doctor could get behind.

"That's wonderful. What sort of research?"

Lagner improvised again. "Primate virology."

Dr. Reed nodded approvingly as she led them inside the entrance and along a well-manicured walking path in the direction of several small administrative buildings. "Excellent. We could use more people working on that." They passed a few wandering visitors and continued toward the largest of the structures, where Samantha Reed reached a set of painted steel double doors and promptly pulled one open.

Holding it open for the others, she led them down a long, bright hallway and into a larger open room with several smaller doors along three of its walls. Lagner and DeSilva presumed them to be smaller examination or treatment rooms.

"One of my trainers is getting the capuchin now and will bring him here so you can have a look at him." She glanced at a clock on the wall and motioned toward another hallway. "We have a few minutes. Why don't we head to my office, and I can make you a copy of his latest workup?"

Lagner smiled. "Sounds great." DeSilva also smiled politely but said nothing, following the women.

"I'm sorry we didn't have things ready when you got here," said Reed as she led them through the next hallway and into an adjoining building. "We have a few people out today, and things are a little frantic."

"Not at all. That's totally understandable."

They entered the next building to find the hall widened. The smell of animals largely disappeared, and their new surroundings took on the look of an office or corporate setting. Several office doors lined the wider hallway, along with an oversized bulletin board that was covered in different memos and announcements.

They turned and entered Dr. Reed's office where she welcomed them to take a seat before easing the door closed behind her. Rounding her desk, she asked, "What sorts of things did you want to look at Dallas for?"

For this, Lagner was ready. "Just any lingering signs that he might still be experiencing similar symptoms."

"You mean like the other animals."

"Correct."

Reed nodded and sat down. Swiveling in her seat, she used her computer to search for the capuchin's information. "I understand. Dr. Souza calls periodically to check the same thing, but it's nice you were able to drop by in person this time."

Behind the woman, Lagner and DeSilva glanced at each other.

"Were there any specific signs you wanted to check for?"

Lagner shook her head. "Just the usual. It's just a courtesy call."

Still staring at her computer and away from her visitors, Samantha Reed blinked. She nodded without turning around and brought up the animal's history. "Let me just print this up," she said.

"Can we get the whole history?" asked Lagner.

Samantha Reed blinked again. "Of course, no problem."

"Thank you."

With her back still to Lagner and DeSilva, the doctor selected the option to print a full report and clicked her mouse. She then turned back around as the nearby printer came to life and made a familiar whirring sound.

"We should have him ready in a few minutes. Did you want to start with a mutagenicity test?"

Lagner stared at Reed from her chair, slowly, gradually nodding. Attempting to hide her uncertainty. "Sure," she replied. "That would be great."

The doctor did not nod with her. Instead, Samantha Reed continued staring over her desk without any response at all. Until after an awkward silence, she asked, "How long have you been working with Dr. Souza?"

Lagner's face was expressionless. "Several months."

Reed grinned politely. "Very nice. In what capacity?"

Nora Lagner suddenly felt a spike in adrenaline.

From the other side of the desk, Samantha Reed noticed a slight shift in Peggy Denton's disposition. She leaned forward onto her desk, studying the woman.

Mutagenicity was not a common medical test or procedure. It was a specific test used to measure cancer mutation rates for animals subjected to chemical testing. Nothing a zoo would ever do.

"You look familiar," she mused. "Where did you go to school?"

Lagner stammered, but only momentarily.

"UC Davis," she replied. It took her a second to recall where Rachel Souza had graduated.

Something was wrong. Dr. Reed seemed doubtful. Had she said something to tip her off?

Whatever the reason for Reed's change in demeanor, it was noticeable. So much that DeSilva suddenly spoke up. "Are those your sons?"

Reed turned to him and then followed his gaze to a set of silver-framed pictures on her desk. She acknowledged, "Yes. Those are my sons."

DeSilva grinned. "Nice looking boys."

"Yes, they are," responded Reed proudly.

"How old?"

There was a slight hesitation in her voice. "Uh, twelve and ten."

"Very nice," said DeSilva. "Do they come here a lot?"

The doctor bobbed her head. "Somewhat."

"I bet they're proud of their mom."

Samantha Reed's eyes were apprehensive. "I suspect so."

"I'm sure they are," said DeSilva. His face suddenly grew serious and dark. "How do you think they would feel if they never saw you again?"

51

Samantha Reed's face suddenly froze.

"What?"

DeSilva's expression had turned from pleasant to menacing in less than a second. He checked the closed door behind them and reached back to withdraw a black handgun from his waistband.

Instantly, Reed gasped and stopped breathing.

Lagner, however, was relieved.

DeSilva remained calm, eerily calm. Bringing the gun forward and placing it on the desk in front of him, with his hand remaining on top.

"Where's your purse?" he asked.

Reed could barely move. She continued blinking fearfully at the gun before her.

"I said . . . *where* is your purse?"

Her eyes shifted. Staring up at DeSilva, incomprehensively at first, until his words finally registered. Her head turned and glanced at the floor.

"Get it," instructed DeSilva.

Confused and shaking, Reed reached down and pulled her sizeable brown purse up and onto the surface of the desk.

"Get your wallet out."

She complied.

"Give me your driver's license."

With trembling fingers, Reed pulled it from her wallet and handed it to him.

DeSilva studied the small card for a long moment before handing it back. "Now we know where you and your family live." He stared at the doctor coldly. "I assume you want them to all wake up tomorrow."

Reed stopped breathing again, slowly nodding her head up and down.

"Then do exactly as we tell you."

The woman's eyes looked to Lagner, who was staring back with zero emotion.

"You said Rachel Souza calls you."

Reed nodded.

"How often?"

"E-every month or so."

"Why?"

Reed could barely speak. "T-to check . . . on the capuchin."

"To check for what?"

The doctor's eyes moved to Lagner's again. "For changes or symptoms. Just like you are."

"Do you have her phone number?"

Reed hesitated but again nodded.

"Good," replied DeSilva. "Get it."

52

Outside the zoo's entrance, Lagner, DeSilva, and Dr. Reed all stood together, watching as the large metal cage was loaded into the back of the pickup truck.

Reed's two assistants said nothing as they set the cage onto the tailgate and carefully slid it forward to the front of the open bed. Together, they crawled back down, where one of them raised the tailgate and pushed it shut with an audible clang.

They had no idea why Reed had abruptly changed her instructions, or why the monkey had to be sedated, or who these two people even were, but it didn't matter. It wasn't really any of their business, and therefore, they simply did what they were told: Bring out the monkey and return back inside.

Nora Lagner, gripping a thick folder filled with printouts and a thumb drive in her opposite hand, turned to watch the men leave. When they were gone, she looked to DeSilva, who in turn spoke to Dr. Reed, who was still trembling beneath her zebra-striped vest.

DeSilva leaned in and spoke in a calm but deep tone. "Remember what we talked about."

Dr. Reed nodded quietly.

With that, the two walked to their truck and climbed in, shutting each of their doors without so much as looking back. They pulled away, leaving Samantha Reed standing where she was. Terrified, watching until the truck disappeared from the parking lot.

"Think she'll keep quiet?"

DeSilva was already on his laptop. "Yes." He reached for the folder of papers on the seat between them and flipped it open. Snatching the first page and holding it up. Carefully entering the handwritten ten-digit phone number into his computer.

"You think it's going to work?"

"I hope so." DeSilva nodded. "Even if Rachel Souza *is* using a burner phone, she's been using the same one for a long time. Which means we can track it."

"What if it's turned off?"

"It needs to be on for an exact location," he answered, "but even if it's not, we can still find out which towers it's been connecting to for the last year. Eventually she'll turn it on."

"What if Reed tries to warn her?"

"Doesn't matter. We don't need a phone call. We just need the phone to be powered up. Even if the doctor tried to warn her, which I doubt she would be dumb enough to do, we should still be able to find Souza."

"Well, if she calls Reed every couple weeks, we shouldn't have to wait long."

"Precisely. Especially since she hasn't called lately." DeSilva turned to Lagner with a dark grin. "And that means she's due."

53

The camouflage truck carrying Reiff and the others arrived at its destination just after sunset, in central Arizona, north of a small area called Ash Fork, where a scattering of lights could be seen nestled between a shadowed patch of low-lying hills.

The main entrance was in the form of an oversized metal gate, guarded by two armed men, with the rest of the heavily barbed fence stretching off in opposite directions.

There was still enough sunlight to see dozens of structures scattered over several acres of land and what Rachel guessed spread out into even more.

The place looked like some kind of compound. Housing at least several dozen people from the looks of the buildings. All appearing well-built and well maintained with cars and trucks parked beside each one.

What stood out to Rachel when exiting the truck was what appeared to be a massive garden set back on the far end of the compound, along with a small playground, and in front of that, dozens of open picnic tables that surrounded a common area, complete with firepits and benches.

She examined several of the homes. Each had porch lights with more illumination coming from inside, from what she guessed were living room or kitchen windows. What also caught her attention were the numerous familiar mounds of woodchips like she had seen at Nick's. Positioned next to or behind each individual dwelling.

Outside, bright flames illuminated the common area where many were sitting and watching as their camouflage truck drove by. While several children ran alongside next to them trying to get a glimpse of who it was.

"Where are we?" asked Rachel as she stared through her side window at the scampering kids.

There was no answer from the driver. Instead, his attention remained forward, until reaching a modest-sized house near the back of the open area before bringing the truck to a stop.

Why is no one else asking questions? She opened the door and slid off the seat down onto a hard dirt ground. She watched Devin and their other rescuer climb over the side of the truck bed and move forward, helping Reiff down before once again throwing his arms over their shoulders.

The driver strode around the front of the vehicle and met them, glancing at a weakened Reiff.

"We won't be able to stay long," said Waterman. "They'll eventually find us here."

The driver, perhaps in his mid-thirties, with a military-style haircut, grinned back at him in the dying light. "Let them. We can defend ourselves."

"But for how long?"

The man's grin widened into a cocky smile. "Till my kids are grown."

"Let's hope it doesn't come to that." Waterman followed the other man's lead, supporting Reiff and heading into the house and a front door that was now open with two women waiting inside for them. The structure appeared modern and prefabricated. Clean and well kept. No doubt like the others.

Inside was a small, plain living room, sparsely decorated, and an even smaller but functional kitchen. Beyond that was a hallway leading back to what looked like a bathroom and a couple bedrooms.

The driver followed them in and watched as Reiff was lowered onto a clean, worn, covered love seat. "You're safe here."

He looked up at the man appreciatively. "I wish there was something I could do to repay you."

The man gave Reiff a cheeky look. "Who said there wasn't?"

Waterman disappeared outside with both men, leaving the other three together in the living room. Henry Yamada was the first to investigate the kitchen, opening the modest refrigerator and checking the cabinets. "There's some food here."

Rachel was holding Reiff's hand and checking his pulse. "Yeah?"

"Not a lot, but it's something."

"Great, why don't you whip us up something to eat?"

Yamada twisted and looked at her with surprise. "*Me?*"

Rachel was digging through her medical bag. "Unless you want to give John his shots."

"Uh."

She paused and stared at Yamada. "I thought you were domesticated?"

"Well, that's kind of debatable."

"You can't cook?"

"I can cook some things," replied Yamada sarcastically. "But I don't see any cereal here."

She sighed before turning back to Reiff. "How are you feeling?"

Reiff winked. "Just another day at the office."

The man looked exhausted. Like he'd been dragged behind a car for the last few days. Just without the scrapes and bruises to go with it. His eyes looked bloodshot, and his body sagged into the couch. It was as if just trying to stay alive wasn't hard enough.

God, what had she done to him? How much more could this man take? She had been so focused on reviving Reiff that she hadn't considered what he would be forced to endure as a result, physically and mentally.

Rachel took his hand and knelt in front of him. "What can I do for you, John?"

He shook his head slowly. "I just need some rest."

She displayed a sympathetic frown and rose back to her feet. She turned and disappeared down the hall and returned with a pillow from one of the beds. She then laid it at one end of the couch and helped ease him down onto it before returning to her bag. "Let me give you something that will help you sleep."

It was all she could do at this point. He was clearly already having trouble sleeping on his own. She could help him medically for a while, but his system would eventually adapt until not even that worked. And how long would that be?

Reiff stared lazily up from the pillow. "No more needles."

She acknowledged and rummaged momentarily to withdraw a small bottle, which she then popped open, and shook two pills into her palm. She motioned for Yamada to fetch a glass of water.

"We don't know how ready your digestive system is, but we don't have a lot of choice. Hopefully, with enough water, it can handle this."

Reiff nodded and twisted his head up, taking the pills and then a few swallows of water from Henry's glass. After a pause, he drank more. Then again, until the glass was empty.

Within ten minutes, he was out.

54

"How do you think he's doing?"

Rachel leaned out one of the bedroom doors to make sure Reiff was still asleep on the couch before leaning back in. "I don't know," she whispered. "It's hard to tell. Last time, we had him in the lab, resting the entire time. Not running from place to place like some animal."

"That's not our fault."

"I know it's not. But it's not his either."

Yamada's voice was somber. "The poor guy must feel like a piece of meat. Like a thankless prize in some sick game. I don't think these people are ever going to stop."

Rachel folded her arms and eased back against the bedroom wall.

"What do we do now?" he asked.

All she could do was shake her head. "I can't lose him, Henry. I can't."

"I know."

"My biggest fear is that no matter what I do, it won't be enough."

"Don't talk like that, Rach."

"Like what? Truthful?"

"I mean fatalistically."

She turned away, rolling her eyes up toward the ceiling. "We're in uncharted territory. Every time we find a solution, a new problem arises. And each solution takes time. A long time. Too long." She shook again. "He could die before we figure this all out."

"We'll get him somewhere. To a hospital or a facility, where they can help."

Right, she thought. *An expert. An expert on what exactly? Cryonic reanimation? Yeah, I'm sure there's a lot of people out there with those credentials.*

"At least he's alive right now," continued Yamada, "so there *has* to be a way we can help him. Some treatment that keeps him stable until we can figure out what to do next."

Her eyes dropped and studied him. Staring and then sighing. "I used to be the optimistic one," she mused.

It was warm. And quiet.

He was standing in a marble-floored entryway of what appeared to be a mansion, wearing a thick gray bathrobe. With stairs on each side winding up to a second story.

He looked around but found no door. Just a rotunda lined entirely with giant bookshelves. Enormous wooden shelves that, for some reason stood completely empty.

And then he heard noise.

Not just noise. A voice. Loud and speaking in the distance.

One of the bookshelves began to change, bending and twisting until turning into a hallway, and he found himself cautiously stepping forward. Walking smoothly toward and then through it until reaching a set of floor-to-ceiling glass doors.

Sliding them open revealed an expansive patio and beyond that, a sizable pool. With crystal-clear water sparkling under the bright sunlight.

The voice was now gone. Echoing as it faded into nothingness. In the pool were a dozen or so gray bathrobes just like his, all floating silently in the water's gentle ripples. Below the surface, the bottom of the pool appeared to be made of metal. A dull gray metal with a strange, ribbed design.

Beyond the pool stretched several acres of beautifully manicured grounds. Like a sea of green grass and bushes dotted with thousands of different-colored flowers for as far as he could see. All surrounded by tall green trees, swaying in the light breeze.

The place looked like some kind of palatial estate. Beautiful and opulent, like a royal palace. The only thing out of place was the deep thumping sound in the distance.

55

It was a little after 4 A.M. when Rachel awoke in a dark room ensconced in complete silence. A fitful sleep, tossing and turning, while her mind roiled in a constant state of worry. Drifting off only for short sporadic dozes.

There was something within the web of her subconscious that her brain could not let go of. Something that felt important.

She closed her eyes and tried not to let it go. Concentrating, focusing, until she finally caught a glimpse of what her mind was searching to find.

It was not a dream. It was a memory.

A distant, ever-so-faint connection that her mind, for some reason, had finally pushed to the surface. A memory of a specific moment in time . . . back in her lab.

It was of John Reiff, standing in her lab, just a couple weeks after being revived the first time. He was standing in the middle of the lab, examining it. Before moving to the far side to observe her animals. Their *test subjects*.

She hated thinking of them that way. But it's what they were. Surviving test subjects that had been used to verify the Machine was going to work. Animals that they, that Rachel, continued studying and caring for long after bringing them back.

She wasn't surprised she bonded with them. They were animals, after all. Small, innocent animals who, like tiny children, had no idea what was happening to them. Which was what eventually caused such an emotional dilemma for Rachel.

But that wasn't the memory she was now experiencing. It was *Reiff* when he saw her lab for the first time.

He was examining the animals in their cages. One by one. The mice.

Then the rabbits and pig. Then the dog, Bella. Followed by Dallas, the capuchin.

She closed her eyes and focused on the image, allowing it to crystallize in her mind's eye. *John Reiff staring at Dallas. And Dallas staring back at him.*

There was a moment there, she now remembered. When their eyes seemed to lock on one another. A moment she had since forgotten but now had come back to her. The two of them looking at one another for a long moment. An odd pause that had only briefly registered with Rachel before.

All the other animals had died, except for the capuchin, from the strange, unexplainable condition. Continually losing heat until their cells and organs eventually slowed to a stop.

Dallas was the only animal who survived it. And it was *his* genes that Rachel used to engineer a similar protection for Reiff. Which now, all of a sudden, had Rachel wondering if there was something else. Another biological connection between Dallas and Reiff that she didn't know about, that she'd missed.

Was it possible? Some other strange relationship between the two that she'd missed, and more importantly, that she might still be able to use to help Reiff?

At first, the return of that memory felt almost esoteric in its connection, but now, as she thought more and more about it, the possibility seemed to be growing stronger. So much so that she could sense the feeling of genuine excitement bubbling below it. As though she had stumbled upon something important. Something crucial. Or was it just the feeling of hope?

No, there was something there. The excitement now had Rachel sitting upright in her bed, staring forward in the darkness. Blinking as she thought it through.

She threw off the covers and jumped to her feet, searching for her bag. When she found it, she fished around inside until her hand found the object she was looking for. She pulled out the burner phone and turned it around, flipping it open. And then turned it on.

Maybe hope was enough.

56

The sun was up within a couple hours, punctuated by noises outside of people moving about and occasional giggles from running children.

Rachel found Reiff on the couch where she left him. Sitting up and watching her as she approached from her bedroom.

"How are you?" she asked in a hushed tone.

"Okay." He turned his head and motioned to a wheelchair that had been delivered sometime during the night. "Can you bring that a little closer?"

She did so and turned it around, lining it side by side with the couch. Carefully and somewhat awkwardly, she helped Reiff into it.

Once settled, he put his hands on each wheel and pushed himself forward. "Been waiting to use the restroom."

"Oh, sorry. Do you . . . need help?"

"Uh, no."

When he was back, he wheeled himself through the living room and stopped in front of a decent-sized kitchen window, where he peered outside out at the activity.

"How did you sleep?"

"I slept okay."

"Still having visions?" she asked.

"To be honest," Reiff said, looking away from the window, "I'm not sure what the hell I'm having."

"What do you mean?"

"Sometimes I don't know what's real and what's not inside my head."

Rachel's heart sank. It was getting worse. She decided to change the subject.

"How about your stomach?"

"It's not bad."

"Good enough to try eating something?"

He raised an eyebrow. "I thought that wasn't allowed."

"Your system seems to be doing relatively well." She moved away from the window and rounded a small counter into the kitchen and opened the refrigerator. "We have a little fruit."

Reiff remembered fruit was the first thing they fed him before and its high water content. "Pre-digestible, right?"

Rachel grinned as she pulled out a melon and looked for a knife. "You remember."

His attention returned to the window as two men strode past, pulling a wagon full of tools and supplies. "These people aren't safe."

Rachel began cutting. "Hopefully, we won't be here long."

"Who *exactly* are we running from?"

"We're not sure." She shrugged. "We have an idea who they are, but we don't know their names. It's the group who was secretly behind what we were doing at the lab."

"How many?"

"We're not positive, but based on what Lagner told Devin, we think anywhere from eight to fifteen. He and Henry are trying to find out. Whoever it is, they're very good at staying hidden." Rachel approached the table with a few slices of cantaloupe. "Here, let's give this a try."

Reiff picked one up and took a bite.

"Taste okay?"

He gave a slow nod. "And I thought the fruit last time was good."

Rachel laughed. "Starvation tends to do that. Just start with a little. Let's see how it goes."

Reiff acknowledged and finished the piece, then took a break. "So, what do these people want, exactly?"

She stared at him stoically through a warm beam of light from the window. "You."

"Why?"

"Our best guess is they want to freeze themselves, but they want to make sure they can wake up again, at least safely."

"So what, they just want to make sure 'I'm okay'?"

"As strange as it sounds, yes. Or at least that's probably what it was in the beginning. By now, they must know about you being refrozen and that something went wrong the first time around."

"So now they want what?"

Rachel sighed. "I presume they want to know *why* you had to refreeze. They must be pretty afraid of doing it themselves now."

"So, they want to dissect me."

"More or less."

"Wonderful. I've gone from being a popsicle to a frog."

"That's just our guess." Rachel picked up her own piece of cantaloupe and winked. "But we kind of don't want that to happen, which is why we're on the run."

Reiff turned in the wheelchair to face her. "Why are you doing this?"

"Doing what?"

"You and Henry."

"What do you mean?"

"You don't need this," said Reiff matter-of-factly. "Either one of you. You could have just walked away and put this all behind you."

Caught by surprise, Rachel stared at Reiff for a long time. "That's a hell of a thing to say."

"It's just a fact. So why didn't you?"

Rachel scowled at him before finally replying. "I can't speak for Henry, but I can't just walk away."

"Why not?"

Her face softened as Rachel struggled with something behind her eyes. "Because," she said, "I *did* this to you."

He watched the emotions rise in her. Revealing signs of an emotional battle within her. Reiff could tell when someone was lying and when they weren't. Their voice, their movements, their behavior. After all this time, the guilt was still plaguing her.

He leaned forward and placed his hand on top of hers. "This is not your fault."

Rachel could feel herself trembling. With a frown, she dropped her other hand on top of his.

His hand felt warm and strong. Comforting. And she stared down at their hands without speaking, surprised to find her finger gently moving back and forth over his thumb. Nervously, she looked up to find Reiff peering at her.

She suddenly pulled back when she heard Yamada enter the room behind her.

"I got to tell you, that bed wasn't half bad," he announced, stopping in front of them at the table. He looked Reiff over and nodded his head. "How are you doing?"

"Good. How about you?"

"No, I mean like, how are you *doing*?"

An amused smile spread across Reiff's whiskered jawline. "I'm hanging in there."

Yamada stole a piece of fruit off the plate and moved behind Rachel, peering out the window. "This is a cool place."

"We're not staying long," said Reiff.

"Why not?"

He motioned outside. "Because we're endangering all of them."

Yamada stammered, "But . . . we're in the middle of nowhere. Maybe we lost the bad guys."

"Do you really think that?"

Their computer expert gave a depressed sigh and fell into one of the chairs at the table. "Fine. What's the plan?"

"Don't know yet. Where's Waterman?"

The younger man glanced around the room and then out the window. "Outside, over there. Talking to the guys from last night."

Reiff began wheeling himself back from the table when he suddenly stopped. Rachel and Henry both turned to him expectantly. It took only a few seconds for them to hear what Reiff already had. A deep thumping sound in the distance.

57

There was yelling outside, and women and children began running past their window moments before the distant thumping became thunderous and roared overhead.

A helicopter.

Men were shouting to each other, and dozens passed, running in the opposite direction of the women and children, toward the compound's entrance and carrying guns.

Reiff was the first to the door, yanking it open and rolling himself forward. Overhead, he could see the chopper come into full view as it swung into a broad turn over the far edge of the property.

This one was not a Black Hawk. It was an AH-64 Apache. An attack helicopter.

Reiff felt a jolt and was immediately wheeled back inside by Rachel.

"What the hell are you doing?"

"You're not going out there!" she cried and jumped in front of him to bar his way. She looked at Yamada. "Henry, help me!"

The younger man paused apprehensively before stepping in to grab Reiff's wheelchair by the back handles.

Reiff leveled his eyes at her. "Get out of my way."

Through the commotion and shouting outside, she shook her head firmly. "Don't you get it? We're trying to protect you!"

"I know that."

"These people will not stop until they get what they want, John. Which is you!"

Reiff's voice grew stern. "Rachel, listen to me—"

"No, you listen to me! I am *not* going to let them have you! We have fought too hard—"

"Rachel."

She reached behind herself and pushed the door closed.

Reiff lowered his voice. "Rachel."

She didn't answer. Her panicked eyes were already searching for an escape for them. Reiff could see it.

"There's no way out of this," he said calmly.

"No!" She shook her head defiantly. "No!" She then turned to Yamada, who could only shrug.

"You're right. You said it yourself," replied Reiff. "They want me, and they're not going to stop. All that's going to happen is a lot of innocent people are going to get hurt."

She stared at him, with the raucous yelling mixed with the helicopter's powerful thumping in the background. And Reiff's words echoing in her head. *They want him, and they aren't going to stop.*

They want him.

She blinked, staring into Reiff's eyes as if frozen.

They want him.

She continued blinking. *Him. They want* him. For a moment, Rachel could feel everything around her slow.

No, they didn't.

They didn't want Reiff. He was just the vessel. The end result. What they really wanted, what they really needed . . . was the answer.

What they needed to know . . . was how she saved Reiff from an inevitable death. They didn't need Reiff for that. They needed her.

Another blink, still staring down at Reiff. Who was in turn staring up at her with a questioning look on his face. Watching as her eyes slowly rose up to meet Henry Yamada's.

"Henry."

"Yeah?"

"You've been watching. You know what he needs."

"What?"

"You know what shots he needs, and when."

Yamada frowned. "What are you talking about?"

Her eyes became almost glassy. "Promise me something, Henry? Promise me you will not let John out of this room. And that you'll get him to a hospital."

"What?"

Reiff's eyes widened. "What?!" He immediately tried to roll forward but couldn't. Not with her full weight leaning against his chair and Yamada still holding it from the back. "Henry, let me go!" he shouted.

Rachel continued pushing against the chair, with her eyes still on Yamada. "It's the only way, Henry. Promise me!"

Before he could reply, Rachel moved all at once. Lowering her body and with all her might, grabbing one side of the wheelchair and lifting it high into the air, toppling the wheelchair over on its side, taking Reiff with it and spilling him to the floor.

Immediately, she turned for the door, pulling it open and slamming it closed behind her.

Outside, the chaos had calmed somewhat. She could see the entrance of the property in the distance, with dozens of men lining the fence and its giant steel gate partially open.

On the opposite side were two black SUVs and several darkly dressed men surrounding them. And perhaps a hundred feet behind them, hovering overhead, was a frightening-looking helicopter with a machine gun below its fuselage and multiple missiles all pointing forward.

Rachel was in a sprint, running over the hard ground as fast as she could toward the entrance. Listening to nothing behind her.

About twenty yards from the gate, she spotted Waterman. Or rather Waterman spotted her, running toward him. He rushed forward and stopped her with his powerful hands on each arm.

"Rachel, what are you doing?"

She was gasping. "Something's wrong with John!" she cried frantically. "We need your help, hurry!"

He looked past her and back at the small house. The front door was closed, but looked like it was shaking. As if trying to open.

"Hurry!" Rachel screamed at him. She pointed toward the house. "*Hurry!*"

Instantly, Waterman broke into a run, headed back the way she came. Leaving Rachel behind.

He would never have dreamed that she would turn and run directly for the open gate.

By the time he reached the house, it was too late. The door was pulled open and the figure of John Reiff appeared snaking outside on his stomach. He spotted Waterman and immediately tried to wave him off, pointing back behind him.

A confused Waterman stopped and stared, then whirled around. But Rachel was already gone.

58

It all happened in a blur. By the time Rachel's adrenaline began to fade, she was in the back of one of the SUVs, pinned between two large men with two more in the front, barreling down a dirt road with the second vehicle close behind.

It was only a few minutes before the driver turned from the main road onto a path amounting to little more than two worn tire tracks. Over giant dips and holes that rocked them all from side to side before cresting a small barren hilltop, flattened on top where another helicopter was waiting. This one did not look military. It looked private. Large and white with thick blue stripes, and its main rotor spinning within a large cloud of circling dust.

Once aboard, they were almost immediately airborne. Rising up over the arid and endless desert terrain, before tilting to the left and heading south.

59

"What the hell just happened?"

Reiff gazed angrily at Yamada. "Ask him."

Yamada held up his hands innocently. "Hey, I wasn't part of that."

"Well, you sure as hell didn't stand in her way."

He stared at Waterman and Reiff. "What was I supposed to do? I was as surprised as you were."

All three were outside, watching the group of men disperse from the fortified fence that had since been closed.

"It was the only way she could think of to stop it," said Yamada.

"By surrendering."

The younger man nodded.

Reiff was in his chair, staring out at the last wisps of dust from the two SUVs. Neither they, nor the Apache, were visible anymore. All gone over a nearby, low-lying ridge.

Waterman slowly inhaled. "Well, shit."

"So, what do we do now?" Yamada asked.

Waterman could only shake his head. "No idea."

Reiff remained quiet and contemplating. Eventually grasping the wheels on either side of his chair and turning back toward their temporary dwelling. He had to admit, Rachel was no dummy. In the end, she *was* more valuable to them. Reiff was just a lab rat;she was the one who knew everything. Which he hoped meant she wouldn't be hurt, for as long as she still knew more than they did.

60

Rachel was too far from the window to discern where they were in the air, but the helicopter eventually began to descend, where it continued over the ground before dropping further into a long, winding, rocky canyon. Setting down on its skids outside a large but obscure entrance directly into the rock wall.

The men on either side of her exited through their own doors, while one led her out with him. Half pulling and half guiding her down onto the ground.

Neither had spoken to her the entire trip. Not in the vehicle nor in the helicopter. They remained silent with stoic, unreadable faces until reaching their destination. Where, to her surprise, one of two of the doors was opened and Nora Lagner stepped outside into the sunlight. Next to her was a dark-haired somewhat handsome man about her same age, and next to him, a man much older. He looked in his mid to late eighties but moved like someone younger. Strong and smooth as he strode forward with both Lagner and the younger man following.

Her two escorts pulled her to a stop as the old man reached them. Up and down, he quietly examined her before speaking. "You were smart to volunteer yourself."

"I'll tell you whatever you want," she replied. "Just leave the others alone."

"You mean leave 'John Rieff' alone."

"Yes."

The old man stared intently at her through a pair of intense blue eyes. "We shall see."

Once inside, Rachel's continuing surprise almost caused her to gasp. The entrance was simple and reinforced with massive, thick steel walls, but beyond that, the complex itself looked more like the inside of a mansion or palace than what she presumed would be some kind of bunker.

Instead, she found a place that an enormous amount of planning and resources had clearly been poured into. In some ways reminding her of Robert Masten's private office at their lab, whose interior had been spared no expense, but this place was on a whole different level.

With expensive marble flooring stretching as far as she could see. Down a broad corridor that opened into an area that felt like the largest living room she'd ever seen. Or perhaps living quarters was a better description. A cross between a vast living room and an opulent hotel lobby.

The area was adorned with an array of expensive-looking furniture, paintings, and sculptures. Feeling like a mix of elegance against a backdrop of modern design in things like lighting, temperature, and more technological aesthetics, like numerous overhead security cameras. A mansion or a museum; she couldn't decide. And in the center, hanging from the ceiling, was an enormous, crystal chandelier.

They continued through the lobby to another area of underground luxury that, along one wall, included a sizeable glass-enclosed room. Inside, she could see an expansive table surrounded by a dozen or so dark leather chairs.

All five people escorted her forward, toward the glass room where one of the henchmen opened the door for them.

"Please," said the old man, "sit down."

She looked around and selected a chair, nervously easing herself into it. "So, what now?"

The old man grinned in response to her smugness. "Well, aren't we testy?"

"You would be, too."

His face grew serious as he sat in his own chair, with an expression that caused Rachel's hubris to disappear.

"Do you know who I am?"

Rachel glanced at Nora Lagner and the other man, who had also taken seats directly across from her before answering. "No."

"Most people don't," he replied. "My name is Douglas Kincaid. Your friends should thank you, especially John Reiff."

"Like I said, I'll tell you whatever you want. Just leave them alone."

"Is that so? And just what is it you are prepared to tell us?"

"Everything."

Kincaid mused again, watching the young woman. She was going to tell him everything whether she wanted to or not.

"If we find out you're lying—"

"I won't."

Kincaid continued studying her. "What precisely do you and your friends know about us?"

"Not much." Rachel glanced again at Lagner, who was sitting across from her solemnly. "Devin Waterman wished he'd pumped Nora for more information." She noticed a slight change in Lagner's expression. "But it's clear you were the group behind everything our lab had been working on. Behind the whole project. And that Duchik was one of you."

Kincaid appeared amused. "Continue."

"It's also clear that you didn't previously know about John's medical issue, and that he had been refrozen."

Kincaid glanced at Lagner and DeSilva. "Something we now know much more about, thanks to Dr. Samantha Reed."

The mentioning of Reed's name caught Rachel by surprise, prompting her to look back and forth between them. "What did she tell you?"

"Enough to know about Mr. Reiff's problems and why you put him back on ice." Kincaid grinned. "Until you found a cure."

There was no response from Rachel.

The old man contemplated for a moment before dropping a hand onto the table in front of him. "So, this is all now going to come down to just how cooperative you are willing to be."

"Just call off your dogs. Leave John and the others alone."

It was then that Nora Lagner noticed something in Rachel. In her voice, as she peered intently at her before a smirk quietly appeared on her own lips. *Rachel had feelings for Reiff.*

"There are many different levels of cooperation," said Kincaid. "Information would be helpful, yes. But your services would be more valuable to us in recreating your cure. If you want your friends to live, *and* if you eventually intend to leave this place."

Rachel had long since given up any concern over what Lagner and her cronies wanted the cure for, or what they intended to do with it. If they wanted to freeze themselves just to wake up somewhere in the distant future, so be it. It wasn't her problem. Her concern was saving Reiff.

"I'll do whatever you want," she said simply.

"Excellent." Kincaid gently slapped the table with an open hand. "Now that that's settled, there is something else you'll need to see."

Without the accompaniment of Kincaid's henchmen, the three took Rachel to an elevator where they all traveled several stories below ground until the doors opened to reveal a somewhat smaller but still spacious cavern lined by raw, machine-chiseled metamorphic rock on all sides, also known as Zoroaster granite. A similar composition to some of the oldest rocks found near the base of the Grand Canyon.

She guessed the cavern to be a couple hundred feet long and about twenty feet high, approximately half of which was completely empty. The other half appeared to be sealed behind a long and enormous wall of clear glass. With some of the glass edges covered in frost on the inside. Stepping out of the elevator, she looked curiously at the transparent wall as she gradually strolled forward.

Next to her, Kincaid faced the glass and placed both arms behind his back. "This . . . is why we need you."

What Kincaid was looking at, beyond the wall of frost and crystals, was some kind of object. Large, long, and metal. Mostly featureless except for the surface area on the far end, where it resembled something akin to etched lines. Or perhaps some kind of ribbed design.

She continued staring, perplexed. And then asked, "What is this?"

Kincaid turned to her with a dubious look as if disappointed she hadn't already figured it out. "It's a spacecraft," he replied simply.

61

Rachel's mouth dropped open. "Excuse me?"

Kincaid turned back toward the object. "You heard me."

"A *spacecraft*?"

Lagner and DeSilva were both standing several feet away, listening, but offered nothing.

"As in . . . an *alien* spacecraft?"

Kincaid nodded. "Alien to us, yes."

Rachel's mouth remained open as she peered through the glass again, longer now and more intently. "Where . . . did you . . . get this?"

"In the Himalayas. Several decades ago."

She was beyond stunned. She was . . . astonished! Eventually turning back to Kincaid. "What in the world does this have to do with me?"

"It seems this crashed on Earth a *very* long time ago, remaining perfectly preserved in the frozen tundra. For hundreds, perhaps thousands of years, until some climbers stumbled upon it. We have maintained it in the same condition ever since."

"I ask again," replied Rachel, still staring incredulously at the object. "But what does this have to do with me?"

"You're not very quick, are you?" asked Kincaid. When he got no response, he said, "This has to do with you because there is a frozen life-form inside . . . and we need your expertise to help us revive it."

62

This time, she was speechless. Trying to comprehend the words the old man had just spoken. So simply and so matter-of-factly.

Kincaid moved closer. "I understand this is a lot to take in, but *this* was the reason for everything. For the project, the lab, Reiff, everything."

Her eyes managed to widen even further. "Wait, what?"

"You're surprised."

"Everything was for *this*?"

"Yes."

She could not believe her ears. It felt like she was actually outside of her body. "A-and you think I can *revive* whatever is in there?!"

"That's the hope."

"Why . . . on earth . . . would you think that?" she replied. "I wouldn't know the first thing about alien biology."

His lack of response made Rachel wonder if he'd heard her. "Did you hear what I said?"

"I did."

"You can't possibly be so obtuse as to think I would know anything about an alien lifeform." She then grimaced. *"Are you?"*

Again, Kincaid remained quiet. He simply stared at her, saying nothing, prompting Rachel to look to Lagner and DeSilva.

"What is wrong with him?" she asked.

They did not comment.

The expression on Rachel's face was turning to bewilderment. Feeling as though everyone had gone crazy except her. Or deaf. "Can you not hear me?"

"I can hear you," said Kincaid.

"Then why aren't you answering me?"

He paused before replying. "I never said it was an alien spacecraft. You did."

Rachel peered back at him, puzzled. "Huh?"

"I never said it was alien."

She blinked and shook her head. "I'm not following."

Kincaid approached and stopped directly in front of her. "The frozen figure inside—" He paused. "—is human."

63

Rachel could not imagine her eyes being able to open any wider. "That's . . . impossible."

Kincaid gave a slight tilt of his head. "Is it?"

Her gaze returned to the glass wall. "There was nothing like that hundreds of years ago," said Rachel. "I'm not a historian but that much I know!"

He nodded. "That's true."

"Then it's impossible."

Kincaid began walking toward the glass. This time, stopping just a few feet away. Close enough to see his own faint reflection. "The metal is made of an alloy we've never seen before. Neither before the collapse or after. A composition that, as far as we can tell, has not been invented . . . yet."

"Yet?"

The old man's outline in the glass continued speaking. "As in not in the present, or in the past." He turned once again to face her. "Which leaves only one other option."

Rachel's head began turning from side to side. "That's just not possible," she mumbled.

"It's not only possible," he replied, "it's reality. Whether you want to believe it or not." He continued staring through his reflection at the giant object behind it. "We can't explain how or why, but we know what it is."

"How . . . do you know it's human," questioned Rachel.

"Because we've been inside."

"Maybe," she stammered, searching for an explanation, "maybe it's alien, and a person crawled inside . . ."

Kincaid frowned and turned around to look at her as though she had just said the Earth was flat. "Let's not go down the road of idiocy."

64

"I want it on the record that I'm not comfortable with this."

John Reiff shrugged at the woman in front of him. "Neither am I."

Standing next to them, Henry Yamada looked nervously at Waterman.

"None of us are," quipped Waterman, "but we don't have a lot of choice."

The nurse, seated before Reiff, completed the injection and smoothly withdrew the needle. Simultaneously pressing down with a cotton swab with her other hand. She kept the swab in place with a thumb while turning to set the syringe down on the table next to her.

She looked to be in her late thirties or early forties, with long brown hair and slightly plump for her size, wearing a pink, short-sleeved nurse's shirt. "No medical professional in their right mind would administer an unknown injection."

"We understand." Waterman smiled. "If it's any consolation, his previous doctor seemed very smart."

The nurse did not laugh. Instead, she looked up at him with a mix of cheerlessness and disdain. She continued cleaning up and gathered her things before standing. "Call if you experience any problems." And with that, she walked to the door, opened it, and left.

"I think you're losing your touch with women," said Reiff.

"The Waterman Touch is eternal."

"My mistake." Reiff looked down at his hand and flexed, opening and closing it.

"So, now what?" asked Yamada.

"We find out where they took her," said Reiff. He looked at Waterman. "Just how big is this 'Network' of yours?"

"Bigger than most people think."

"Good." Reiff then turned to Yamada. "Got your laptop?"

65

They were now in a large computer lab, where dozens of monitors filled a wall before them in a rectangular checkerboard pattern.

On his keyboard, DeSilva brought up the first frame of a video, causing all the screens to light up simultaneously as one giant monitor. He glanced back at Kincaid with a questioning expression, and the old man nodded at him.

DeSilva began playing it.

The video was jumpy and jostled back and forth, through a warped or curved viewpoint normally seen when a three-dimensional image was compressed into a two-dimensions. After several seconds, Rachel recognized the curved image in the video as the gray-colored spacecraft she'd seen several floors below, or at least one end of it.

The camera in the video felt like it was on the tip of a pole or some kind of snaking device as it approached a small black hole in the ship's metal hull.

Slowly, it pushed through before a light behind the camera illuminated, basking the interior in bright white glare.

The inside looked downright spooky. A large open cavity that appeared mostly circular, with several objects inside, all completely covered in ice.

The ice was thick and reflective, layered over every object and surface in sight, with scattered and glistening patches of frost on top.

What gave it a spooky appearance was the ice itself, draping from object to object like frozen cobwebs sparkling under the snake's bright illumination.

Rachel could not identify the shapes beneath the thick ice but assumed they were parts of the ship. One partially covered area resembled an oval doorway, but she couldn't be sure or see much beyond it. Frankly, she had little idea at all of what she was observing.

The remote camera continued forward, up and over what looked like a flat open-ringed depression in a wall, until it reached a giant hunk of icy mass on the opposite side. The ice was covering something bulky that, again, she could not make out. It was then that the camera's movement stopped and focused on the frozen mass.

Kincaid quietly tapped DeSilva's shoulder and he paused the video.

"This video is almost forty years old," he said, surprising Rachel.

She squinted and studied the image on the giant screen more closely. "You haven't been inside in forty years?"

"Of course, we have. Remotely. But nothing has changed."

Rachel studied the strange mass of ice on the screen. "Why all the suspense? Why not just tell me what it is?"

"Where's the fun in that?" replied Kincaid, who then tapped DeSilva again to continue the video.

In the video, the camera gently nudging closer. In small spurts, closer then pausing, then closer and pausing again. Each time, the thick ice seemed to reveal more, like looking through an extremely warped piece of glass, with the shapes inside shifting and bending from the camera's angle.

With a few more movements forward, something on the inside became visible. The camera angle then twisted slightly to the left, allowing a shape to be seen more clearly. It was a face.

Rachel almost gasped. She assumed she would be shown the figure inside, but the suddenness at seeing its frozen, ghostlike face startled her. And after relaxing and studying the image, there was absolutely no doubt about it being human.

"Wooow," she breathed.

She faced Kincaid. "And you think this was here for how long?"

"We think about 1200 A.D."

Rachel could not believe it. It was extraordinary. There was no question that the thing was a spaceship, even to her. The interior was thoroughly covered in ice, but through small patches, she could make out what looked a lot like computerized instrumentation.

What Kincaid told her appeared to be true at first glance. And still, she couldn't quite grasp what she was seeing. Let alone what it meant.

Everything she believed her work to be about for the last several years was nothing but a farce.

"So, the whole thing was a sham," she muttered aloud. "The lab, the project, everything. It was never about our own cryonic goals. It was all for this."

"I wouldn't go that far," answered Kincaid. "The two are not mutually exclusive. One technology, two objectives."

"Wait." She peered at all three of them, Kincaid, Lagner, and DeSilva. "So, you're saying this *is* about you?"

The old man sighed with a condescending tone. "You *still* don't get it?"

Rachel's eyes narrowed. "Evidently not."

He gave her a long stare before finally asking, "What value is a successful cryonic suspension if you don't know what you're going to wake up to? Waking up in the future with a body that's healthy again doesn't mean a lot if the world is still in chaos. If you cannot be sure that you won't be harmed, or worse, immediately upon being revived."

Rachel finally got it. "Like waking up in the middle of a fire."

"That's one way to put it."

"And so, you want my help reviving this person."

"Correct. And as you know, you only get one shot. If they die in the process, that's all she wrote."

Rachel thought of Reiff. They'd almost lost him the first time. Bringing him back a second time was nothing short of a miracle. But Kincaid was still correct. Accidentally killing someone while trying to reanimate them was a very easy thing to do. Too easy.

"We have big plans for the future, Ms. Souza," he said, turning back to the frozen face on the screen. "And to be sure you are not 'waking up in the middle of a fire' it helps to have someone who already *knows* the future."

66

Rachel's mind was now racing in multiple directions. She finally understood their obsession with finding John. And why they didn't let up. Why they couldn't let up.

He's still the key. Kincaid himself admitted as much. They can not freeze themselves unless they are sure they can be revived safely and healthfully. And now . . . now they have what Kincaid claims is someone from the future? Good God!

As if reading her thoughts, Kincaid continued, "We don't know how or why this ship got here. And frankly, it doesn't matter. What matters is that you help us bring its occupant back to life."

She continued staring in amazement until her lips finally moved and asked the obvious: "How do you know they're alive?"

"Because it looks like they're also in a cryo chamber, more advanced than ours, and as far as we can tell, undisturbed. If the ship crashed with him still frozen, even if the cryo unit was damaged, there's a good chance the conditions in the mountains were cold enough to keep him preserved."

"That's debatable."

"Everything is debatable," said Kincaid.

"Maybe this person is from some other planet but only looks human."

Kincaid shook his head. "The man's features are *very* human. And we've also been able to make out some wording inside the ship, beneath the ice. Written in English."

Somehow, every new detail Kincaid added only increased her disbelief. "How in the world could a ship travel back—"

"I told you; we don't know, and we don't care." Kincaid stepped forward, grasped an empty chair by its backrest, and pulled it out for her. "Some of us have been waiting a long time for this moment. We're not interested in dawdling."

She looked at the chair but remained where she was.

"The sooner you help us," he said, "the sooner you and your friends are free to go."

Rachel then turned when DeSilva asked, "Where's all your data?"

"My data?"

"Your research data, to find Reiff's cure?"

"It's with all my equipment," she replied. "At Nick Bailey's place. But I also hid a copy online."

DeSilva leaned from his own chair and pushed the empty one in front of a nearby computer monitor and keyboard.

Rachel took the hint and stepped forward, lowering herself and scooting forward. She used the keyboard and typed in a long, convoluted address. When the site came up, it did so as a blank screen providing only a small log-in box in the upper left-hand corner. Without a word, she typed in her username and password and hit enter.

A page then appeared, displaying dozens of folder icons, all listed in cryptic naming conventions. Rachel selected one near the bottom and began downloading a copy.

"How long will it take to recreate the cure?" asked Kincaid.

Rachel eased back and watched the download. "Creating a Cas9 protein isn't hard, especially when you already know the RNA and DNA targets. And I used a common bacterium that replicates quickly."

"How long?"

"Depends on what kind of equipment you have here."

"We have a complete medical facility."

"Then somewhere between twenty-four and forty-eight hours."

Their "facility" was more than she expected, much more. A large, expansive room on sublevel four that could easily be described as a mix between a research lab and a hospital room. A surprise even to her, compounded not just by the size and myriad of systems available but by the sound that could be heard upon their approach.

It was unmistakable as soon as the four of them stepped off the elevator. A muffled, distant shrieking that only grew louder the closer they got to the double doors in front of them.

Rachel already knew what it was, and it made her stomach churn. With each and every step until they reached the doors and opened them.

She noted only briefly the sophistication of the facility, and instead turned her attention to the far corner, where a half-height metal cage was located. Inside, the tiny capuchin was going berserk behind the thin gray bars. Screaming and incessantly pulling and tugging, pausing only briefly upon seeing the familiar face of Rachel Souza.

She could only look at the small animal mournfully. Heartbroken and sickened. It was true. They had found Dallas.

Rachel never noticed the open, empty area of the room in the opposing corner. Where the Machine would soon reside.

67

It was after midnight when Douglas Kincaid checked the security feed in Rachel's assigned room. Small and comfortably decorated, with a bed, sitting chair, desk table, and private bathroom. Generic pictures of landscaped photographs hung on the walls beneath natural-hued LED lights, all still on, allowing Kincaid a clear view of Rachel sitting quietly on her bed.

Her back was against the wall with both knees pulled to her chest and her chin resting on top for hours now.

She was having doubts; that much was clear. Not about protecting her friends but about helping Kincaid, and DeSilva, and most of all, Lagner.

Nora Lagner had a direct hand in Rachel's friend and colleague, Perry Williams, being murdered, and she knew it. Once Williams learned about the actions of Liam Duchik and his cohorts—the group consisting of Kincaid, DeSilva, Lagner, and several others.

Rachel had now agreed to help, wholly and unconditionally, but that was *before* she knew the full extent of what Kincaid and his colleagues were truly involved in. And now that she knew, it was clear the woman was having reservations.

But Kincaid didn't care. He had come too far. He was so close he could taste it. So close he could actually envision the moment their time traveler reopened his eyes and began speaking. So close he could almost feel the preparations for his own decades-long cryo sleep. Awakening in the future with his mind and body fully restored. Youthful and completely repaired after dozens of years of frozen, age-reversing therapy. Achieving what no other individual on earth had ever achieved: victory over death itself.

Kincaid's eyes remained fixed on the screen, watching as Rachel's own face stared straight ahead, with her body ever so slightly rocking back and forth.

The proteins had been created and were now in an incubator, allowing the bacteria to multiply, replicating over and over in their petri dishes. And she would finish the job. He was certain of it. There was no question when it came to the lives of her friends. She would willingly give them the cure and help reanimate their long-awaited patient. There was not a shred of doubt in his mind.

But he needed her to do it quickly, for multiple reasons. Not the least of which was to get what he needed out of her before she began to suspect that she would never, under any circumstances, be allowed to leave the compound alive.

Little did Kincaid know that someone else was also watching the video feed from Rachel's room. Not so much watching, but rather having it onscreen while Nora Lagner toiled away on her own computer.

There was something strange about Rachel Souza's behavior that Lagner couldn't quite put her finger on. Subtle reactions that told her the young woman was still hiding details or withholding something. Made even more apparent in the way Rachel spoke when referencing Reiff.

She was sure there was something more.

Rachel Souza was a captive. A prisoner. And what prisoners wanted above all else was freedom. In Rachel's case, an end to being pursued. From constantly having to be on the run, continually looking over her shoulder at everything she did and everywhere she went. It would be mentally exhausting for anyone.

And yet, what Rachel wanted more than anything else was for them to leave Reiff alone. And, of course, the others. But specifically, Reiff.

Was it love that Lagner was sensing in Rachel? Maybe. A woman with those feelings for a man would typically want to be reunited with him. Through either escape, which was impossible, or rescue. But Rachel did not appear to be thinking of either. She seemed much more . . . resigned. Resigned to the fact that she was going to be there for a long while.

For her to fold completely and agree to whatever Kincaid wanted told Lagner that Rachel did not believe him and there was something else going on in Rachel Souza's brain.

Lagner's eyes were not focused on the video feed of Rachel's room but instead on the rest of her computer screen as she worked. Rachel was still hiding something; she was certain of it. Something about Reiff. And as Lagner continued scrolling through the thousands of data files downloaded by Rachel, she was determined to find out what it was.

68

What if Kincaid is wrong? Rachel thought to herself. *What if the frozen astronaut is no longer alive? Even if he is, what if she can't revive him?* If what Kincaid claimed was true, and the man was from the future, their cryo procedures could be completely different, especially if their technology or medical protocol had radically changed.

There were a thousand questions running through her mind, with all of them eventually leading back to the same place. Both hers and her friends' lives could now be hanging in the balance. Hanging upon something she may have absolutely no control over.

Everything about their original cryonic project had suddenly taken on a dark, almost sinister feeling after finding out about the body inside the ship. And now it felt like she was about to assist in something truly bizarre. Something she did not, in any way, want to be part of. But what choice did she have? And could she do it without revealing Reiff's current condition?

Things were spiraling out of control. She surrendered to Kincaid in an attempt to save Reiff, but had she? What would happen if their frozen astronaut was already dead? Or if he wasn't and Rachel killed him trying to revive him. Or even worse, what if Rachel *was* able to revive him? What would Kincaid do once he had what he needed from Rachel? Once he had extracted every last piece of information. And how would Kincaid even *know* when he'd gotten everything from her?

She was growing increasingly fearful. Even of going to sleep. All she could think about now were Kincaid's next steps; what would happen once the Cas9 cure was ready?

Several hours later, in the early morning light, a familiar white box truck appeared at the top of the canyon ridge. It momentarily snaked back and forth over the dirt road before angling downward along the canyon wall. Carefully making its way toward the compound's main entrance.

When it arrived, two of Kincaid's men climbed out of the truck cab and onto the hardened ground.

No sooner had they moved to the rear of the truck than two more emerged from the compound to join them, accompanied by Daniel DeSilva.

The truck's rear cargo door was raised to reveal a load of oversized electronic and mechanical parts. The Machine dismantled into a dozen pieces, where they were being moved inside and reassembled within the compound's medical facility.

Inside the main doors, Kincaid watched as two giant pieces were wheeled in over his temporarily covered marble flooring in a straight line toward the waiting elevator.

Over the course of four decades, and against nearly all odds, the wait was finally over. While outside, through the open doors, Kincaid allowed himself to smile when he heard the sound of another approaching helicopter.

The rest of The Nine were returning.

They didn't want to miss this.

69

He was in a large room with clear walls and a soft sandy floor.

The sand felt soggy, and he looked down to see water appearing from below it. Rising, covering the sand, and gradually continuing up his foot and ankle. Then his shins.

There was sunlight coming from the other side of the walls, but he could not see through them. They were angled and warped, preventing him from viewing anything outside. He stared closer, examining the walls themselves until realizing they were not glass. They were ice.

Everywhere he looked, every bit of surface area was covered in a thick sheet of ice. The only exception was the water around his knees, which continued to rise.

He heard screams and quickly turned around. Dozens of people were frantically trying to squeeze through a tiny doorway and escape the quickly filling room.

The clear liquid accelerated faster like a miniature tsunami. Reaching his hips, then his stomach, then chest. And then the room began to change. Turning into something else entirely: the inside of a bus.

He found himself paralyzed with both hands tightly gripping empty seats. Frozen in place as the icy water rose above his shoulders and stung the exposed skin on his neck.

He was going to drown. Again.

70

Waterman emerged from one of the small bedrooms to find Reiff on the couch where he'd left him. Awake and slumped, with bloodshot eyes and a glassy look on his face.

"You okay?"

Reiff nodded wearily.

"You don't look so good."

"I'm fine."

"Did you sleep?"

"A little."

"How much is a little?"

Reiff stared up at his friend through heavy eyes but said nothing.

They were interrupted by pounding on the front door, causing Waterman to reflexively draw his gun. He raised the weapon and silently aimed.

After a tense lull, the pounding returned, this time louder and harder, followed by several muffled words.

"Waterman, you in there?"

The older man looked at Reiff with a raised eyebrow.

"Waterman!"

He cocked his head and, recognizing the voice, stepped forward. He lowered the gun and reached to open the door with his left hand. On the other side was a rumpled and very dirty Wayne Coleman.

Agitated, Coleman strode inside with a huff and looked around. "Nice to see you're getting pampered."

Waterman looked him up and down and wrinkled his nose. "You smell like you've been sleeping in the forest with a family of skunks."

"I smell as bad as anything else out there, in case someone was following me." Coleman removed his jacket, and then pants, and tossed them both outside before slamming the door, leaving him standing in the small living room in a T-shirt and boxer shorts.

The racket brought Henry Yamada from his own room holding his laptop. He stopped cold and stared at the undressed Coleman. His eyes moved to Waterman and then Reiff. "Okay, I don't know what's going on here, but whatever it is I'm *not* in."

"Very funny."

Yamada wafted the air in front of him. "Wow, you smell terrible."

"Where's the shower?"

All three men pointed down the hallway, where Coleman nodded and stormed away without a word.

Yamada looked back at Reiff and Waterman. "He just get here?"

"Yep."

He nodded and continued forward, setting his laptop down on the small kitchen table. "Internet connection's not great here but it works."

"What do you have?"

He turned his screen around so they could see. On it was a still image: a giant lime-green circle against a black background. In and around the bright circle was a scattering of different green lines and vectors, along with tiny icons that looked like aircraft. "This is from your air traffic controller friend," he said to Waterman.

Both men squinted at the screen. "Radar, eh?"

"Yes. It looks like whoever took Rachel briefly popped up on Phoenix's radar."

"Heading where?"

"Southeast."

"How far?"

"I'm not sure. And neither are they. It was a helicopter and it dropped off the radar near the Tonto National Forest." He brought up a topological map of the area. "It's unclear where it went from there. Their guess is that it landed somewhere within this fifty-mile radius."

"Fifty miles," mused Waterman. "Wonderful."

"Your man is working on getting access to satellite images, but it's difficult."

"Can't be that difficult, Lagner and her cronies have obviously been using them to track us."

"Let's hope what's good for the goose is good for the gander."

Waterman nodded before turning back to Reiff still on the couch. "In the meantime, we should get you to a hospital."

Reiff's eyebrows narrowed. "What are you talking about?"

"She told us to get you medical attention."

"I'm fine."

Waterman nodded. "Yeah, you look it."

"In case you hadn't noticed," replied Reiff, "I'm kinda going through something here."

His friend could not help but laugh. "That's *kinda* the point."

"I'm fine," he repeated. "I just need a little time."

Waterman folded his arms. "For what, your sleep to get better?"

"Yes."

"It ain't gonna get better, John. It's only gonna get worse."

Yamada turned from his computer. "He's right."

"I'll be fine," said Reiff. "My system just needs to recalibrate."

"I don't think that's how it works."

"You a doctor?"

Waterman shook. "No."

"Then I win."

Waterman sighed. "If you get much weaker, winning this argument is going to be the least of your worries."

Reiff responded by reaching out and pulling his wheelchair closer. He then leaned forward, and without help, angled himself up and into the vinyl seat. He looked at Waterman. "No problem."

He then wheeled past his friend to the edge of the table and stopped next to Yamada. "Let's have a look at that map."

71

Their medical lab, or clinic, was bustling with activity as the last parts of the Machine were reattached and carefully measured to ensure perfect alignment.

In front of the massive device, DeSilva had erected a makeshift console where all data and power cables connected. Providing a complete digitized view of the Machine's internal cavity, populated with several hundred miniature microwave sensors and transmitters.

He used the computer to slide the door closed on top and began typing to initiate a full diagnostic check, which would take close to an hour as each transmitter was individually checked and calibrated.

"Well?"

DeSilva glanced over his shoulder at Kincaid. "So far so good. Everything is checking out, but we won't be sure for another few hours."

Kincaid nodded. Next to him stood the imposing figure of Colonel Cannon himself. With deep-set brown eyes and a familiar military-style high-and-tight black haircut, his sharply dressed stature exuded an attention to detail.

Behind Cannon was Nora Lagner, observing quietly from the background. The remaining three members of The Nine were still en route.

Lagner noted the absence of screeching in the room and turned to view the far corner of the lab. Inside his cage, a heavily sedated Dallas lay slumped and immobile. Observing the others through a pair of weary amber eyes.

The room's broad metal door opened and Wicks, their head of security, pushed Rachel Souza inside by her arm, then pulled her to a stop, and without a word, disappearing back through the doors.

She looked at Dallas with a sad expression and then turned to the others, and finally the metal behemoth behind them.

From his console, DeSilva peered around the others at Rachel. "Anything you'd like to share about our little prototype here?"

She shook her head. "Henry Yamada was the expert, not me."

DeSilva turned back smugly, as if ignoring her reply. Continuing to monitor the diagnostic test in progress.

The older Kincaid turned to Cannon. "Once we're sure the system is ready, we can begin the extraction."

Cannon nodded but Rachel spoke up. "Extraction?"

"Of our astronaut. Removing him from the ice must be done carefully." Kincaid then asked, "Anything we should consider in transporting his body from the ship?"

"Like what?"

The old man shrugged. "I don't know. Temperature changes, anything like that?"

Rachel shook. "If you're worried about thawing, even a moderate amount would take hours. As long as you don't stop and take a nap in the process any temperature change should be immaterial."

Kincaid ignored her sarcasm and turned back as the colonel spoke.

"How long to remove the ice?"

"Not long. The outer layers should go quickly as we chip it away. After that, we'll melt the rest away. Our guess is an hour or two."

"Just don't get too close to the body with them," said Rachel.

Kincaid acknowledged the comment and continued: "Once that's done, the extraction should be fairly rapid."

The colonel turned to Rachel. "How long to rewarm him once he's in the Machine?"

"Minutes," she replied. "Which is why it has to work perfectly. Overheating of the tissues and organs can be terminal. So can underheating."

"Did you have that problem with Reiff?"

"Yes. But fortunately, most of the damage was in non-vital areas. I doubt we would get that lucky again."

"What about the second time?"

"I don't know. We didn't have access to the necessary equipment."

Lagner turned to her with a raised eyebrow. "So, he could have internal damage and you wouldn't know?"

Rachel hesitated. "It's possible." She turned and spoke to DeSilva. "Too much heat is better than too little. As long as it's not excessive."

"Why is that?"

"Because some tissues can heal. But if you don't get the vascular system liquified enough to pump, revival is near impossible."

"We are aware," acknowledged Kincaid. "Don't forget we have all the data from both of Reiff's restorations now."

Rachel shrugged and looked away, staring at Dallas, unmoving behind his metal bars. "Do you need me for anything else right now?"

"Not at the moment."

With that, she turned and walked across the room to the metal cage and knelt down in front of it.

When they were sure Rachel was out of earshot, Cannon lowered his voice. "What about the ship?"

Kincaid answered quietly, "As soon as we have him out, we can begin."

"Excellent."

The astronaut was merely step one. Extracting and reviving him. A prospect they already knew was risky. And one that would require time, especially if successful. Whether his recovery would take as long as Reiff's recovery did, they didn't know.

Step two, however, could be initiated almost immediately after extraction, which was the defrosting of the ship itself. It would take much longer as they had to be careful. Using a more organic thawing process called "gradual thaw," that was as simple as turning off the industrial chilling system that had kept the ship frozen all this time.

Rachel Souza was shown only a small portion of the ship in the video they played for her, but there was more of the vessel the group of nine were interested in. Much more.

72

It was time.

All preparation and testing of the the Machine were successful. After decades of waiting, it was now time to breach the ship.

It began with three of Kincaid's men, including Wicks, entering the glass enclosure on one end through an oval-shaped door resembling an old-style submarine hatch. Donning heavy jackets and pants, they turned the large handwheel counterclockwise to break the door's seal and pull it open.

Standing back from the giant enclosure, Kincaid and the rest watched the men pick up a heavy bag and enter. Moving around the front cone of the ship and positioning themselves along the ship's long body. Where they set the bag down and began pulling out cutting tools in the form of arc welders.

Different holes drilled into the ship over the years revealed the front to be far thicker than the sides. Those were thin enough to allow an arc welder to pierce the alloy skin. It was ideal as the heat from the welders could then be used to carefully melt areas of ice inside.

Wicks stepped forward between his men and used a dark waterproof marker to outline the designated area, calculated from hundreds of videos of the craft's interior.

Breaching the ship would be the easy part, and in truth it had been meticulously planned almost a decade in advance. Making the excruciatingly long wait all the more difficult to endure. The truly challenging piece had been developing the science behind a successful cryonic suspension and resuscitation. *That* had taken Kincaid and his cohorts the better part of thirty years.

And now it was all happening. He could hardly contain his excitement, noting the other members seemed to appear more successful at containing themselves, including two more of The Nine, who arrived less than an hour before the big event.

Nina Sandhu stood nearby at five foot six with thick black hair and an olive-skinned complexion, and had left Brussels shortly after Rachel was captured. A parliamentary member of the European Commission and former director of the west European region of the NIH.

Anna Lu, from Singapore, was shorter by a few inches with thin, straight, shoulder-length hair. She was of Chinese lineage and another former high-ranking member of the NIH. Lu was, without a doubt, the cornerstone behind The Nine's almost inexplicable ability to procure the technical systems and resources needed for their decades-long project. Her ability to beg, borrow, or steal, along with the sheer ruthlessness in doing so was beyond impressive and stood in direct contrast to the becalmed, almost placid expression she wore outwardly.

To Kincaid, the two women could not have been more different. Sandhu was loud, expressive, and excitable, while Lu was just the opposite. Thoughtful and quiet, and extraordinarily calculating.

Now together, they stood next to each other watching as Wicks and his men slowly and methodically cut a door-sized hole in the side of the ship.

While watching them, Kincaid could not help but muse in a brief moment of reflection. Wicks and his men were young, all between the ages of twenty-five to forty. And all with a military background. Loyal and obedient.

And yet, what bemused Kincaid the most, even puzzled him, was how little interest they *still* had in what The Nine were doing. Wicks and his men knew about the ship, they knew about the frozen man inside, they knew about Rachel's lab and the project, and of course, they knew about Reiff. In other words, they knew most of what Kincaid and the others were involved in, and yet the men still showed little to no interest.

A large part of that no doubt revolved around their compensation. Kincaid and the rest were in the process of making Wicks and his men rich. But it didn't just involve the amount, it was also the duration.

The Nine were not stupid. They were more than just seasoned; they were as greedy and self-serving as anyone. They knew how fleeting true loyalty was, and how often young lions lay in wait for the old lions to become vulnerable, or lionesses as the case may be.

Kincaid, Lu, and Sandhu were all in their seventies and eighties. They had been on the planet long enough to know how much darkness lay within the human heart. And how best to protect themselves from the deceitful agendas of the very humans serving them. Riches, to be sure. But not all at once.

The young rarely concerned themselves over the imminence of mortality, and Wicks and his men were no different. They did not care about The Nine's ridiculous quest to prolong their lives. They just wanted the money.

And The Nine gave it to them. With a long string and carrot. Simply put, Wicks and his men were paid out over time. More than enough each year to live a life of luxury, especially in the current world, but it was not enough to be truly rich, until they themselves were old men.

A gradual prolonged payout was much better at ensuring allegiance and loyalty. And much better at ensuring silence. The Nine had made it abundantly clear that the moment Wicks or his men opened their mouths about what they were up to, the money would disappear in the blink of an eye. And they themselves would become targets.

Kincaid blinked out of his momentary trance when the two men in front of Wicks finally completed their cutting. Reaching the bottom and promptly pulling away as the rectangularly shaped door wavered momentarily and suddenly fell inward with a resounding crash.

73

Altogether, as if choreographed, the six observers moved forward toward the frosted glass. Stopping just a few feet away and trying to peer inside the frozen vessel while Wicks and his men carefully climbed in.

From outside they could see the obscured, ice-covered objects within and watched the men step carefully over the slippery piece of charred hull lying flat and still steaming from its edges, before they disappeared out of sight.

There was a long bout of silence, with all six waiting breathlessly, until Wicks's head reappeared in the doorway and nodded.

At that, Kincaid turned to Rachel. "Ready?"

"What?"

He motioned toward the ship. "To go in?"

"Uh . . . I didn't—"

"You, of all people, will need to examine how our patient is preserved."

Rachel thought for a moment and turned toward the glass, nodding. "Right."

She had not noticed the heavy parkas left outside the enclosure by Wicks's men before donning their own, which she and Kincaid now picked up and stepped into. They zipped up then retrieved a pair of gloves and slipped them on, leaving Rachel standing still and staring apprehensively at the submarine-like hatch.

She glanced back at the others, DeSilva, Lagner, Sandhu, and Lu, all of whom were watching her. There would be plenty of time for them to see the ship, she surmised. The priority was extracting their patient.

Kincaid did not share her apprehension. He was through the door in seconds, turning to make sure she was following. With a deep breath, she did, and gripped the sides of the doorframe to step over its high lip.

Immediately, she felt the slipperiness beneath her boots and adjusted her balance, leaning forward slightly and moving close enough to the wall of glass to put one hand on it for support. Step by step, she followed the older Kincaid as he made his way along the ship's hull to the freshly cut opening.

Once in front of it, he gripped both sides of the entry and took a big step up, assisted by Wicks. Next came Rachel, pulled up and shuffling inside, where she carefully navigated herself forward.

The interior was larger than she was expecting. Significantly larger than it appeared in the video. Leaving her staring into a spacious open cavity where Wicks's men were already at work chipping away large chunks of ice draping the area over their patient.

Rachel peered up and examined the rest of the craft, realizing the ship was primarily cylindrical. At least on the inside, showing that the person the men were trying to dig out was actually oriented on his side.

As each chunk fell to their feet and tumbled away, more and more of the silhouetted figure became visible. Revealing that he was in some kind of capsule or pod, perhaps eight feet long and oval-shaped and transparent, seemingly made of glass.

Now larger pieces of the ice were breaking free. Large enough that Wicks's men could pry them away with their hands and toss them out of the way. Once the upper half was exposed, they began on the bottom. Making quick work until the entire outside of the capsule was exposed.

Next came the refiring of their two arc welders. This time used in slow repeated passes to carefully melt away the final film of ice.

As it melted and ran down the capsule's surface, the face through the glass became clearer. Eerily clear, with his eyes closed under a head of dark crystal-filled hair and light blue skin, he appeared surreal. Almost peaceful.

Rachel took a step forward, noting something about the man's face. He seemed to be wearing a mask. Clear and thin, and molded over his nose and mouth. Form fitted, almost like shrink wrap. And from it, a clear hose running down his bare chest.

What was the mask for? What kind of suspension was this person in? To Rachel's knowledge, none of the cryonic patients over the last half century had been frozen with the use of a mask. Which meant whatever process was used on this person could be very different from anything she had ever done.

The apprehension and worry were morphing into dread. Over-whelmed with a sense of fear that they could be woefully unprepared for what Kincaid wanted her to do. And what it could therefore mean for her.

In an almost nervous spell, she continued staring at the person on the other side of the glass. Wondering what year he had come from and how different their revival procedures might have been. Too far into the future would surely mean trouble.

Nervously, she stepped forward and pushed her way past one of the men to examine the figure more closely. His entire body was bare, with the only clothes being a pair of black synthetic shorts. The clear tube at-tached to his form-fitting mask snaked down to some kind of connection near his feet. He was clearly tilted on his side; had the ship been upright in its proper orientation, he would have been lying flat on his back.

Rachel studied him carefully. Her heart beating at an accelerated pace as she tried to discern *some* detail that would tell her what she was dealing with. There was nothing else connected to the man's body. No intrave-nous tubes, no electronic sensors, nothing.

It was then that she noticed something. Not about the body, but about the capsule. Along its right side, that was also made of clear glass.

Rachel twisted her head and checked the opposite side of the pod's interior wall: both were clear.

She then caught sight of something that their astronaut appeared to be lying on top of. It resembled a fabric, like a thin mattress positioned under him. Dark gray with something like cross stitching.

Rachel turned and spotted some of the same fabric through the cap-sule's side wall. Then back to the other side, where she saw the fabric again. But there was nothing on top of it.

Her eyes widened excitedly, and she pushed herself away from the curved glass. Stepping back carefully and peering intently at the rest of the draping sheets of ice. This time, she looked closer, more intently, through its warped translucence.

Dear God! There are more pods. More capsules. And they are all empty.

Rachel whipped her attention back to Kincaid, who did not appear surprised in the slightest. Instead, he had been watching her the entire time.

74

"Okay, this is what we have." Henry Yamada turned his laptop back around for Reiff and Waterman to see. As well as Coleman who was now fitted in a borrowed long-sleeved shirt and jeans.

On Yamada's screen was an overhead image from a satellite. A still photograph revealing sections of green and brown craggy terrain as seen from orbit. "This is a shot sent to me from Devin's friend Arney at the base. An aerial view of the Tonto National Forest."

"Hi-yo, Silver," muttered Coleman.

Yamada glanced at him curiously. "What?"

"Never mind."

Coleman looked at Waterman and shook his head. "Kid doesn't know who Tonto is. I weep for the future."

Yamada ignored the quip and turned back to his screen. He zoomed in on the high-definition picture until the craggy lines became small canyons. He continued zooming and the dark green ground cover revealed itself as miles of trees, and then eventually an object among them. A white oval-shaped outline of a helicopter's fuselage.

All three men leaned in for a closer look.

"Well, well, well."

"He could only sneak a few images," said Yamada, bringing up the second one, "but together they give us a direction. And it's a straight line from us."

Reiff remained fixed on the screen while Waterman spoke over his shoulder: "So we don't have a final destination?"

"No." Yamada brought up the third picture. "But Arney said the chopper dropped off the radar not far from this position, so it stands to reason that it landed somewhere in the vicinity."

"Unless it just continued under the radar," said Coleman.

"It's a possibility."

Reiff continued staring, blinking several times. He was beginning to see double of some things. "Can you get in closer?"

Yamada expanded the picture as far as he could.

"Looks like an Agusta," said Reiff, "which would put its range at roughly five hundred miles." He leaned back in his chair and gave his eyes a rest. "How far away is Tonto from here?"

Yamada brought up a digital map and measured. "Looks like a little under two hundred miles."

"So a round trip would take up a good eighty percent of its range."

Waterman nodded in agreement. "So, dropping off radar was probably due to landing."

"Seems likely."

Yamada zoomed all the way back out. "Okay, so we just need to figure out where it landed."

There was nothing quite like it. A sensation both extraordinarily exhilarating and extraordinarily frightening at the same time, and a view almost beyond description.

The worst part was the climb.

Almost two hundred feet straight up. Up a perfectly vertical column of reinforced, structural steel lined on each side with cables of thick black coax, secured several inches behind hundreds of horizontal steel pegs for his hands and feet.

Climbing cell towers was not for the faint of heart, no matter how immune to heights a person was. In the end, all that protected a technician from a horrifying fall was a half-inch steel safety cable running from top to bottom. The same cable Elijah Jackson's harness was currently fastened to. Every time he climbed he remembered the immortal and chilling words from the man who trained him. *It's not the fall that's so bad, it's the sudden stop at the end.*

It wasn't just the risk; it was also the climb. Long and arduous, working both hands and feet until reaching the various splitters, couplers, or antennas at the top.

Today the tower was positioned atop a modest mountain overlooking the distant and sprawling city of Albuquerque, New Mexico. With his jacket zipped and heavy boots, Jackson was almost a third of the way up the tower when his ears heard the familiar chime from his phone through the whistling breeze.

He took a break from his climb and relaxed, thankful for the interruption. Double-checking his safety harness, he relaxed and let go with his hands, flexing both sets of fingers before unzipping his pocket and stuffing his hand inside.

Carefully, he withdrew the phone and turned it over, checking the message.

It was from his wife. FYI, we're out of asparagus.

Jackson studied the message and sighed before returning the phone safely to his pocket and, peg by peg, began his long climb back down.

It took fifteen minutes to reach the bottom and unhook, where Jackson then dropped his toolbelt on the ground and turned toward his work van, sitting idly in the breeze.

Once inside, he reached across the cab to grab his backpack from the passenger seat and proceeded to dig through it, finally producing a second cell phone. He tossed the backpack onto the seat next to him and powered it on.

Once booted, he activated the encryption app and began texting.

> Catbird here.
> *Greetings, Catbird. It's Gunny.*
> What's up, Gunny?
> *Need some help. Need to trace a signal.*
> What's the number?
> *Don't have one. It's a burner.*

Jackson furrowed his brow. Need more details.

> *Looking for a number active near Ogden, Utah, a couple weeks ago, and now active near Tonto Forest.*

Jackson glanced up from his phone, thinking. Gonna take some time.

> *Understood. Need it as soon as you can.*
> Copy.

Jackson stopped typing and exited the application. He then held down a button to power off the phone while he continued pondering. He'd have to get into the servers. He would also need to think of a way to disguise his poking around as being related to one of his work orders.

He looked through his side window and peered up at the tower. The climb back up would certainly give him time to try to figure it out.

Jackson stuffed the phone back into his backpack and zipped it up, then climbed out of the vehicle. He could not help but smirk. Over the irony of them spoofing his wife's phone number when they sent him the first message.

She of all people knew how much he hated asparagus.

75

Rachel climbed back outside the ship and stopped, turning when Kincaid followed her out. She looked at the others still observing from the other side of the glass wall.

"I take it everyone already knows."

"Knows what?"

She shook her head irritably. "When were you going to tell me?"

"Tell you *what*?"

"Don't play games with me," Rachel shouted. "That there are more capsules!"

Kincaid was unaffected by her outburst.

"It's not your concern," he replied.

"Excuse me?"

"Not your concern," he repeated. "As in irrelevant. Now get to work."

Rachel held up a hand. "You're telling me that you don't think this is 'need to know' information?"

"Not to you."

"Did it ever occur to you that nugget of information might shed just a little light on their cryonic suspension system?"

"No."

She stared back, almost aghast.

"We don't know," said Kincaid, "whether anyone else was in the other capsules."

Rachel did not believe him. "You've had forty years to find out."

"There was only so much we could do without the risk of breaking something. Keeping the body frozen and undisturbed was priority one."

"Oh really?"

"Yes."

Rachel folded her arms. "I don't believe that."

"And I don't care."

The sharpness of Kincaid's response dazed her.

"I don't need you to believe me," he said. "I only need you to do what I tell you."

"So, I'm just a mule to you."

"That's exactly right."

His apathy caused her to fume. "Forty years and you have no idea whether someone else was in those other pods."

"I will tell you again for the last time, we don't know. We couldn't take the chance of compromising the ship or the person inside until we knew we had a way to revive him."

"Thanks to John Reiff."

"Reiff helped us kill two birds with one stone."

"Perfecting cryo suspension both for you," said Rachel, "*and* your astronaut."

"Like I told you before, no one in their right mind would choose to wake up in the future without knowing what it holds." He motioned back through the hole in the ship. "And our astronaut may be the person who can tell us."

She leaned and peered through the opening again, and then shook her head. "I don't know if I can do it."

"Do what?"

"I don't know how far into the future of cryonics we're looking. How he was preserved, what they used, what they didn't use. Their process could be so different, or so advanced, that we're the equivalent of medieval doctors using leeches and we end up killing him."

"We have no choice," replied Kincaid. "We have only what is available to us, if he's still alive."

His comment made her think. Of a conversation Rachel had had with Reiff. *Was the cryonic state a state of being alive or dead?*

Kincaid had had enough of her distraction. He narrowed his eyes and pointed at the ship. "Now do it."

76

By the time they returned inside, Wicks was standing before the capsule with a large handheld device, pointing a laser through the glass. He turned to Kincaid as he approached. "Nothing special inside, just regular old air."

"Good." The old man glanced briefly at Rachel before instructing his men to look for a way to open it.

"When he's out, I need to take a tissue sample."

"What for?"

"To look for cryoprotectants. It might give me at least some idea."

Kincaid turned back to his men, who were examining the edges of the pod. After a couple of minutes, Wicks turned back with a shake of his head. "Don't see any way to open it. Might be automatically controlled by the ship."

Of course, thought Kincaid. *By the ship that's frozen solid.* "Break it."

Rachel turned in surprise, only to have Kincaid ask, "Got a better idea?"

Wicks motioned his men to pick up the welders. They retrieved and fired both up, each reproducing their white-and-blue flames. Following Wicks's instructions, the men reaffixed their goggles and one began cutting a vertical line down the center while the other cut horizontally.

They could watch tiny, jagged edges of glass appear before quickly melting away under the intense heat until both welders were extinguished after forming a cross, and the men stepped back. It was then that Wicks reached into the large duffle bag and retrieved a heavy, curved crowbar.

He checked back with Kincaid, who nodded, before gripping the bar tightly and hitting the glass enclosure at full force.

The first crack was small, but the second strike produced a much larger fracture, traveling out in multiple directions like long frozen strikes of lightning.

The third impact was the charm. Punching a small hole through the clear surface and sending shards crumbling inward.

Wicks leaned forward and put his nose to the hole, sniffing the air. Stale but nothing alarming. He looked back to Kincaid who again nodded.

The capsule's entire canopy was destroyed and pulled free within minutes, using the crowbar around the edge to clear any sharp edges. The tool was then dropped, and all three men maneuvered inward, reaching with gloved hands to grasp the body. Pulling it forward produced an eerie peeling sound from the dark fabric behind it.

Leaning the stiff body forward, Wicks removed one glove and peeled the thin, see-through mask away, dropping it.

Kincaid had moved forward to assist and lifted a charcoal-gray body bag, carefully laying it out to allow his men a place to lower the figure. Checking the capsule for anything else, they wasted no time, promptly lifting the open body bag by its thick handles and moving in short, controlled steps for the opening.

They were out of the ship and out of the giant glass enclosure within minutes. Heading for the elevator while the others in the cavern stood grouped around the elevator entrance for a glimpse of their frozen patient. Blue and featureless, save for a head of dark hair and a pair of shorts.

In less than five minutes, they had reached the medical lab and eased the bag onto a waiting table, where Rachel rushed around them and procured a scalpel and clear slide. Carefully, she cut a delicate layer of skin from the man's blue-tinted leg and laid it flat on the tiny pane of rectangular glass.

She turned and moved across the room to a low countertop supporting multiple machines. The Raman spectrometer was similar to the handheld device but faster and more accurate. Producing, in less than thirty seconds, a full display of graphical plot points for all detected chemical compounds.

Rachel studied the results and turned around to view the body again. Without a word, she retrieved the slide from the machine and moved farther down the counter to a heavy compound microscope. She remained hovering over it for nearly a minute, studying the sample through the powerful lenses.

She raised her head, pausing a moment to turn around, peering at Kincaid with a look of genuine surprise.

"What is it?"

She moved her head from side to side. "There's no sign of cryoprotectants," she said. "And no crystallization in the tissue."

"Meaning what?"

Rachel didn't answer. All cryonic patients frozen in the last fifty years were subjected to crystallization. The unavoidable microscopic icicles that developed in each and every cell of the human body. Icicles that often damaged the cell beyond repair. Cryoprotectants were the special chemicals developed over the ensuing decades in an attempt to minimize the crystallization and resulting damage, often compared to a car's antifreeze.

It was one of the reasons why John Reiff was so unique. And why he had been the one revived during the course of the secret project Rachel and Henry had originally been a part of. But at the time, they didn't know anything about Reiff. Neither his name nor where he came from. He had been presented to them, through people like Nora Lagner and Liam Duchik, as simply a John Doe. A random medical donor that just happened to demonstrate an abnormally low level of naturally occurring crystallization compared to other cryonic patients.

That was all before they found out Lagner and Duchik were part of the group behind the entire experiment, having already done things to Reiff's body in order to achieve those low crystallization levels.

But their "astronaut" was different.

Rachel had never seen a frozen patient with zero crystallization, or cryoprotectants, or vitrification. Not once.

She was still staring blankly at Kincaid when his growl snapped her out of it. "What . . . is it?"

Rachel could only shake her head. "This may not go well."

"Why not?"

"However this man was frozen, it was much more advanced. Way beyond where we are."

"So?"

"I told you," she said, "not knowing exactly how he was preserved could be detrimental when it comes to how we attempt to revive him."

"Or," replied Kincaid, "it makes it easier."

Rachel stared at him in silence. *Easier?* Her eyes fell to the table where the body was lying, contemplating Kincaid's words. Not his words, the concept. Was that possible? Could it, in fact, make their job easier?

The extensive damage to the cells had always been the biggest hurdle for cryonics, from the very beginning. And what made reviving Reiff even possible. He had the least amount of cellular damage of anyone. But reviving him was almost a miracle in itself. Could a patient with no cellular damage at all make it easier to reanimate even without direct knowledge of how he was preserved?

She continued staring forward, considering the possibility. Before blinking and looking at the giant device waiting behind Kincaid and his men. "Get him into the Machine."

11

Together the three men lifted the body up and over the top of the machine, pausing to readjust their hold before slowly and somewhat awkwardly lowering their patient inside.

The others had all rejoined them, with DeSilva moving directly to the console. Onscreen, the digital outline of their frozen subject appeared within the cavity, surrounded by 1,024 carefully positioned transmitters and sensors, represented onscreen as tiny blue circles.

Wicks and his men looked for further instruction but were brushed out of the way when Rachel climbed up on top and bent over at the waist to lean inside. One by one, she attached over a dozen patches to the man's ice-cold arms, legs, and chest. All leading back and connecting to the Machine through thin fiber-optic cables.

She checked the distance from the patient to each interior wall to ensure he was straight, then rose back up and nodded at DeSilva.

After she moved out of the way, he instructed the computer to close the lid and seal the cavity.

Rachel looked at Nora Lagner, standing near DeSilva, and motioned her over. Instructing her to bring the defibrillator closer, which she did. Rachel then looked at the others. "Get back out of the way," she said. When they were clear, she gave DeSilva a final okay.

He acknowledged and glanced one last time at Kincaid before initiating the countdown.

Rachel moved quietly to the console and took a deep breath. The entire heating process would take less than three minutes. The blink of an eye to some, but still more than enough time for something to go horribly wrong.

With Reiff, they were barely a minute in before problems arose, causing them to heat longer than planned. She hoped the improvements made since then would result in a better outcome.

When the countdown hit zero, the three-dimensional image on the screen began to light up as the thousand transmitters suddenly energized, filling the entire chamber with carefully measured microwave radiation. Using the adjacent sensors to individually adjust according to the density of organic matter between them, be it liquid, tissue, or solid bone.

Unlike the first time, most transmitters on the screen remained a steady blue, which was a positive sign. Some changed to orange and even red, indicating unsafe levels of heat, but the majority quickly adjusted and, one by one, eventually returned to normal.

Rachel pointed over the console to Lagner. "Charge the defibrillator!"

The other woman responded and flipped the large button to On, immediately illuminating several lights on the unit's front panel.

Most of the transmitters were holding steady.

"When we're done," she said to Wicks's men, "get him out as soon as the lid opens, and back onto the table."

"Thirty more seconds," announced DeSilva, "temperatures look good."

Rachel now left the console and moved to a nearby shelf, retrieving a stethoscope and blood pressure cuff. She approached and stood between the Machine and the waiting table before rounding the table and placing her instruments on a shelf directly beneath it. She then stepped in to take Lagner's place in front of the defibrillator.

"Ten more seconds . . ."

There was no sound from inside the massive contraption when it was over, until the hiss of the lid pushing up and sliding to the side, followed immediately by a column of rising steam.

"Okay," Rachel called, "get him, quickly!"

Wicks and his men were immediately back on top and reaching inside, grappling until they could get a firm grip and lifting the astronaut back out. One at a time, they slid carefully down the device's exterior until all three managed to get him to the table with a delicate thud.

Rachel had both paddles ready. "Clear!" she yelled and placed them on his chest, pausing only a moment before releasing a massive jolt. Swiftly, she returned the paddles to charge again and grabbed the stethoscope and cuff. "Get the blanket!"

Lagner fetched the nearby thermal blanket and in one smooth motion, unfurled it over the body, watching as Rachel checked for a pulse.

There was a long silence. Rachel moved her hand to various areas of the body, checking, before Lagner noticed something out of the corner of her eye. An area of blanket over the man's chest began to move.

Through her stethoscope, Rachel could hear a faint heartbeat.

After listening to both lungs, she removed the scope from her neck and glanced up at Kincaid, who appeared almost frozen himself. A pin drop could have been heard in the room.

The old man's eyes remained wide and expectant, waiting for her to speak.

"I guess he wasn't dead," she stated.

78

Within minutes, the man's skin began to change color. From its previous blue to a light or ashen gray and eventually to a faint, pale shade of pink. Suggesting that his vascular system was working.

But what surprised Rachel the most was how quickly the other readings improved. Progressing even faster than Reiff's second revival, and seemingly smoother.

Oxygen levels, blood pressure, and pulse were all inching toward normal levels faster than Reiff's had. And so far, after more than an hour, no signs of seizures, even small ones, which were early indications of muscle or nerve damage.

"How soon will he wake up?" asked Kincaid.

Rachel frowned. "How should I know?"

"Because you've done this before, multiple times."

She shook her head in disagreement. "Not *this*."

"How long?" the old man pressed.

She gazed down at the patient, having been moved to one of the facility's beds, motionless and resting in a slightly inclined position. An IV tube running down to his left arm. "Probably days," she finally said. "There's a lot happening internally. Trillions of cells are gradually coming back to life, all trying to reestablish communication with each other. Along with a nervous system that is most likely screaming in protest over what happened to it and presenting a signaling overload. At least that's what we've seen in Reiff."

Standing on the opposite side, Kincaid considered her words. "It's going well though, yes?"

"Yes," she admitted. "So far."

The old man nodded and looked around at the others. All standing in a semicircle, quietly observing.

Over time, everyone eventually filed out of the room, leaving Rachel monitoring the man's progress. The only person to stay was Nina Sandhu, who remained quietly sitting on the other side of the bed.

As Rachel studied the screen of the Dinamap, noting its updated readouts, she observed Sandhu rise and study the man's unconscious face. She reached down and gently raised his eyelids one at a time, checking his pupils, then reached down and flexed his wrist back and forth, then his fingers.

She was testing his motor function.

"You have some medical training," said Rachel.

"A long time ago," she replied without looking up. "In a previous life." She then corrected herself. "In a previous career."

"What specialty?"

"Neurology."

Rachel was surprised. "Where?"

Sandhu gently raised the man's arm and lowered it again while feeling his elbow. "Baghdad."

"And after that?"

The woman glanced at Rachel with a sly expression. "Doesn't matter."

"Okay then"—Rachel's sarcasm returned—"would you like to take over here?"

"You're doing fine." After a pause, Sandhu added, "I can see why Reiff survived, twice."

Her comment surprised Rachel, leaving the younger woman staring back at Sandhu. "You know about Reiff."

She nearly scoffed. "Of course I do. Who do you think was reading the reports you submitted?"

"I thought a lot of people were."

"Some." She nodded.

Rachel turned back to their patient. "Then you know that what we've done so far with him is the easy part."

"Oh yes," answered Sandhu, finally looking at Rachel. "The brain is very complex. There's no guarantee he won't wake up in a vegetative state."

"Agreed."

"Fortunately, John Reiff didn't."

"John Reiff wasn't frozen for hundreds of years."

"True," commented Sandhu.

"Then I'm sure you also appreciate just how rudimentary this new technology really is."

"Of course I do. The first version is always flawed. Which is why we had Reiff."

Rachel's face became infuriated. "That's all he was to you, a lab rat."

"Yes," answered Sandhu frankly. "A lab rat, guinea pig, test subject, whichever you prefer." She grinned at Rachel with a look of hubris. "Everything must be tested, must it not?"

Rachel's eyes narrowed. "Someone should have tested it on *you*."

To her surprise, Sandhu laughed. "I'm far too valuable for that."

"But Reiff wasn't."

Sandhu gave her an almost curious look. As if Rachel were stating the obvious.

"You people are disgusting."

Sandhu's brown eyes intensified. "Oh really. We're disgusting. *We are.* Not the mindless sheep that inhabit the planet. Lemmings who do nothing but talk about the same things over and over and over. Who spend most of their lives angry and arguing about nothing that will ever make one ounce of difference."

Rachel stared at the woman in confusion. "What are you talking about?"

It was then that Nina Sandhu shocked Rachel. "Do you even know why the *Great Collapse* happened?"

The question left her peering blankly at the woman, as though transfixed. "Because . . . of the wars—"

Sandhu rolled her eyes. "Dear God, that's exactly what I mean."

"What?"

"The standard 'sheeple' response, over and over. The same naive talking point I've heard a million times." She looked down at the unconscious man between them. "That's why we're doing this. Because of people like *you*."

Rachel did not reply. She remained fixed as Sandhu continued.

"The sheep don't know the first thing about what really goes on on this planet. That the entire world is run by nothing but powerful, corrupt elites, and it always will be. And you know why?"

"No."

"Because *you* believe exactly what you're told. All of you. That one side is good, and the other is bad. That your neighbor is evil and heartless while you are honest and moral. My God, it's the oldest playbook in history. Just keep the peasants arguing with each other so they never bother to look behind the curtain to see what's really happening. Who's really pulling the strings."

Rachel stared, dumbfounded. "So . . ." she finally said with a hint of disdain, "you're one of those behind the curtains."

"Hardly," sneered Sandhu. "We're sick of them just like everyone else. Even more so, with their constant greed and endless narcissism, while sitting atop their ivory towers of phony righteousness. *They're* the reason the world collapsed, from seeds sewn decades and decades before you were ever born. But the sheep keep listening to them, keep electing them, because that's what they are told to do." A grin crept across Sandhu's lips, as though not even realizing it. "So, if the world will never change on its own . . . we will do it ourselves."

79

"We have a problem."

DeSilva's hands paused and he swiveled away from his monitor to face Lagner. "What kind of problem?"

"Rachel Souza is lying to us."

"What about now?"

"About John Reiff."

DeSilva sighed and lowered his hands.

"I've been looking through the files she downloaded. All of her testing documentation."

"And?"

"And there's still something wrong with Reiff. Something serious. It's all there in her files. Copious notes, recorded in extreme detail through hundreds and hundreds of tests. Including the details about how those animals at the zoo died. And now we know exactly what it was, and why that capuchin monkey is still alive."

DeSilva folded his arms, curious. "I'm all ears."

His colleague reached for a seat and sat down in front of him. "Ever hear of something called 'thermogenesis'?"

"No."

"It's the molecular process responsible for generating a body's internal combustion. In other words, our metabolism. The animals Rachel delivered to the zoo and to our friend Dr. Samantha Reed, all began showing signs of thermogenesis breakdown shortly after being delivered. Resulting in a gradual loss of body heat. Which eventually begins to affect all kinds of things, from muscles, to organs, and eventually the brain. That's why," said Lagner, "they all appeared to be freezing to death. Not because they were producing something cold but because their systems could not hold onto the heat they were creating. Slowly becoming self-reinforcing as they held on to less and less, prompting their cells to work harder and harder, which meant losing even more energy, until they effectively froze to death."

"Huh."

"And *that* is why John Reiff had to be refrozen. Because the same thing was happening to him, and quickly. Rachel Souza didn't know what else to do, so they froze him again until she could find a solution."

"We already surmised that," said DeSilva. "But why didn't it happen with the monkey?"

"I don't know. And neither did Rachel. If I had to guess, I suspect she still doesn't know. But she did eventually find DNA markers in the monkey that seemed to protect against it."

"So, she still doesn't know *why* the cure works?"

"I doubt it. I think she only knows that it does."

"How?"

"With the help of hundreds of mice. Some of the first animals we successfully reanimated, followed eventually by different animals in increasing order of size and biological complexity."

"Okay," thought DeSilva aloud, "so she used mice to find the cure for Reiff. And the problem is what?"

Lagner settled into her own chair with a guileful smile. "The problem," she said, "is that while she may have found a solution to the thermogenesis breakdown, a bunch of the mice she was experimenting on began demonstrating signs of a whole new problem."

"What problem?"

"I'm not sure exactly. That part is less clear. But you can bet that Rachel knows."

Daniel DeSilva slowly bobbed his head. "And she's keeping it quiet."

"Precisely. Something is still seriously wrong with Reiff, but something tells me she may not even know what's causing it this time."

"And why do you say that?"

Lagner shook her head. "I don't know, I need to do more reading. But it's clear they were in a hurry to revive Reiff for some reason."

"And you're absolutely sure about this?"

"It's all in her notes," said Lagner. "I can show you."

80

Douglas Kincaid was sitting at the crystal table in his quarters, leaning back in his chair while holding a small glass of celebratory eighteen-year-old scotch.

"Let's not rush things," he said to Anna Lu, swirling the dark liquor in the palm of his hand.

Lu was glowering. "Not rush things?"

"We have time. Nothing happens in a day."

She hated platitudes. "We are more than six months late," she said tersely. "They are tired of waiting."

"It'll be fine."

"Tell me," she said, "how will it be fine? Because they will relent or because my head is the first on their list?"

"Don't be so dramatic," replied Kincaid. "They're men of reason. They know things like this can take time."

"Even reasonable men get tired of waiting."

"It took us longer to find Reiff and Souza than expected. But we have them now. At least one of them. The one that matters. And our astronaut is alive. That is a colossal step forward."

"They don't care about the astronaut. They care about the ship."

Kincaid took a sip of scotch. "Yes, I know that. And the ship is now defrosting. But we cannot just give it away without having first crack at it."

"Our agreement with them said nothing about 'first crack.' You forget that if it were not for them and all their resources, none of this would have even been possible."

Kincaid was growing irritated. "I have not forgotten. But no one in their right mind would have expected us to just hand it over so quickly, without our own examination."

Lu maintained her demeanor. "And what exactly is included in this examination of ours?"

"For Christ's sake, Anna. It's a ship from the future! What the hell do you think we want to examine? How about everything!"

"They will not wait for that."

Kincaid abruptly leaned forward. "I don't really care. This is still the U. S. of A. They can't just come in and take it!"

Lu did not respond. She remained solemn, looking at him through a pair of unreadable eyes.

Kincaid regained his composure and finished the scotch in one swallow. "Tell them we need a little more time," he said. "We're very close now."

Again, there was no answer from Lu. No words, no expression, not even a nod. Her only movement was to turn in silence and walk back toward the door, leaving Kincaid seated and watching her depart.

When Anna Lu opened the heavy door, she was surprised to see DeSilva and Lagner standing on the other side, seemingly about to knock.

81

The heavy parka was picked up off the floor and pulled open, allowing entry one leg at a time with each foot wiggling down and into both over-sized attached rubber boots. Thick fur-lined gloves slipped over each hand before turning to grip the large metal handwheel and turning it counterclockwise. The metal hatch opening was then pulled open.

The chill inside had less of a bite and felt slightly warmer, lending to less frost spanning the giant glass wall, and the ice beneath each step becoming slushy.

Entering the ship, Rachel slipped on one of the partially melted patches but caught herself with a quick grab at the burned opening.

Carefully, she plodded forward across the melting floor until reaching the open capsule, or at least what was left of it. Broken pieces of glass still littered the floor, some glistening from the cavern's overhead lights outside.

She stepped on several shards with a loud crunch to draw closer to the opening. The oval-shaped capsule was empty.

Rachel placed a gloved hand on each edge, careful to avoid remaining fragments, and leaned inside.

She examined the top half before dropping her head and looking toward the bottom, spotting the thin, crumpled mask and tubing their patient had been wearing.

Bracing herself, she reached down and picked it up, noting a small hole or nozzle halfway down in the side of the capsule where the hose had been attached.

She stepped back and moved closer to the door where she could get a better look at it. Removing one glove, she rubbed her thumb and index finger back and forth over the surface. The material was very thin, resembling a clear latex but with a rubbery feel to it. The hose was small, perhaps a quarter of an inch, and felt the same. And it was just as clear as the mask.

Rachel stuffed it delicately inside her parka and put her glove back on. With one final look around the inside of the icy ship, she turned back the way she came.

In the lab, the spectrograph revealed something surprising. Microscopic frozen droplets inside the tube of what the machine was identifying as hydrogen sulfide.

During the early stages of their project, she remembered reading about different experiments from the early 2000s. Long before the collapse, when scientists discovered that exposing animals to small amounts of hydrogen sulfide gas put them into a state of suspended animation. Also referred to as "biostatis."

But there wasn't much data in the years following the experiments, at least not that Rachel and her colleagues could find. Unless it was destroyed in the cyber wars along with ninety percent of all other digitized information. She and the others had ultimately moved on, but now she began to wonder.

Could their astronaut have been suspended through means other than cryonic freezing? Or something complementary to it? If so, if he was suspended through other means, then through what means was his reanimation supposed to occur?

A tinge of nervousness returned to Rachel's gut. Was it possible? Was he suspended in a completely different manner? Had they perfected the use of hydrogen sulfide and put him into hibernation with gas, and then froze him? And again, and more importantly, did that mean there was another way he was supposed to be revived? Or, she wondered, was the gas part of the reason why their astronaut seemed to revive so easily?

Rachel reached forward and picked up the clear, soft mask. Cautiously examining it in her hands. There were no cryoprotectants in his system, and no ice crystals. Meaning no discernable cellular damage. Was there a way that using the gas provided that protection, or something entirely different?

It was as far as her wondering made it before the door to the medical lab suddenly burst open and an angry Kincaid entered, followed by his stooges DeSilva and Lagner.

82

"You've been lying to us!" growled Kincaid.

Rachel was taken aback, putting the mask down and looking back at them. "What?"

"You heard me!" the old man shouted, crossing the room as if ready to attack, and causing Rachel to press back against the counter.

"What are you talking about?"

"Enough!" bellowed Kincaid. "You said you would tell us everything! *Everything!*"

Rachel's eyes moved nervously between them, then to the unconscious astronaut on the bed before returning to Kincaid. "I-I don't know what you mean. He's alive. I revived him just as you instructed."

"I'm not talking about him, I'm talking about Reiff!"

"Reiff? W-what about—" It was then that she caught the glint in Nora Lagner's eyes. One of smug satisfaction.

"What's wrong with Reiff?" demanded Kincaid. "What are you not telling us?"

She swallowed nervously.

The old man pressed closer until he was nearly on top of her. "Tell me *now!*"

Rachel put a hand out and pushed him away, then straightened. "I don't know."

Kincaid raised a bony finger in front of her face. "Stop with the lies."

"I'm not lying! I mean it. I don't know."

"What the hell does that mean?"

"It means I don't know. Something is wrong, yes, but I don't know what it is."

"Bullshit!" growled Kincaid.

"I'm telling you the truth. I *don't* know."

"And you didn't tell us. Because . . ."

"Because she knew the same thing would happen to us once we were revived," said Lagner.

Rachel looked briefly at the woman but did not comment.

"So *that* was your plan."

"My plan," said Rachel, turning to point at the occupied bed, "was to help you revive *him*."

"You said you would tell us everything."

"Everything I knew," she countered. "But I can't tell you what I don't know. Like what's happening to John."

"Don't play games with me, you bitch." He raised his hand and snapped his fingers. "Or I'll have you disappear just like that."

Rachel looked past them to see Sandhu and Lu enter the room. All of them looked like they were ready to kill her. She slid farther away along the counter. "I just need more time to understand it. I think it can be treated. That's why I didn't say anything," she lied.

"Is that so?" challenged Lagner. "And just what kind of treatment would that be?"

Rachel's mind was racing, trying to think of an explanation the sounded plausible. Her eyes found Sandhu, and she thought of something the woman had said. "I think . . . it's just a neurological effect. Maybe Nina can help."

Sandhu's eyebrows rose in surprise, only to fall skeptically. "I haven't practiced in years."

"Then we can find someone else," Rachel offered. "I just need more time."

Kincaid leveled his gaze at her. "*More* time?"

"Yes."

"And how," he replied in a bilious tone, "do you plan to do that from here?"

She didn't answer.

"John Reiff could be anywhere," said Kincaid. "If he were a smart man, he would already be gone. Disappearing into this hellhole of a world never to be seen again."

"He wouldn't do that," Rachel replied.

"No? Are you sure? If he's as intelligent as you imply, he would know to stay the hell away from you, and me!" He moved closer again. "Believe me when I tell you that I am by far the most dangerous person you will ever meet."

She said nothing and Kincaid glanced behind himself at the others. "Go ahead, ask them."

He pressed in so his face was just inches from hers. Speaking in a near whisper. "If I find out that you've lied about anything else, or that you cannot *fix* what is wrong with John Reiff, you will pay. In ways you cannot even imagine."

Rachel remained motionless, staring fearfully into Kincaid's cold eyes, and shaking.

Until something sounded.

A loud buzzing behind Kincaid, somewhere near the others. They all glanced at each other before Nora Lagner instinctively reached into her pocket and withdrew her phone.

It was vibrating as it rang.

She looked at Kincaid and slowly raised it to her cheek. "Hello?"

Lagner remained quiet, listening, before the color on her face became ashen. "It's John Reiff."

83

The heavy crunching over the dirt and gravel came to a stop, leaving nothing but soft whistling from a cool evening breeze behind them.

"You sure about this?"

Reiff looked up at Waterman. "They're not going to let her go," he said. "Not without an incentive."

"You mean a trade."

Reiff nodded and looked out over the top of the open ridge line, peering down the dirty road into the canyon, not far from where Yamada estimated the helicopter had landed. The precise meet location was provided by Nora Lagner.

At the bottom of the canyon, a dust trail appeared behind a small dark object, a truck, making its way toward them, up the winding dirt road along the towering canyon wall.

Waterman, alone with Reiff, lowered a hand onto his friend's shoulder. "Feel like I should say something deep or profound."

"Such as?"

"Like . . . when life gives you lemons . . ." he started but paused and shook his head. "Nah, I got nothin'."

"Well said."

The truck continued up the road until cresting the top, where it stopped about fifty feet from a lone John Reiff. Behind him, Waterman gave one more look at his friend from the window of his own vehicle.

Wicks and one of his men climbed out of their oversized black Ford and carefully scanned the ridge with its brushes and trees bristling in the breeze. They then carefully approached.

As they neared, both men drew guns from their holsters and pointed them at Reiff. "Anyone takes a potshot at us," warned Wicks, "at least one of us puts a hole in you."

"If anyone was going to drop you," replied Reiff, "they would have done it as soon as you got out of your truck."

Wicks smirked at that and studied Reiff in his wheelchair. The man was ragged and looked like he'd been dragged there. "What they want with you, I have no idea."

84

They entered the cool interior of the compound with Wicks's subordinate rolling Reiff through a set of wide double doors, where they found everyone waiting for them. Members of The Nine as well as Rachel Souza, who was standing a step or two in front of them and peering at Reiff with a sad, solemn expression.

Beleaguered, Reiff still managed a grin as he looked up at Rachel. "Isn't everyone supposed to jump out and yell 'surprise'?"

She shook her head, unable to suppress an exhausted chuckle. She strolled forward and stopped in front of him. "Why are you doing this?"

"We don't have a lot of choice anymore." Reiff looked away and scanned the faces before him, stopping on an old man who was staring intently at him. "I'm guessing you're Kincaid."

The man stepped forward. "So, you already know my name."

"It's about all I know. Maybe you can tell me what all this is about."

Unlike Rachel's, Kincaid's chuckle was clear and audible. "You haven't figured that out?"

"Been a little preoccupied."

The old man placed his hands behind his back and nodded. "I should think so." He glanced up at Wicks, who was standing behind Reiff. And who, at Kincaid's signal, turned and closed the two reinforced doors behind them.

Reiff peered over his shoulder when he heard them close. "The deal was a trade."

"And it will be"—Kincaid nodded—"when I'm ready." He turned and looked Rachel over. "We still have work to do. Now that you're here."

Kincaid's expression in no way reflected the thoughts going through his mind.

This is John Reiff? This? The man is in a wheelchair and looks like he's been in a barroom fight and lost. He's slouching, feebly, as if he can barely sit up. This is what I and the rest of The Nine can look forward to after coming out of our cryo freeze?! Good God.

He kept the sudden disappointment and unease from showing on his face. Or the anger. Rachel Souza had deceived them more than he ever imagined. *A slight neurological effect? The man is a wreck.*

It was right there and then that Kincaid finalized Rachel Souza's fate in the blink of an eye. He was done with her. The woman was no longer anything more than a tool that he would use until he had extracted everything he needed. And once he had that, she and Reiff would be eliminated. Where he would witness it firsthand and know that they were gone forever.

He was done, totally and utterly finished. The moment he had what he needed.

In the medical lab, the small capuchin stirred lazily in his cage, with barely enough energy to turn his tiny head. Staring out through his glazed amber eyes toward the sound of abrupt rustling in an otherwise silent room.

On the bed, the human was beginning to move. First his head, then small movements in his hands and fingers. And finally twitching from his legs beneath the sheets. With eyes that trembled, as if struggling to open, before the human became still again.

Reiff was shown to his room, one floor down, not far from Rachel's, and just as sparsely decorated. He glanced around, noting the bed, small table, a fake plant, and locked door. No bathroom, leaving him with the impression the room wasn't designed for guests. Likely repurposed from some other use.

It was not long before Rachel appeared to get him, opening the door with Lagner and Wicks behind her. The latter of whom eyed him callously their entire trip down a narrow hallway while Rachel pushed him, until reaching the waiting medical lab.

Inside, Reiff noted the large, well-provisioned room. Medical devices of all kinds, many he did not recognize, and a cage in the corner. *They'd found the capuchin.* On the opposite side of the expansive room was a machine that he recognized. The Machine as they called it, and not far from it, a still figure lying on one of the two beds.

When he looked up at Rachel, she simply said, "There's a lot to explain." Before continuing forward and aligning his wheelchair with the second, empty bed. With some effort, she helped him out of his chair and somewhat clumsily onto the waiting mattress.

She helped get him situated and asked in a soft voice, "How are you feeling?"

"Like a hundred bucks."

Rachel rolled her eyes and turned around to power up the second Dinamap machine, then raised his hand to clip the pulse oximeter onto his index finger. "When's the last time you had one of the therapy injections?"

"This morning."

"Good." She continued speaking while wrapping the blood pressure cuff around his arm. "I've recreated the serum so we can give you another dose tomorrow." Rachel finished fastening the cuff and pressed the button to begin inflation.

While it proceeded to inflate and take a reading, Reiff looked to his right at the other bed. "Who's that?"

"He," said Kincaid, appearing behind Lagner and Wicks, "is none of your concern."

Reiff was unfazed. "You seem a little tense."

Kincaid stopped at the foot of his bed and glared. "All I want from you . . . is cooperation."

"Fine."

The compound was an interesting place. Reiff had never seen anything quite like it. Certainly nothing as swank. "Nice bunker you got here. Must have taken years to turn it into a fortification."

"More than you know. From an underground cavern," replied Kincaid.

Reiff examined the large room. Noting the walls still consisted primarily of rock. "I can see that." They were natural, though clearly carved into their current shape. The floor and ceiling, however, were manmade.

Expensive marble below and what looked like polished concrete over-head. The rest of the room could have been taken straight out of a modern hospital or research lab.

Rachel disappeared for a moment and returned with a syringe and special container. "I want to take some blood samples and run some tests."

Reiff nodded and watched as she set them down and began wrapping a rubber strap around his free arm. He then looked at Kincaid and motioned to the other bed again. "Let me guess, your second defrosted victim?"

"I told you, it's none of your business."

Sandhu appeared at the door and entered, strolling forward past her colleagues with a brief glimpse at Kincaid before studying Reiff. She stood beside him, examining his bloodshot eyes. Reaching down and lifting one eyelid and then the other. "When is the last time you slept?"

"Yesterday morning."

"And for how long?"

"Beats me."

"Having trouble remembering things?"

"Don't we all?"

"Try again," replied Sandhu.

"Some things."

"Like what?"

Reiff shrugged. "Like why I thought this was a good idea."

"Because running is futile," injected Kincaid.

"Right." He studied Kincaid as Rachel calmly drew the blood from his arm. "So, what is it you want from me?"

"Answers," replied the old man. "And a cure."

"I see. Because you're afraid it's going to happen to you, too."

"You're very sharp, Mr. Reiff."

"So, I guess the sooner you get your cure, the sooner you let us go."

"Precisely."

Reiff laid his head on the pillow behind him. "Great. Glad we're on the same page."

He then closed his eyes. The old man was stressed about something. All of them were. About something important. The tenseness in Kincaid's jawline and posture were hard to miss. While the others appeared stressed but quiet and obedient. He didn't know why, but Reiff's guess was that it had to do with him and the unconscious man lying next to him.

And it was clear Kincaid was lying. There was no way he was ever going to let either one of them out of there.

85

Early evening arrived and presented a stunning blue and pink scattered sky as the sun finally dipped below the horizon. Leaving just enough light available to see with. Enough to still see the main entrance to the compound at the bottom of the canyon, through the crosshairs of a Bushnell Banner 6–18x50 mm sniper scope.

Now from the far side of the ridgeline, positioned between a grouping of pointleaf manzanita bushes, Devin Waterman leaned back and lowered the rifle, laying it carefully on its side. He then rolled over and sat in a low sitting position.

"Well?"

He shook his head. "Still nothing."

A nervous Henry Yamada stared at him expectantly, only to watch Waterman scoot a few feet over the dirt ground to position himself comfortably against a rock. He then fished into one of the pockets of his desert fatigues and withdrew a small package of beef jerky.

Waterman bit it open, pulled a large piece out, and began to chew. He then reached out and offered some to Yamada.

"No, thanks. I can't eat."

"Not hungry?"

Yamada gave him a sidelong frown. "That's not it."

The older man nodded and laid the open package on the rock behind him, then raised his chin and peered past Yamada. There was still enough light to make out Coleman's outline nearby.

"So, what are we supposed to do now?" asked Yamada. "It doesn't look like anyone's coming out."

"We wait."

"For how long?"

"No idea."

"Aren't you a little worried?"

"Of what?"

The younger man rolled his eyes. "Of them coming after us."

"Not particularly. I'm guessing Kincaid and his goons have a fairly small security detail."

"Why is that?"

"Because of how remote and secluded this place is. It's clearly intentional." Waterman bit off another large piece of jerky and talked through a full mouth. "Probably means they don't want a lot of attention. From anyone. You can't live in secrecy *and* have a giant security team. Gotta keep it small and tight."

Yamada let out a sigh.

The older man stared at him through the dwindling daylight with a raised eyebrow. "What's wrong?"

"I'm just not sure why we're here."

"For support."

"Support to do what?"

"To wait."

Yamada rolled his eyes.

"Now what?"

He held up his hand in a helpless gesture. "I don't get it. I just assumed we were supposed to be the cavalry or something."

"A three-person cavalry?"

"I thought there would be more of us," confessed Yamada.

"How many were you expecting?"

"I don't know!"

Waterman picked up his jerky again, smiling broadly at his young compatriot. "Nah, we're not the cavalry," he said, motioning down into the canyon. "The cavalry's already inside."

86

After dozens of neurological tests, Reiff was wheeled back to his room by Wicks and promptly pushed inside. Turning, Reiff looked at the other man who merely gave him a long brooding glare.

"Problem?"

Wicks glanced over his shoulder to see if anyone was behind him. "I haven't forgotten about you, or your friends."

Reiff wasn't following.

"The two men you killed at the missile site were my friends," said Wicks.

"What missile site?"

"Don't play dumb."

"Okay, how about ignorant?"

"Shut up," he growled.

"I don't know anything about a missile site."

It had no effect on Wicks, whose only reaction was to reach for the door.

"Wait!"

He stopped and briefly stared at Reiff, who said, "I'm a little hungry. You got any fruit out there?"

Wicks pulled the door closed with a bang. Leaving Reiff listening to the sound of a key being inserted on the opposite side and locking the door. Then only silence.

Wicks looked to be ex-military. In his late forties or early fifties. Strong, in good shape, and probably still near the top of his game physically. His M9 Berretta was the most commonly carried handgun in the military, at least it was before Reiff's accident. Wicks was also left-handed and had an almost imperceptible limp when he walked. Maybe a birth defect, or from an injury, perhaps from combat.

The door that Wicks had just locked was a simple keyhole knob. No deadbolt reinforcement, strengthening Reiff's suspicion that his room had previously been used for something else. Maybe a storage closet?

The large open area they'd brought him in through appeared to be the main entrance and well-fortified, judging by its doors. But it couldn't be the only way in. And the only other security person Reiff had seen was the younger man who wheeled him in but had since disappeared. Judging by the small group inside the compound, Reiff suspected Kincaid's entire security detail was made up of a dozen men at most. Especially considering the group's need for secrecy. But so far, Reiff had only counted six members of Kincaid's cadre, leaving three missing. And of course, Duchik, who would have brought the number to ten.

Rachel was in the lab staring through both lenses of the powerful microscope when she looked up. She could hear Kincaid's breathing as he hovered behind her in close observance. Too close. The man needed a mint.

"Do you mind?" she said over her shoulder.

Without apologizing, Kincaid eased back. "Tell me what you're doing."

She withdrew a small rectangular slide and slid another into place. "I'm examining the cultures to see if the bacteria are ready."

"And?"

"They're close. Once the system is closed and food is removed, bacterial growth is very predictable and happens in four phases: the lag phase, log phase, stationary, and decline. We're nearing the log phase," she said as she returned to the lenses, "also known as the exponential phase. Where the cultures reach peak concentration. That's when we harvest and create the serum therapy."

"Good. Good." Kincaid nodded.

Rachel pushed herself away from the microscope and rolled farther down the counter to another machine, known as an ESR analyzer. She examined its screen and read the results.

"What is it?" asked Kincaid.

"The results of John's blood test."

"And?"

Still facing away from him, she rolled her eyes before turning around. *It says he's pregnant,* she thought sarcastically. "It measures protein levels common with inflammation markers," she said, "which often rises when someone suffers from serious sleep deprivation, just like blood pressure."

"And?"

"Both remain consistent."

"What does that mean?" Kincaid looked optimistic. "Reiff is getting better?"

"Not better," she replied solemnly. "But hopefully not worse."

"So, you'll continue giving him the serum?"

Rachel nodded, pondering the question for a moment before opening her mouth to continue, but stopped when she heard something.

Together, they turned and looked behind Kincaid, at the beds. The one closest held their astronaut patient. And he was moving.

Rachel leaped to her feet. The patient's right hand twitched again before going still. Then one knee moved, beneath the blanket. Followed by the other.

But it was the eyes that made them jump. Eyes whose lids had managed to open revealing small glints of green irises and black pupils, glazed and dilated. Staring up at the ceiling lights for a long moment before slowly rolling to the side and looking at them.

87

Rachel quickly responded, leaving a stunned Kincaid lingering behind her, watching as she rushed forward and grabbed the man's wrist.

The pulse felt strong, sending her eyes immediately to the Dinamap's display. All readings looked normal. Much faster than she expected.

It took several minutes before his eyes appeared to normalize and adjust. And even longer for any sort of recognition to kick in. Which when it did, suddenly and reflexively caused his eyes to widen in fear.

"Easy! Easy!" shouted Rachel, as the man's entire body seemed to move at once. In a conscious panic. Hands, legs, and feet, all suddenly jumping and jerking together, haphazardly but instinctively, as though trying to escape.

He was uncontrollable and Rachel whirled around to Kincaid while trying to hold the man still. "Get my syringe!"

Kincaid's face did not register.

"*My syringe!*" she yelled, looking past him, searching for it and finding it on the counter. She pointed and nearly screamed. "*Now!*"

Kincaid stumbled and turned, managing to grab it and hand it to her, where she immediately took it and lunged across the patient to grasp the IV line. Quickly pulling off the cap and injecting the sedative into the clear tubing.

Almost immediately his thrashing began to slow. Still uncontrolled but less severe and fading, until they finally subsided altogether. In less than a minute, he was unconscious again, prompting Rachel to step back, out of breath, staring at the man's motionless figure.

"Holy shit," mumbled Kincaid.

She tried to calm her breathing. "Now that," she said, "I was not expecting."

When he came to the second time, he was still under a light sedative, allowing his eyes to open in a somewhat drowsy or listless state. And this time he was being recorded. In a video feed being broadcast to another room where the other members were observing.

When the man's eyes opened again, there was no shock or immediate panic. But instead, a lazy view of the lights overhead before eventually finding the faces of Rachael and Nina Sandhu. Kincaid himself was standing out of sight behind the bed's headboard.

Rachel touched the man's hand and leaned in, speaking gently. "Can you hear me?"

There was a long pause until his head gave a barely perceptible nod. His lips twitched as he tried to speak but produced only incoherent mumbling.

"Wrrrrr nu."

Rachel grinned sympathetically and softly squeezed his hand. "It's okay. Everything is okay. Take your time."

His eyes rolled lazily away but eventually returned to her. "Wrrr," he repeated. After a pause, he tried again. "Wrrreeerrrr."

She peered past him at Kincaid and replied apprehensively. "You're in a hospital." It was the same lie she told John Reiff the first time, and she still resented saying it.

There was a guttural sound in his voice before he tried to move his lips again. "Ooooo."

Both women tilted their heads, trying to understand.

"Hoooooo."

He was asking who. And this time Rachel looked to Sandhu for a response.

"We're doctors," replied Sandhu. "We're helping you."

Technically not a lie, but not the truth either. It was just as difficult now as the first time with Reiff. They lied to him because they had to. To minimize any possible psychological stress. They had no idea what condition Reiff would reawaken in, physically or psychologically. But they knew his system and mind would be highly susceptible to any form of stress, and the last thing they needed was to add to it. Their new patient was no different.

The man continued staring at them. Still through a sedated haze. Trying to process the sudden flood of stimuli.

After several minutes, he spoke again. Gradually regaining control of his mouth and voice.

"Wheeeere."

He had just asked that. Did he not hear or understand, or was he asking something different? They both assumed it was the latter.

"You're in Arizona," answered Sandhu.

The man blinked, continuing to stare at them. "Waaaa," he mouthed. "Haaapppaa."

Rachel had no idea how to answer, and was relieved when Sandhu stated simply, "We're not sure."

Again, accurate, but ironic, given that it was about all *any* of them knew.

The man became quiet, and somewhat listless. Making it unclear whether he was still processing or heading back toward unconsciousness. Behind their patient, Kincaid looked at Sandhu and nodded firmly, signaling her. She quickly moved to the other side of the bed, faster than the man's fading attention could follow. Producing another syringe, she injected it into the IV tube without hesitation.

The patient's eyes rolled and slowly closed, and the blackness returned.

88

Kincaid was overjoyed, but fearful. Their astronaut had reawakened faster than anticipated, and even hoped. It was an extraordinarily exciting moment, but along with it came an immediate worry.

The Nine were well aware of the protocol used by Rachel Souza and her team at their lab. On how best to ease a patient back into a state of limited reality. In other words, into the present. Not unlike patients recovering from a coma.

Too much information too quickly could be disastrous, overloading an already struggling cerebrum. Especially if a significant amount of time had passed. And in their astronaut's case, "significant" was an understatement.

Kincaid, along with Sandhu and Rachel, joined the other members in the observation room. Six people surrounding Rachel as though she were being interrogated.

"So what do we do?" asked Cannon.

Rachel looked at him and shrugged. "How do I know?"

"Because you've been through this before."

"I told you before, this is different. Reiff's time lapse was twenty-two years, not a thousand. And we knew the answers to his questions." She looked sarcastically at Kincaid. "Do you know *his*?"

Everyone was silent.

DeSilva finally folded his arms and exhaled. "We have to tell him as little as possible. At least to start." He turned to Rachel. "When you revived Reiff not a lot had changed from what he remembered. That's not the case here."

"True," she replied.

"The best option," voiced Kincaid, "is to keep him in an empty room.

Just having him see the instrumentation in our med lab would be enough to tell him something is off."

"Unless . . ." wondered Rachel.

"Unless what?"

She tilted her head. "Unless you wake him back up inside the ship."

The others turned and looked at each other, contemplating.

"I presume you're going to defrost it," she added.

Kincaid acknowledged.

"So, wait until it's at a normal temperature and wake him up there. It will all look normal to him."

Kincaid did not answer. Instead, he peered at Anna Lu. "That will take too long."

Rachel was surprised. "Too long? You've been waiting forty years. What's a few more days, or weeks?"

Kincaid did not answer, his eyes still fixated on Lu's expressionless face.

"He also wants to know what happened," said Colonel Cannon.

That was something no one knew the answer to. For forty years they could not take the chance of disturbing the ship for fear of flipping the wrong switch and somehow killing the astronaut inside. They were forced to wait and agonize for years until they developed the technology with a solid chance of reviving him.

"If you lie to him," said Rachel, "he'll know it." Everyone's attention returned to her. "We made that mistake with John, which resulted in us having to tell more and more lies to try to cover up the first ones. All it did was create a giant web of problems."

Kincaid nodded. "We're aware."

"What about the stress of telling him the truth?" asked Lagner.

"Given how quickly he's recovering, I think it's probably the lesser risk. You have no idea who this man is, or how he's going to react. The last thing you want to do is compound that stress with a bunch of lies and half-truths. Especially given your intent is to pump him for information."

When Kincaid shot her an icy glare, she returned a sarcastic smirk. "You yourself admitted as much."

Rachel was dismissed and took it upon herself to return to John's room to check on him. Through the same open walkway, illuminated by dozens of overhead lights, until reaching his locked door. The key was still in the lock where Wicks had left it.

She unlocked and pushed the door open, finding Reiff inside on his bed, staring at her. He didn't seem surprised.

"Everything okay?"

"Sounds like some things are afoot out there."

Rachel couldn't help but chuckle. "You are not going to believe what I'm about to tell you."

89

After twenty minutes of bringing him up to date, Rachel leaned back in Reiff's wheelchair, which she was sitting in. He was speechless.

"You're kidding," he finally managed. "And you're sure this *ship* couldn't be from the present?"

"I don't think so. I couldn't see a lot of detail inside with everything frozen over, but what I did see, like the capsules, makes me seriously doubt it. The real proof for me was the man inside, and how effortlessly he recovered. That's way beyond where we are now."

"Hmm," said Reiff.

"Is it possible a ship like that could be built today? I don't know. Maybe forty years ago before the collapse. But Kincaid said it had been buried in the ice for a very long time. I suppose he could be lying, but I doubt it."

"What would he get by lying about that?"

"My thought exactly. Nothing."

Reiff continued thinking. "How in the world could something like that end up in the past?"

"I have absolutely no idea. If anyone has even a guess, I'm sure it's Kincaid. I'm sure he wouldn't have dedicated all this time and energy if it wasn't authentic."

"Agreed," mumbled Reiff. "Something tells me I'm not so valuable anymore."

"Of course you are. You're their insurance policy."

"How do you figure?"

"Trying to understand how this astronaut was suspended so perfectly will take a while. Years at least. And I don't think they have that kind of time."

"Why is that?"

"Just a hunch," replied Rachel. "This whole thing just has a feeling of urgency to me."

"I'm getting that feeling, too."

"As for you and me, we're just hostages now. And as long as you don't keel over, I think we're going to be here awhile."

Reiff did not respond. He agreed with her, mostly. Except for her last sentence.

When their patient awoke again, it was in a small, featureless room, devoid of anything but a bed, a monitoring machine and IV, and a small video camera positioned out of view. And once again, the faces of Nina Sandhu and Rachel Souza.

They brought him out slowly, just as before, and waited patiently for him to become lucid.

He opened his eyes to see the same two faces staring down at him. This time clearer than before. Two women, both partially silhouetted by the half dozen ceiling lights above them.

He felt groggy and wondered if he was still sedated. But the rest of his body felt good. Worn and somewhat achy but not much pain. With a mind that was struggling to think straight. Logic and basic thought process felt laborious, with memories that were a patchwork of random and seemingly unconnected images.

He tried speaking again. This time with a mouth and lips that felt more cooperative.

"Who . . . are . . . you?"

"My name is Nina," the older woman replied. "And this is Rachel." She smiled warmly at him. "Do you remember your name?"

He thought for a moment. "Murrrray."

Nina grinned. "Hello, Murray. How about a first name?"

He struggled, this time having to scour his brain. "Thomas."

"Excellent."

From overhead, Rachel Souza looked down at him. "Hi, Thomas," she said, "how are you feeling?"

The man closed his eyes as if running through an assessment of himself. "I feel okay."

"Any pain?"

"A little."

"Where?"

Murray slowly swallowed. "All over."

"Okay. We can give you something for that." All of this was so much like Reiff.

He nodded but didn't answer. Instead, his eyes moved back and forth, examining his surroundings. "What . . . hospital?"

It was decided they would tell him the truth, but not all at once. In small doses. "It's a private hospital and right now we just need you to rest."

If they had to, they would limit the questioning via sedative. Knocking him out again if necessary. A rather blunt approach, but effective.

They had to control the narrative. At least until delivering the first major shock. To make sure he could endure the news. But unfortunately, their approach was not quick enough to prevent the man's next question.

"How are the others?"

Sandhu was quick on her feet. "They're fine," she said. "And don't worry. You're going to fade in and out of sleep for a while. Don't fight it."

She reached behind him and gently pushed on the syringe's plunger, putting him back out.

When his eyes closed, the door to the small room opened and Kincaid and DeSilva entered.

Sandhu folded her arms. "We're going to need a plan B."

90

There was nothing but blackness, save for a slim ray of light reflecting on rippling water.

And then he was under it. Frigid and murky. Moving with a strong unseen undertow. Icy enough that he could feel his extremities beginning to freeze, first in the blood vessels as they started crystallizing.

Strange, muffled sounds became clear again as he broke the surface and continued ascending through the night air. Closer and closer toward the strange sounds until they gradually became a roar. Constant and thumping.

High above, the blackness gave way to small pinpoints of light. Stars. Impossibly far and twinkling as if trying to speak to him.

And far below, the black waves, passing beneath him . . . until their reflective rippling surface was replaced by something else he could not see.

John Reiff opened his eyes. Tired and weary, now unable to remain asleep for more than a few minutes at a time. Leaving him with dozens of visions that felt both like dreams and hallucinations mixed together.

But tonight it wasn't what he saw that lingered. Deep in his chest, in his heart, it was a feeling. An emotion. A mood from the dream that left a dark and foreboding sensation.

Something bad was coming.

91

Rachel was awoken just after 5 A.M. with a firm shake of her shoulder. Hard and startling. When she came to in the darkness, she could make out the shadowed outline of Sandhu.

"Get up," instructed the woman. "He's awake again."

Their walk down the wide concrete hallway felt surreal while Rachel tried to shake the cobwebs from her mind. Past the familiar double doors of the med lab, the same right turn, then left, and then the second longer hallway. Back to their patient's tiny room to find it brightly lit with him sitting upright on his bed, as if waiting.

His face was like stone. Unreadable but fully awake this time. And to his left, a limp dangling clear tube. He had removed his IV line.

"Hello, Thomas," said Sandhu with a forced smile. But the man's expression didn't budge. No change at all as he stared at them with a clear intensity.

"Where am I?" he asked flatly.

"We told you, you're in a private hospital. We're helping you—"

"You're lying to me."

Sandhu stopped and looked uncomfortably at Rachel. "It's more a clinic," she offered.

Murray gave her a long stare before his eyes moved to Rachel. "Where are they?"

"They?"

"The other crew," he said, his voice growing hostile. "Where is Helena?"

Sandhu's response was not immediate. "Who is Helena?"

The expression on Murray's face quickly changed as he studied the women from his bed. Why wouldn't they know who Helena was?

He thought back to their previous conversation. When they asked his name, it wasn't to see if *he* knew it, it was because they *didn't* know it.

The hostility in his voice rose. "Who are you?" he demanded, and began looking around the empty room, spotting the camera behind him. "You're recording this? He turned back to the women. "Why?"

Rachel could feel her heartbeat hasten. *He knows something is wrong.* She watched his eyes travel to Sandhu's left arm and down to her wrist, momentarily studying her watch. When he looked up again, his expression was contorted in a mix of confusion and surprise.

"What is happening?" he asked, almost absently. "Who are you?!"

Sandhu stalled in a brief panic, prompting Rachel to step forward and raise her hands in a cautionary gesture. "I'm Rachel, and she's Nina. We're trying to help you, I promise."

He didn't believe her. As if suddenly noticing the small sensor, he ripped it from his finger and then threw off the bed cover, sliding himself toward the edge of the bed.

"Wait!" snapped Rachel. "Easy. We just brought you out, we have to make sure you're ready."

Murray disregarded her and slid forward, placing both feet on the floor, and promptly fell with a thud when his legs gave way.

Behind the women, the door to the room abruptly opened and Kincaid entered, closing it behind him. He held a hand up and tried to calm Murray with an authoritative tone. "Take it easy. Everyone just take it easy. We're here to help you."

"Who the hell are you?!"

"My name is Douglas. I'm in charge of this . . . clinic."

"I don't care what you're in charge of, you stay away from me!"

"We're not here to hurt you, I swear it. We just want to help."

"Then tell me what the hell is going on!"

"You've been revived"—Kincaid nodded—"just like Rachel said. That's the truth. Do you remember being suspended?"

Murray stared at the old man, blinking several times. "Yes."

Kincaid sighed. "Something went wrong," he said. "And your ship crashed."

After a long pause and still on the floor, Murray responded: "Where?"

"In the mountains."

He looked between the three of them before finally lowering his voice. "Where are the others? Where's Helena?"

"We don't know."

"What do you mean you don't know?"

Kincaid hesitated. "You were the only one we found inside."

The man shook his head. "That's impossible. If you found me, you would have found them, too." He blinked, still appearing puzzled. "They were with me."

"Including Helena?" asked Kincaid.

"Yes."

"I'm sorry," the old man replied. "No one else was there when we found you."

Murray's gaze dropped to the floor, questioning. "They must have . . . gotten out then."

"How many others were with you?"

"What do you mean *how many*? You know just as well as I do." He studied Kincaid, baffled, and then the two women. "Why don't you know how many?" Murray then looked up and around the room again. "Wait a minute. Where am I? Where's Ramsey?"

"Ramsey?"

Murray's eyes narrowed. "The flight director."

Kincaid stared at him for a long time and exhaled. "Let's get you back up onto the bed. We need to explain some things."

92

Together they helped Murray up and back onto the edge of the thick mattress, helping him into a sitting position.

"We," began Kincaid, "were not part of your team. We were the ones who found you."

Murray's confusion only appeared to deepen.

"So we don't know the details about your mission."

The man's brow furrowed. "Everyone knows about our mission."

"We don't," said Kincaid. "Tell us."

Murray was staring at the three as though they were delusional. "*The* mission," he said. "To Proxima."

When still nothing registered, he squinted. "Where did you say you found me?"

Kincaid hesitated. "In the Himalayas."

"The Himalayas? What the hell were we doing there?"

"Again, we don't know."

"Why didn't the Foundation recover us?"

"The Foundation?"

"Yes, the Founda—" Murray changed from curious to concerned. "You don't know who the Foundation is?"

Kincaid and both women shook their heads.

"The *Foundation*," he said again. "The consortium." Still nothing. He began to look suspicious. "Where am I? What country?"

"You're in the States. In Arizona."

Murray shook his head. "If we were in Arizona, you would definitely know about the Foundation and the mission." His posture began to grow defensive. "Where am I *really*?"

Kincaid looked at the two women who said nothing.

"*Where am I?!*" Murray suddenly yelled. "Tell me right now!" He checked the room for something to grab. Something to use as a weapon. Finding little around him, he reached behind and grabbed the metal stand supporting the video camera. Trying to pull it up and over the headboard with both hands, causing Kincaid and the two women to rush forward.

"Stop!" yelled Kincaid. With some effort, they managed to wrest it from his hands. "*Stop!*"

Christ, the man was ready to fight.

"Please, just stop," pleaded Kincaid. "Just . . . let us explain." He stepped back from the bed while holding the stand and camera. "Just . . . listen."

He stared at Murray with a look of exasperation, then raised his hand and ran it down over his face with a loud sigh, trying to think of what to say. "We're not trying to hurt you," he said, pausing again. "Nor are we lying to you. You *are* in Arizona."

"Then you should already know—"

Kincaid raised his hand again, cutting the man off. "Just . . . listen." Another deep breath. "You were frozen when we found you. In a suspended state. And some *time* had passed."

"How much time?"

"A *lot* of time."

Again, Murray's eyes squinted. "How much is a lot?"

"Enough that we don't know who the Foundation is."

Something occurred to the man on the bed, and he immediately looked back at Sandhu's watch. "I haven't seen a watch like that in a long time."

She glanced down at it; a stainless-steel quartz watch with a pink-gold crown.

Murray's eyes rose and scanned the items in the room again, stopping this time on the Dinamap machine to his right. His face became uneasy as he examined it. "What year is this?" he asked.

"I think it might actually be better if you told us when your mission was."

The man cocked his head suspiciously. "We left in 2132." He watched as the other three tried to hide their reactions. "What year is it?" he asked again.

Kincaid took another deep breath. "2046."

93

The man stared back as if not hearing correctly. "What?"

"I said the year is 2046."

"You mean 2146."

Kincaid slowly shook his head.

Their patient gazed at them with complete bewilderment.

No one replied. They merely waited for it to sink in.

Murray shook his head and put a hand over part of his face, trying to make sense. "I'm hallucinating . . . from the drugs." He turned and looked at the IV line. "What did you put in that?"

"Just water," replied Rachel, "and electrolytes."

He shook again. "No. You're drugging me. You're playing games."

"We're not," said Kincaid.

"You are!" growled Murray. "Why else would you say these things? You're trying to trick me into something." His eyes darted around the room again. "This isn't America," he said, "this is a *foreign* interrogation."

Kincaid moved his head from side to side. "Believe me, it's not."

Murray's face hardened, peering intently at him through steely eyes. "Murray. Lieutenant. 584–12–97."

"What?"

"Murray," he repeated. "Lieutenant. 584–12–97."

"You've got to be kidding."

The women turned toward Kincaid. "What's going on?"

The old man sighed. "It's his name, rank, and serial number."

"Huh?"

Kincaid shook his head, frustrated. "Listen to me," he said to Murray. "My name is Douglas Kincaid. This is Rachel Souza, and this is Nina Sandhu. We are in *Arizona*, and in the United States, which consists of forty-two states, the last of which seceded six years ago in 2040. Today's date is May 11, 2046." Kincaid fished his phone from his pocket. "Look," he said turning it around, "the clock on this phone is synched to the only remaining atomic clock, in Colorado. Look at the date and time."

Murray's eyes glanced at the small screen before returning to their steely gaze. "Murray. Lieutenant. 584–12–97."

"Jesus," cursed Kincaid. He opened another app on the phone, bringing up a map and their GPS coordinates. He zoomed out to show a blue dot indicating their location, in Arizona.

"Murray. Lieutenant. 584–12–97."

Kincaid turned to the women in exasperation and could read their faces. Yes, the phone apps *could* be faked. But why would they? He was hoping, stupidly it seemed, that Murray would be more receptive. But if that's the way he wanted to go, then there was something that couldn't be faked.

He turned and approached the door, forcefully yanking it open and shouting outside, "Get a wheelchair!"

94

This time, the door to Reiff's room opened to reveal Daniel DeSilva on the opposite side, staring into the room at Reiff, who was lying still on his bed.

He glanced up and watched DeSilva enter without comment and seize Reiff's wheelchair.

"You break it, you buy it."

"Shut up," replied DeSilva, who turned back for the door, pulling the chair.

Once outside, he gave one last look at Reiff before pulling the door closed behind him.

"Hey, you got any fruit out there?"

When he returned to Murray's room, DeSilva entered with little interest from their patient. The man was now watching them through an apparent lens of indifference.

Kincaid positioned the wheelchair close to the edge of the bed and waited, but Murray did not move.

Finally, Kincaid lowered his head and said the magic words. "Care to see your ship?"

Once in the hallway, they turned left and wheeled Murray through the long and featureless concrete-reinforced hallway in the opposite direction of the med lab. Heading for the elevator. Still accompanied by the women, they filed inside and hit the button to descend, then waited almost a minute to reach the sixth level.

When the metal doors opened, they all moved out into the wide-open cavern and stopped once they were in full view of the long, thick glass wall.

Murray immediately fell silent, staring solemnly at the ship. He raised his hands to the large wheels on either side and rolled himself closer, stopping a few feet from the glass and gazing through it, spellbound. The frosty hull was completely intact, though dented and scraped in a few areas. But what was unequivocally clear was the series of long, dark streaks along the bottom.

They were burn marks. Signs of a reentry.

Slowly he moved along the wall, until reaching the closest point to the giant hole cut open in the port side by Kincaid's men. Through the opening, he could see some of the interior and the faint glistening of melting water.

At least part of what Kincaid said appeared to be true. The ship did look to have been frozen. Perhaps for some time. But so what? It didn't prove anything else. The best lies always contained threads of truth.

"So, it crashed and was frozen for a while. Big deal. The others must have gotten out. Maybe they had to abandon it for some reason."

"You're most likely correct about the second part," said Kincaid. "But you were frozen in that ship for more than a while."

Murray turned to him. "How long?"

The old man didn't answer.

"Ten years? Twenty?"

Kincaid folded his arms. "Try a thousand."

95

Regardless of whether Murray believed him, he was not prepared to hear that. Kincaid's words felt like a dagger through his chest, and his brain.

No. It isn't possible. It is not *possible. For so many reasons.* The most important was because if it *was* possible, it left him with one painful and agonizing realization. *Helena was gone!*

He sat quietly in the chair for a long time. His head down with his stubbled chin resting upon his chest.

No. No. No, he repeated in his head. *It cannot be. It simply cannot be.* The phrases echoed over and over until he couldn't hear anything else. Including Rachel's voice behind him.

"Murray?"

The man didn't answer. He could only stare at the concrete floor, shaking his head from side to side. He didn't want to believe it. He couldn't believe it. But something, somewhere, deep inside told him it was true. Against all rationality and logic . . . it was all somehow true.

After a long while, his head slowly rose to examine the ship again. End to end before his attention finally shifted to the strange cavity the ship was in. That *they* were in. Surrounded on all sides by red-and orange-colored rock.

"What is this place?" he finally said.

"A series of large caverns," answered Kincaid, "formed eons ago." He peered up at the ceiling along with Murray. "Used by Native Americans during enemy attacks."

The cavern they were in was much larger than the one Murray had seen above. "How did you get the ship in here?"

"It wasn't easy."

Murray continued gazing at his spacecraft. "You . . . kept it frozen all this time?"

"For forty years."

When he became silent again, the older Kincaid stepped forward and stood beside him.

"What was the mission you and your crew were on?"

Murray didn't hear him. He had slipped back into a state of denial. He was not ready to believe them, any of them. Even if it looked to be true, even if so much time had passed, it should have been into the future, not the past.

He closed his eyes, racking his brain. Thinking through every detail he could recall from the individual memories returning to him from the fog.

He wasn't one of the scientists. He didn't know the physics involved. He only had a rudimentary understanding of the system, which operated using a new combination of electromagnetism and fusion. It was what caused the "warp," allowing manipulation of space and time itself. And allowing the ship to travel not through space, but around it. He couldn't remember precisely, but what he could remember was a conversation about it. With Helena. Who had tried to explain it to him.

The details were over his head, but what his mind did recall was her lying next to him, trying playfully to explain the unexplainable. Something to do with Einsteinian physics.

He then remembered something specific she'd said to him. Something about how traveling through space at high speeds causes time dilation, or time travel, into the future.

He tried to remember her wording. Something about relativity. That general relativity carved a path forward in time, but special relativity suggested a path in the opposite direction.

Was he remembering correctly? He wasn't sure. She said their engine operated in the world of general relativity. That special relativity should not come into play. No, she said that it couldn't. Not with the way the warp engine was designed.

He opened his eyes as a jolt of fear traveled through his body. Dread at the possibility she was wrong. That they were all wrong. That somehow the engine did not work as expected. That everything Kincaid said was true, and it made him sick to his stomach.

96

The man looked like he was having a nervous breakdown before their eyes. Prompting Kincaid to have him quickly returned to his room and bed, where he now lay motionless and silent, staring absently up at the ceiling.

The door to his room was left open, where Kincaid and others spoke softly out of earshot.

"This isn't going well," stated Cannon. Next to him, Sandhu and Lu listened while glancing periodically back through the doorway.

"No shit," replied Kincaid.

"He's showing early signs of psychosis," said Sandhu.

"Meaning what?"

"Meaning his physical system may not be ready to handle all of this yet."

"Then when will it be?"

Sandhu shook her head and looked around. "That's probably a question for Rachel."

Rachel had returned to the med lab to run new tests on John Reiff's blood draw. Worried the signs of his system possibly stabilizing would prove false.

She was in her chair, waiting for the results from the hematology analyzer, when she decided to run another DNA sequence.

She added a drop of Reiff's blood to the 1.5 ml microcentrifuge tube and rolled her chair several feet to the sequencer. Opening the door and replacing the existing tube. Then with the press of a few buttons on-screen, began the process.

She sat wordlessly at the machine, lost in thought, when a set of results appeared onscreen. She studied them, then looked down at the previous tube still in her hand. They were from the test she had run a couple hours ago, from Murray.

It took her only seconds to realize what she was looking at and abruptly leap from her chair. Rushing for the door, and upon finding the outside hallway empty, she raced toward John's room.

When the door was unlocked and thrown open, Reiff was still positioned on top of his bed, with a look of consternation on his face. "They took my wheelchair."

Rachel hastily pushed the door closed behind her and moved immediately to his bed, lowering herself onto the edge.

"We're in trouble," she said frantically.

"I'm aware of that."

"No"—she shook her head—"you don't understand. Not soon. I mean *now*."

"What happened?"

She began to answer but caught herself and looked around his tiny room. "Do you think Kincaid has bugs in here?"

"No. I've checked."

"Good." She then pulled out a printed piece of paper from the sequencer and placed it on the bed in front of him. "This is a DNA report. From the last test I ran."

"Okay."

"Not your DNA," she said. "Murray's, the astronaut."

Reiff waited for more.

"He has the same markers," she said. "The same proteins."

"Same proteins as what?"

"As *you*."

Reiff's eyes narrowed. "What?"

Rachel could feel her heart pounding within her chest. "The same protein clusters," she said, "that I took from the monkey and used on the mice to develop a solution. For you. To keep your body from refreezing. The *therapy*," she cried. "The therapy I've been administering to you!"

"And the astronaut—"

"The astronaut has them!" she burst out, cutting him off. "He has the same proteins in his DNA!"

Reiff's expression was puzzled. "How is that possible?"

"I don't know, but he has them!"

"Did Kincaid give him the therapy?"

"No. The therapy takes time. And the new bacterial cultures I created for Kincaid only just became ready."

"How long does it take for these changes to occur?"

"A lot longer than a day!" cried Rachel.

"Are you saying what I think you're saying?"

She nodded. "I don't know how, but that man has a copy of *your* cure in *his* DNA!"

Reiff was as surprised as she was. But quickly moved past the question of "how" it was possible, to ramifications. "If that's true," he said slowly, "then Kincaid no longer needs us."

Rachel nodded fearfully. "Neither of us."

Reiff continued thinking before looking at her again. "You're sure about his DNA?"

"Positive. I took his blood myself and ran the test myself." She then pointed to one of the spikes on the paper. "And there is no way I would mistake that pattern."

"What about a false positive?"

"It's a possibility, but a small one."

"How small?"

"Extraordinarily small," she said. "Impossibly small."

"And what if this guy is *not* from the future?"

She turned and peered at the door as if looking through it. "Then I have absolutely no idea how he has the strands of DNA that I created. I mean an exact match."

"And what are the odds of that?"

"Zero," she replied, "of an exact match, with the changes I made. Which means his changes came from *my* bacterial cultures."

Reiff continued thinking. "Does Kincaid know?"

Rachel shook her head. "No one does."

"Not yet."

"Not yet." Rachel nodded.

"You need to delete that data."

"I already did. But if Kincaid or any of the others do their own test, they'll know."

97

Nina Sandhu's instructions were clear: Keep Lieutenant Murray engaged, mentally. Leaving their patient alone at this stage could allow him to slip into a deeply depressive and unrecoverable state. They could not let that happen.

Together, she and Kincaid sat on either side of the man's bed. Doing anything they could to keep him connected to the present, even if it was mentally and emotionally painful.

"Who is Helena?" asked Kincaid.

The man's eyes remained unmoving. Staring up at the ceiling with only an occasional blink.

"My wife," he answered softly.

"Your wife was on the ship with you?"

"Yes."

Kincaid looked past him to Sandhu, who encouraged him to continue. But before he could, Murray turned his head and looked at him.

"You said you found the ship in the mountains," he said, "buried in ice."

"Correct."

Murray hesitated briefly. "Did you find . . . anything else? Outside the ship?"

"You mean like remains?"

"Yes."

Kincaid shook. "No. Nothing."

"How far did you search?"

The old man thought for a moment. "Probably a few hundred yards."

Murray's gaze turned back to the ceiling.

"Why do you think your ship was in the mountains?"

"I don't know. If there was a serious malfunction, the ship's computer would have attempted a safe return to the surface."

"But why the mountains?"

Murray considered the question. "The computer relied on GPS for navigation during launch, and it would have done the same for reentry. But . . ."

Kincaid waited until he understood what the lieutenant was implying. "But if the ship malfunctioned and you traveled *back* in time, those GPS satellites would no longer exist."

Murray nodded in acknowledgment. "Leaving the ship to fly blind, unable to calculate its exact coordinates or altitude." His thought continued. "Which means it would have had to try to use its cameras in ways they were not designed to be used." With eyes still fixed on the ceiling, he then said, "Probably a miracle the ship wasn't completely destroyed."

"The others must have survived," offered Kincaid.

"Their capsules didn't empty themselves." Murray's gaze returned to Kincaid. "How far up was the ship?"

"What do you mean?"

"Elevation," he said. "Was it low enough to make it down the mountain?"

"It's possible. If they had some kind of gear or protection."

A glimmer of hope appeared in Murray's eyes. Briefly, before fading into irrelevance. "Even if they did survive the climb down, they would have died a long time ago—" Without warning, he turned and pushed himself onto his elbows. "Wait, how do you know we came back a thousand years ago? Maybe it wasn't that long."

"It was a while," answered Kincaid. "A long while."

"How do you know?!"

"Because we found fragments of animal bone and other organic matter near the ship when it was being dug out. Carbon dating put your arrival at around 1200 A.D."

Murray visibly deflated, lowering himself back down. "How did you find it?"

"Hikers," said Kincaid. He left out murdering them.

Murray merely nodded before closing his eyes. Images of what they must have gone through began flashing through his mind. All of them being revived from their cryonic suspension and wondering what happened. Jesus, did they even know where they were? They had to have known. The ship's computer would not have been frozen yet. It would have shown that they had only been suspended for a few days instead of years. But would the computer have known what the malfunction was? Or what year they had arrived in? He doubted it.

But it *would* have recognized the planet as Earth. Even if it failed to understand why all navigation and communication systems were no longer responding.

None of that mattered to Murray. What mattered was whether Helena and the others made it to safety. And if they did, what kind of a world did they find? A world a thousand years in their own past.

The ramifications of survival were too horrific to contemplate. How would they have survived in that world? If they survived at all? Hopefully they had taken supplies with them.

Murray's eyes suddenly opened and this time he sat up completely in bed. With bulging eyes, he stared at Kincaid. "I have to see the ship!"

98

Barely strong enough to stand, he managed to step inside the opening on wobbling legs, using both hands to grip the edges of the cut door and steady himself.

Inside, Wicks and his men donned parkas and were carefully chipping away at the last layers of thick ice in an effort to accelerate the ship's thawing.

The four men turned when the others entered and watched Murray's eyes examine the frozen interior. Immediately, he stumbled across the slick floor to the empty cryonic capsules.

All six preservation chambers were now exposed and undamaged, with the only exception being his own. He moved to one of the chambers next to his and reached down, finding a manual button and releasing it. The clear shield opened and slowly rose up and over his head. There was nothing inside.

Murray checked the others through their glass faces before turning and peering straight up at the arching ceiling. His eyes followed the curve of the interior before ending on the doorway and ladder not far from where two of Kincaid's men were working to remove ice from a wall of instruments.

Struggling to keep his balance, Murray moved past them, through the door and into the next section of the ship, where he found DeSilva, Lu, and Cannon, all clearing more of the ice. All of whom paused when they saw him.

He ignored them with a sense of urgency and stumbled past, searching for something along the icy walls. Past a set of exposed tables and chairs ringed almost entirely by a wall of stainless-steel counters and storage cabinets. "This was your living quarters, right?"

He ignored DeSilva and continued searching, slipping and grasping one of the exposed chairs to maintain his balance while counting each cabinet until identifying the one he was looking for.

He reached out and snatched some of DeSilva's tools without speaking and scrambled up a small slope of the floor to get close enough to place his chisel against the ice, and he began hammering.

Piece by piece, the last frozen remnants chipped and fell away, exposing the double doors in front of him. Murray then dropped the tools and reached up with both hands, yanking multiple times before they broke free and opened.

Dozens of items fell out. Several metal boxes, items of frozen clothing, picture frames, and a number of other personal effects. And with them, several frozen metal binders.

Kincaid and DeSilva stood by watching as he picked them up and pulled the first one open. "Binders?"

Murray did not look up. He merely flipped through what appeared to be some kind of synthetic or reflective pages.

From several feet away, Kincaid and DeSilva could see most of the pages were covered in text. When he reached the end, he dropped it and opened the next. Again, turning page after page.

What he was looking for was in the third binder, and upon finding it, he abruptly became still. Unmoving and reading.

"What is it?" asked Kincaid.

Murray did not answer until he finished. When he did, he turned and looked at them with the mist from his warm breath visible in the air. "They survived the crash."

"You're sure?"

Murray turned away as if not hearing them and reread the message. When done, he raised his head and gazed quietly forward.

Helena had survived. They all did. And she left him a note among his belongings before evacuating the ship.

Thomas,

We are alive with only minor injuries. Not sure what happened. Ship malfunctioned and crash-landed. Don't know where. Somewhere in the mountains. Communication and life support systems are down so breaching your capsule is too risky. Can't stay here long. We are going for help and will return for you.

Love,
Helena

Murray lowered the binder and returned to view the ship's insides. He then picked up the chisel and hammer and stumbled back toward the doorway and the horizontal ladder. Entering the next section revealed more ice-covered objects, much larger and almost entirely featureless. All carefully positioned like giant puzzle pieces to fill the entire level.

Along the wall nearest to the door were more cabinets, all closed with various symbols or emblems on them, many of which were now legible. The one Murray rushed to displayed a familiar red cross on one of its doors. Chipping away at it, he finally wrestled it open.

It was empty, just as he had expected. *At least they had emergency supplies.*

Kincaid and DeSilva remained in the doorway, watching. Observing the giant puzzle-shaped objects. "What are those?" asked DeSilva.

Murray turned around and examined them, pausing when noting a subtle difference in their alignment. Several were crooked as if stuck or jammed against one another. "They're supplies," he said.

"For what?"

"Inflatable habitats. Food stores. Light mobility vehicles." He continued examining the misaligned gaps between them. *They couldn't get them out.*

"What were they for?"

Murray turned. "What do you think?"

Kincaid shrugged.

"It was a one-way trip," he said, the mist still escaping his mouth as he spoke. "Two other supply ships were supposed to be right behind us. These were emergency provisions for establishing a survival camp if necessary." He reached up and pounded his hand against one of the giant pieces. "They must have shifted during impact. Helena and the others probably couldn't get them out. Or had enough time." His expression slowly grew solemn. "And they were probably wondering why there was no rescue team to pick them up."

The other men remained silent.

"They would have come back to revive me . . . if they were able. Unless they couldn't make it down the mountain. Or back up."

"I'm sure they made it down."

The lieutenant nodded without looking back. "I hope so."

Kincaid let several moments pass before asking, "What can you tell us about the capsules?"

He turned to look at the old man. "What?"

"Your cryonic pods."

Murray looked back at the opening and ladder. "They're computer controlled."

"How do they work?"

"With gas, to put us into a state of bio suspension. Then we were frozen."

"What kind of gas?"

"Hydrogen sulfide primarily, along with some others. I don't know the exact mixture. The computer's artificial intelligence does."

"And what about the revival process?"

"They used another gas for that. Followed by a gradual thaw." A thought occurred to Murray, and he peered at Kincaid and DeSilva. "Why, how did *you* do it?"

They were interrupted when Wicks stepped into the room and cleared his throat. When Kincaid turned, Wicks motioned back behind himself. "I think you're going to want to see this."

Together, they all returned to the living area, where the women were standing next to Wicks's men at the far wall, in front of a large instrumentation panel. They turned and parted when the others approached, allowing them to see between them.

On the wall, beneath a host of small screens, icons, and corresponding buttons, was one that had illuminated.

99

They all looked at Murray who appeared just as surprised. Staring at the single round bright blue light.

"What is that?" asked Lu.

The lieutenant blinked and remained gazing at the small light. "It's a power indicator."

Several sets of eyes widened.

"This thing still has power?" said Cannon.

Murray looked up and around the interior. "It has a thermal nuclear power source," he answered. "Designed to last a long time." He returned his attention to the wall. "A very long time."

They all nearly jumped when another light on the wall illuminated.

"Good God!" cried Cannon. "This thing's not dead!"

Murray stepped back and peered up again. Scanning more carefully the curved walls surrounding them. Wondering if it would continue. The power source was built to last a lifetime, as was the rest of the ship. Not just the hull, but nearly everything in it. Hardened for the conditions of deep space *and* redundant. Virtually all systems had fail-safes, including the main computer system. All designed to withstand both the conditions and extreme temperatures of deep space for long periods of time.

Without speaking, Murray began to wonder if the computer system somehow put itself into a suspended state when the rest of the ship began to freeze over with ice.

It did not take long to get his answer. When one of the small screens on the wall suddenly flickered on and a string of characters appeared.

System in power up . . .

100

When the next lines appeared, half of the group behind Murray gasped.

Subsystem One powering . . . Followed shortly by *Subsystem Two* powering . . .

Everyone turned to him as module after module appeared to load itself into the computer's memory. With each module illuminating more buttons and icons across the surface of the wall.

"Holy shit," breathed DeSilva.

The lieutenant, however, was not paying attention. Instead, he twisted his head, watching as strips around the interior began to turn on. Slowly accompanied by more screens on the far side of the curved room and finally . . . the small tabletops themselves.

A loud alarm shrieked, and Murray turned back to the main screen to see error reports begin to appear in bright red letters.

> Life Support Systems malfunction!
> Communication Systems malfunction!
> Navigation Systems malfunction!
> Cryonic System malfunction!
> Cryonic System 1—Unoccupied
> Cryonic System 2—Unoccupied
> Cryonic System 3—ERROR!
> Cryonic System 4—Unoccupied
> Cryonic System 5—Unoccupied
> Cryonic System 6—Unoccupied

The alarm continued blaring until, after a long pause, more reports began to appear:

> Power System online.
> Propulsion System online.

Electromagnetic Shield online.
Warp System online.

Lines continued appearing as the computer completed its boot-up process. Running through test after test. When finished, all reports disappeared, leaving only the identified malfunctions, all of which continued blinking in bold red letters.

They were all examining the ship in awe. Watching in wonder as section after section was systematically illuminated and previously unseen details became visible. Everyone that is, except for Anna Lu.

Instead, she watched the others as their faces became almost hypnotized. Especially Kincaid.

The old man was gazing all around like a child in a candy store, and eyes just as wide. Raptured in both shock and amazement at what he was seeing.

He was speechless, completely and utterly speechless. He had never dreamed the ship was still in working order. That anything worked at all. He assumed the crash or time itself had rendered it completely unusable. And now, even though some parts were clearly damaged, some were clearly not. And the implications . . . were enormous.

A ship from the future, even partially working, was priceless. Beyond valuable on every level. Advancements in technologies, for metals and alloys, mechanical and computer designs, space technology, and power systems!

Good God, Kincaid thought to himself. He had just won the mother of all lotteries. Everything about the ship was more advanced than anything they currently had, *everything.* Leaving him absolutely stunned. Stunned but excited.

Lu continued watching them. Each one of her colleagues, and then Wicks and his band of mercenaries, with her eyes finally stopping again on Kincaid.

She could read his thoughts simply from the expression on his face.

Old and worn but with those same intense blue eyes. Studying every inch of the ship's interior like a hungry animal. Or worse, like a shark.

His eyes finally fell and noticed her looking at him. Studying him. Studying his face. And he grinned at her.

Lu knew what he was going to say without having to ask, through the slow smiling shake of the man's head.

He was telling her no. They were not ready to hand over the ship to the Chinese. Not now, perhaps not ever. What it represented was simply too extraordinary. She knew Kincaid. He would ask her to find a way to put the Chinese off longer. Temporarily at first, until he could figure out a way to make it permanent.

The thought made her ill. Not nauseous, not irritated, but physically sick to her stomach. Because she knew the Chinese would not wait. They would take it by force if they had to.

101

It was called the *Fujian*. The first Chinese-built supercarrier, weighing in at over 85,000 tons of displacement with ultraefficient and ultrapowerful steam turbines. The first with electromagnetic catapults, the ship not only carried an incredible array of Chinese-made aircraft but could launch dozens of them in exceptionally rapid succession.

Classified as a Type 003, the three-hundred-meter-long *Fujian* was unequivocally the largest and most advanced aircraft carrier to be built outside the United States, only years before the *Great Collapse*.

Almost three decades later, only three more Type 003s had been completed, but none with the same power and armaments as the *Fujian*. Which, thanks to its monstrous steam engines, was now surging past Isla Tiburón, one of the Gulf of California's largest islands, like a floating city of destruction.

None of the aircraft carrier's exterior lights were on, leaving the vessel's massive bridge illuminated in an eerie red glow. A powerful backdrop for its stalwart captain, Hae Wang, who, in his late fifties, stood tall and sullen. One of the finest commanders in China's New Liberation Navy and a man deeply dedicated to the betterment of his country, no matter the cost. Fixed like a statue under the red lights, as the dark shadow of the island quietly passed on the ship's port side at almost forty knots.

The Gulf of California itself stretched for another 120 miles to the north, with thousands of feet below its dark rippling surface, ending near the small town of Puerto Peñasco. Which was less than fifty miles from the Arizona and Mexico border. And they would launch long before reaching Puerto Peñasco.

102

With all the excitement in the spacecraft, what no one noticed was Nora Lagner's absence. Less interested in the ship at the moment than something far more pressing, at least to her.

She was in the med lab, alone, standing and quietly studying the machines before her, specifically the sequencer. A few feet away, on one of the lab's monitors, she had a video pulled up of the room and Rachel Souza. Who had been using several of the machines for testing before discovering something and exiting the room in haste. Lagner had seen it all: Rachel in front of the sequencer studying different results before printing out a page, briefly fiddling with the machine, and running out.

Lagner was now staring at the same machine, trying to deduce what had happened. She studied the device before touching her index finger to its small screen. It immediately displayed the welcome screen with several icons representing the system's various functions.

She spent several minutes navigating in and out of the different windows, trying to understand the multitude of options, before finally locating the administrative tools.

Lagner selected the icon titled "History." When the next window opened, she was surprised to find a blank list. In other words, no history at all.

Her eyes rose and stared forward, immediately realizing what had happened. Rachel Souza had erased all the machine's previous tasks and results.

Now Lagner turned and peered at the room's open door. What was it that needed to be deleted? And why so quickly?

She scanned the room and stopped on the small medical refrigerator on a nearby counter. Inside were several groups of different vials. Samples. From the monkey, from their astronaut, and from John Reiff.

"How much of this facility have you seen?"

Rachael stopped to think. "Three levels. The main floor, this floor, and the one with the ship."

"The elevator had seven buttons," said Reiff. "That's a big cave."

"Kincaid said the cavern was naturally formed. It might even be bigger."

Reiff nodded. "I wonder how many ways out of here there are. The ventilation system alone would need multiple openings to the outside, but finding them would take time. What about the first and main floor? Did you see any stairs?"

"Not that I recall."

"What about Wicks and his men? How many have you seen in total?"

She tried to think back. "When I surrendered, there were two SUVs, so at least eight."

"At least. I've only seen three," said Reiff. "So the others are somewhere else. Most likely nearby."

"Maybe in another part of the compound?"

"Maybe." He mentally recounted his trip through the main level, trying to remember what he saw. The marble flooring, marble pillars, leather couches, tables, hallways. He recalled a glimpse of a short glass wall with four clear panes that were dark. He didn't see any stairs.

"We're on level three," said Reiff. "And you said the ship is on six. That means the systems responsible for maintaining this place are on four or five."

"Or two."

"I doubt it. You'd want as much insulation from the noise." He placed his hand on the nearby wall and concentrated. "I don't feel any vibrations. My guess is the systems are on five."

"Okay. What does that mean?"

Reiff answered as if talking to himself. "Any additional venting would most likely terminate there."

"So a way out?"

"Too difficult," said Reiff. "The main entrance is the most expedient exit." He then swung his legs over the edge of the bed and stood up.

103

On the spacecraft, Murray stared at the screen before him, still surrounded by the others, at the three words displayed in the center.

Please provide identification . . .

Next to him, Kincaid turned around to Wicks and his men and dismissed them. Watching the five men turn and exit the section of ship.

Without speaking, Lieutenant Murray carefully removed the glove on his right hand and peered at a metal wall nearby. Slowly reaching forward, he pressed it against a blank metal plate.

Nothing happened.

Murray frowned. He removed his hand and once again pressed it against the plate.

Still nothing.

Even after a third attempt, there was no response on the computer screen.

"Hmm."

"What is it?" asked Kincaid.

"Doesn't seem to be working," he murmured.

"Is there another way to access it?"

Murray nodded with a disturbed look. "Yes, but I don't know how to do it." His eyes remained thoughtfully on the screen. "Wallace was the engineer and computer expert."

Kincaid turned to DeSilva, who was also pondering. The younger man inched forward and reached out to touch the bare wall between the plate and the screen. "It's still ice cold. Maybe not all the circuitry is thawed yet."

"Possibly," said Murray. "Guess we need to wait."

"For how long?"

He gave Kincaid an irritated look. "How should I know?"

The old man bobbed his head and stepped back. *Fine.* They would wait. In the meantime, there was still more to discover about the ship, and the last of the ice to remove. Content for the moment, he examined Murray. "What year?"

"Pardon?"

"What year did you leave?"

Having all but succumbed to the reality of what happened, even if he did not fully understand how or why, Murray replied. "2132," he said simply. "Eighty-six years from now."

Eighty-six years, thought Kincaid, surprised. It wasn't as far into the future as he expected, but it was enough. Eighty-six years' worth of advancement. Not just advancement but actual knowledge of future events. Of everything that was going to happen over the next eight decades! He was instantly reminded of an old quote he'd heard many times: *The future belongs to no one.*

Douglas Kincaid strongly disagreed.

They spent another hour inside while Murray explained what the giant puzzle blocks throughout the rest of the ship contained. Not just emergency provisions but machinery and digging tools, 3-D printers, graphite composites, solar panels, water filters, everything the group would need to survive and build upon the surface of their new planet. One of the supply ships supposedly had a 3-D printer the size of a truck that could create small structures in a matter of hours with an adobe-like material made from the new planet's soil.

According to Murray, future space telescopes had become strong enough to identify details on the alien surface, not just the nitrogen, carbon dioxide, and oxygen in the atmosphere. Details like forests, running water, lakes and valleys, and animals. Large, very odd-looking animals.

The planet's atmosphere had a similar composition to Earth's with lower nitrogen levels and higher oxygen. Not perfect but easily adaptable with special filtration systems, whose components were also in Murray's ship. Along with an advanced ground-based laser communication system for contacting Earth upon landing.

It was all there. All still in the ship. Some components were possibly damaged, but the technology behind it was all there. And more than that, they had someone to show them how it all worked.

Kincaid was elated. It was far beyond what he or any of the others ever dreamed. The cost of the last forty years had been worth every penny.

104

After leaving the ship, most of the heavier cold-weather gear was discarded for the last time. The warming of the craft was gradually accelerating, reaching a temperature that would soon require little, if any, of the parkas at all. At least for shorter stints inside.

And once the ship's computer could be accessed, the amount of *information* waiting to be seized would be nothing short of godly.

A level of knowledge whose ramifications still appeared lost entirely on Wicks and his men. Who simply followed them out of the craft and were removing their own gear, near the end of the cavernous room and where Nora Lagner was found waiting for Kincaid.

Kincaid approached, and she quickly pulled him aside while their colleagues conversed in exclamations of excitement.

"You're not going to believe this," Lagner whispered.

"Believe what?"

"What Rachel Souza just discovered."

The old man rolled his eyes. "Now what?"

She handed two pieces of paper to the old man who studied them. "What is this?"

"DNA results," she said. "From Murray and Reiff."

Kincaid looked up and then down again as she pointed to two areas of sequencing patterns with her finger. The patterns were circled and repeated on each page.

"What am I looking at?"

"The DNA edits Rachel is administering to Reiff," answered Lagner. "The cure she found with her mice."

Kincaid blinked, staring at the first page before pulling it away and studying the second. "And this one . . ."

"That," she stated, "is Murray's."

His expression remained puzzled. "Is this . . . ?"

Lagner nodded smugly. "They both have it."

"How is that possible?"

"I don't know," she said, peering back at Murray, who was standing near the others. "I haven't administered anything to him, have you?"

"Of course not."

The two simply stared at one another. The conclusion was obvious, even if confusing as to "how." Their astronaut from the future already had a copy of Reiff's cure, in his own DNA.

They now had Rachel's cure, which she had just replicated. And they also now had a cryonic system far more advanced than their own: the capsules in the ship. Far more efficient, and a computer that could explain precisely how the new systems worked.

Kincaid slowly displayed a menacing smile. "It looks like our hostages just became disposable."

It was at that moment that everything in the cavern, everything in the entire compound except for the ship itself, suddenly went dark.

105

Everyone in the room froze, bathed in the faint glow from the ship's illuminated interior.

"What the hell?" Kincaid muttered.

Their power system was completely redundant, overly so, able to provide more than three times the required power from four different generators. They had never had an outage before, leaving the large room eerily quiet following the disappearance of the background noise from ventilation ducts overhead.

Five bright lights promptly appeared as Wicks and his men turned on their small tactical flashlights. Pointing them around the room while Wicks approached Kincaid and Lagner.

"This is not an accident."

"Of course not, you idiot," yelled Kincaid. He peered upward into near-total blackness. "He's right above us. Go!"

Wicks ignored the insult. Instead, drawing his gun and breaking into a run past his men and toward the elevator behind them. Upon reaching it, he instinctively pushed the button before remembering *all* power was out and instead motioned his men toward an unseen stairwell nearby.

All five men entered the stairwell and began ascending the metal steps in a thunderous cacophony of pounding boots. Reaching the door one level above and quickly spreading out around it.

The door was open.

Wicks and one of his other men positioned themselves on both sides of the doorway, pointing their flashlights through the opening. The place was filled with mechanical equipment. The critical systems for producing all air, water, heat, and power required for the compound. Dozens and dozens of bulky machines of varying types and sizes located below a maze of overhead piping and ducting traveling in all directions.

Beyond the machines on the farthest wall, the ten familiar cryonic pods could be seen in the glow of the men's flashlights, sitting dark and silent.

With guns still drawn, the men slowly eased inside the door, lowering themselves and spreading out without a sound. Each stepping in a careful heal-toe fashion to minimize noise. All at once, they began fanning out and moving around the machines, using them for cover before quickly searching between them. Searching for Reiff.

"He's mobile," whispered Wicks to his men.

Rachel's heart felt like it was going to jump out of her chest. Scared to death and listening to the distant murmuring.

Next to her, at the top of the next flight of stairs, Reiff kept his eyes glued to the open doorway beneath them. Watching the faint glimmering from the flashlights gradually growing weaker as the men all moved deeper into the room.

Reiff put a finger to his lips and began descending in the dim light, showing Rachel how and where to step; on the outer edge of each stair where most of the support was located.

Down past the open door, continuing to level six, where reaching the next doorway, they could see Kincaid and the others inside. They had all moved closer to the ship and were talking quietly.

When they were clear, Reiff immediately pulled Rachel through the shadows with him, past the doorframe, and once again proceeded downward.

"What's going on?" asked Murray.

"Nothing. Just an electrical problem."

"Who is upstairs?"

Evidently, Murray heard his exchange with Wicks. "No one important."

"Sounds pretty important."

"Just a problemed patient we have," replied Kincaid with a sigh.

Murray eyed him suspiciously and turned to face the others. Studying them before turning back to Kincaid. "Where's the other woman?"

"What woman?"

"The other doctor," Murray said and pointed to Sandhu. "The one who was with her when I woke up."

Kincaid didn't need this. He could feel his blood pressure rising as he stared back at the man idly. "It doesn't matter."

106

Level seven was pitch black. With its door closed but unlocked, allowing Reiff and Rachel Souza to step inside the cool interior with absolutely no idea what they were walking into.

He began to ease away from her when she grabbed him and pulled him close again. "I can't believe you can walk!" she cried.

"Yeah, it's a miracle." Reiff moved away again and disappeared into nothingness. Extending his hands in front of himself, feeling his way while taking one small careful step at a time.

"Wait!"

"What?"

Rachel edged forward, searching for him. Upon finding him, she grabbed tight. "Don't just leave me there."

"I was two feet away."

Unexpectedly, Rachel felt herself pulled into him and a sudden pressure on her lips. "Did you . . . just kiss me?"

There was a long pause. "No."

"Yes, you did."

He began to pull away when she grabbed him again. "Wait," she said and pressed her lips against his.

"That was my chin."

"I can't see where you are!"

"Shhh," he said and found her hand, leading her forward in the darkness. "Keep your hand out in front of you. Tell me when you feel something."

"Wait, wait!" She tugged at him to stop and used both hands to search her pockets. She found what she was looking for and produced a slim device, the burner phone Yamada had given her. She flipped it open, and the tiny screen lit up, revealing Reiff's face.

"You're kidding. They let you keep your phone?"

"They didn't care, it doesn't work down here."

Reiff took the phone and looked at it. "You have two percent battery left."

"I didn't charge it."

He didn't reply. He instead turned it outward in an effort to see, but the tiny screen only revealed a few feet in front of them. But it was at least enough to avoid walking into a wall. "Follow me."

Together they shuffled forward, in small cautious steps, until eventually reaching something in front of them. It looked like the corner of a large metal rack. A heavy reinforced edge with wired shelves. And on top, what looked to be thick plates of something.

"What is that?"

Reiff examined them closely and turned outward again with the phone. "Looks like extra pieces of marble flooring." He moved along to the next shelf and found dozens of pieces of pipe and plastic conduit, and beyond that, several large rolls of wire.

"What is this place?"

"Their supply room," answered Reiff.

He moved to his left and found another vertical rack. This one holding stacks of large, closed boxes. He pulled one forward and tilted it against his chest, opening the top flap with his free hand. He rummaged around and withdrew a squat steel canister.

"What's that?"

He read the label on the can and stepped back to look at the other boxes. "Freeze-dried food."

Rachel stepped in beside him to examine the can. "How long can that stuff last?"

Reiff shrugged. "In a place like this, probably twenty-five years." He returned the can and pushed the box back into place, then turned to face Rachel when the tiny screen in his hand abruptly blinked out.

Standing in the darkness, he tried powering it back on, but to no avail. "Don't suppose you have your charge cable on you."

"I don't."

"It was a joke." Reiff found her hand in the darkness and returned the phone. "Wait right here."

She grabbed him again. "Wait! Where are you going?"

"Shopping."

107

Wicks and one of his men returned to level six, where the others were. He pulled Kincaid away and spoke in a hushed voice. "The fuel lines on the generators were pulled off."

"And?"

"We can't find them," replied Wicks. "It'll take some time."

"Great. While Reiff wanders around doing God knows what."

"He's not going anywhere," said Wicks, "all exterior doors require power to open and he doesn't know how to open them manually."

"Fine," replied Kincaid in frustration. "Then go find him!"

His head of security nodded and began to turn when he paused. "You want him alive?"

"Not at all."

Reiff would be upstairs, where he had more places to hide. Probably waiting for Wicks and his men to restore power and providing him a way out. Wicks guessed they would find him and the Souza woman somewhere on the top floor, allowing him and his men ample time to clear each floor and gradually drive Reiff into a veritable corner.

Wicks began by sending three of his men down to clear the supply room while he and his fourth man returned to level five and ensured it was still clear. Once finished, they would all then move up together, one floor at a time, and flush Reiff out.

Wicks's three-man team reached floor seven with guns and flashlights drawn, entering the room and spreading out again.

The supply room was not as large as the others, limited by a natural tapering of the cavern as it descended deeper into the earth, but the area was still sizable. Sporting several dozen tall metal racks lined in five long

rows and housing the compound's extra supplies, from building materi-
als like paste and cement filler, replacement parts, food, heavy tools, and
spools of extra wiring. Enough to repair and keep the place running for
a lifetime.

The three men edged closer until reaching the racks and traveling
down three of the five rows. Together with both lights and guns sweeping back and forth, passing pipes and conduit, boxes and boxes of supplies, and multiple racks holding stacks of wood and sheets of drywall.

Slowly and methodically, they continued forward. Moving without a
sound while pausing at each new set of racks to bend down and check
beneath them.

They all suddenly turned when a sound was heard behind them, coming from the stairs.

One of the men motioned at the other two to investigate, while he
stayed behind continuing to use his light to search up and down the rack
in front of him.

Men two and three moved back across the room, returning to the doorway. Nothing else could be seen in the darkness. No more sounds emanating. Only silence and their own heavy breathing.

They peered through the doorframe, shining their lights inside and
up the stairwell. Finding and hearing nothing, one of the men edged
through the doorway and checked to his left.

Nothing.

He leaned in further, taking a small step and looked up the metal
stairs above him. He then turned back and checked the bottom of the
stairwell to his right, including the corner closest to him.

Still nothing.

He turned to the other soldier and shook his head, then returned to
face the room behind him. "It was nothing."

Together they reapproached the tall racks, walking in the bright beam
of the first man's flashlight. Having to use a hand in irritation to block the
blinding glare. "Lower your light!"

The first man did not answer.

"Dammit, Sanchez, get it off me."

There was nothing but silence.

Both men slowed and tried to peer through the glare. "Sanchez?"

Sanchez was no longer standing where they left him.

It took only seconds for the men to realize something was wrong and bolt to opposite sides, behind the racks and out of the glaring light.

"Sanchez! Can you hear me?!"

One of them reached the row where the man had been standing and where his light was still shining from. No one was standing behind the flashlight, which was lying horizontally on a shelf. No body on the floor, nothing.

The two remaining mercenaries immediately went silent. No more noise or calling out. Instead, they remained motionless, listening. There was something in the distance. A strange soft raspy sound at the far end of the room, where the rows of racks ended. Neither man budged.

They continued waiting, hushed and still. Waiting for sounds of movement from Reiff. But nothing came.

Almost in tandem, they slowly began forward again, pressing along the outside rows and peering through the giant racks between them, carefully scanning through the countless shelves.

They made it almost twenty feet, until one of the men reached a section storing large amounts of plywood and drywall. Several shelves high and reaching nearly to the top.

Unable to see around the giant slabs of wood, he stepped out and looked up just in time to see the flash of a thin gray pipe swinging down out of the darkness, striking him hard on top of his skull and sending his limp body collapsing to the floor with nothing more than a guttural grunt.

The sound of a heavy slump on the floor caused the third man to freeze.

"Engle?"

Unlike the others, the last man didn't pause or wait, but instead bolted forward around the corner of his rack, toward the far aisle, gun outstretched and flashlight illuminating in front of him.

He reached the last row of racks in three seconds, and was greeted by the same pipe, smashing down on his gun hand driving him sprawling onto the concrete floor. Lost in the darkness, the gun absorbed most of the blow, and left the third mercenary empty-handed. And instantly back on his feet with his bright light searching and finding Reiff's figure in front of him.

The man ducked, barely avoiding the next swing of the pipe, which struck the rack with a reverberating clang. He was immediately on Reiff.

Dropping his light and grabbing the pipe with both hands, trying to wrest it away.

Reiff grimaced, trying to force the man backward, but he was still weak. He tried again, but the other man was stronger, pushing forward and slamming Reiff painfully into the hard rack directly behind him.

He was too strong and too fast.

Reiff improvised, keeping one hand on the pipe and using the other to drive four outstretched fingers into his assailant's right eye, then stepped back and followed it with a foot into his groin.

The man's grip on the pipe weakened allowing Reiff to rip it free, whirling it up and over and striking the man's shoulder with a loud crunch. His attacker yelled and fell to the floor in the glare of the flashlight, splayed out onto the floor and, to his surprise, on top of his own gun. He quickly rolled off and searched for it with his hand, finding it and aiming at Reiff with his good eye.

Once again, the pipe found its target, which was the top of the man's head, but not before a stray shot exploded from the gun's barrel.

108

The gunshot was heard by everyone. Echoing through the door and up the stairwell, reverberating past Kincaid and the others, before reaching Wicks and his fourth merc above them a fraction of a second later.

Wicks's first instinct was to radio down, but he cursed under his breath remembering their radios didn't work underground.

He and his remaining man both rushed to the door and stopped, listening, waiting for another report. When none came, they flew down the metal stairs, past the others on level six, continuing to the bottom where they stopped on either side of the last door. To his surprise, there was nothing but silence and darkness inside. If Reiff was dead, Wicks's men would not be waiting in the dark.

His man next to him began to move in when Wicks stopped him. "Wait!" he whispered. "Turn your light off."

The younger man stared back as if not understanding.

"Turn it off!" spat Wicks and he reached for the man's flashlight, promptly extinguishing it.

Reiff was not upstairs. And with their lights on, Wicks and the soldier next to him were easy targets. If the other three men were unconscious, or worse, it meant Reiff was alive and likely armed. And just waiting for a good shot.

Wicks motioned to his man. "Get upstairs," he whispered, "and get some backup. Everyone on site, now!"

The soldier nodded and turned, rushing back up the stairs.

"Tell me what the hell is happening."

Kincaid, like everyone else, was facing the open doorway, frozen in fear as the pounding in the stairwell could be heard again and one of Wicks's men passed the opening in a blur. Followed eventually by Wicks himself who backed into the room and positioned himself inside the frame of the door, peering back down the metal stairs.

He glanced over his shoulder and found everyone staring at him fearfully. "Reiff's downstairs."

"No shit," spat Kincaid. "Get down there and kill him!"

Wicks turned only long enough to stare sarcastically at Kincaid. "Don't be an idiot, three men are already down. We have him trapped."

A gunshot suddenly rang out and ricocheted off the stairway wall, causing Wicks to jump back. He grabbed the heavy door and slammed it closed for protection.

"We can't stay here."

Rachel stared at Reiff, who had now turned on a flashlight and laid it on a shelf, aimed directly at their doorway.

"Why not?"

"Because we're sitting ducks down here," answered Reiff. He used his thumb to release his gun's magazine and checked the number of rounds in it. He moved to the door and took a darting glance up the dark stairwell. "We have to get out before any more come."

"How?"

He grabbed her hand and pulled her toward him, guiding it to the back of his belt. "Stay behind me," he said. "And don't let go."

109

Oddly, out of everyone in the room, Murray seemed the calmest. Curiously staring at Wicks who remained at the door listening.

"Who's Reiff?"

"I told you it doesn't matter."

"Obviously, it does."

"He's our lab rat," growled Cannon behind them. The large man was leering at Kincaid. "A very dangerous lab rat."

"What does he want?"

"To kill us," answered Kincaid.

Nearby, Nina Sandhu slowly shook her head. "No," she said. "He wants out."

No one responded. They simply turned back to Wicks who had his ear to the door. He then held up a hand, motioning them to be quiet. Listening to what he thought were faint sounds on the other side.

Inside the stairwell, Reiff eased toward the closed door, with just enough light left from below to make out the number "6" on the wall.

He reached out and slowly wrapped his left hand around the handle, while with his right lowering his gun and delicately pressing its barrel against the metal door.

On the other side, Wicks's eyes shifted back and forth as he listened. There were no more gunshots from below, only the fading ringing from the first. His hand was still on the door's handle, and he readjusted his grip, wrapping it around the cold stainless-steel metal . . . and slowly turning.

To his surprise, it didn't move.

First came confusion. A momentary question as he wondered if he'd automatically locked the door when he closed it. But looking down he could see he did not. Then came the fear, in a flash of panic. It wasn't locked. Someone one was holding it from the opposite side. Reiff was on the other side of the door!

Wicks instinctively leaped away from the door, his hand moving off the handle and instantly joining his right hand around the grip of his gun. Steady, at shoulder height, ready for Reiff to burst through.

Kincaid's people would provide a perfect, momentary distraction, right before he took Reiff's head clean off from the side.

Time slowed, and there was no sound.

Wicks's index finger contracted against the trigger, removing what little slack there was. The next movement from his finger would be firing the gun. In rapid succession.

Wicks's heartbeat slowed, as though frozen in that one single second, waiting. Until . . .

Nothing.

Another second passed, and then another.

There was nothing. No sound, no movement, no opening of the door. Nothing.

After dozens of agonizing seconds, and then a full minute, Wicks inched forward and reached to place his left hand back on the door handle. Gripping the handle's cold steel and turning once again.

This time it rotated. Surprising him and forcing him back yet again. After another long pause, he moved back to the door and again found the handle free. This time, filled with adrenaline, he grabbed it and quickly threw it open, stepping back out of the way with his gun aimed high.

There was nothing. Nothing but the sound of a squeak from the metal hinges as the door gradually began to swing closed again. Providing more than enough time for Wicks to see that the stairwell was empty.

110

The Changhe Z-18 was a powerhouse of the new Chinese Liberation Air Force. With three WZ-6C turboshaft engines and a carrying capacity of up to thirty troops, it was still one of the fastest flying rotor transports in the world. And admired by Captain Wang as he looked out from his bridge, into the darkness and onto the aircraft carrier's deck, where the shadows four Z-18s were now at full power and each of the aircraft's tail ramps were closing.

They didn't need thirty men per chopper. Ten was more than enough, leaving adequate lift for the four rotorcraft to retrieve Kincaid's spaceship and fly it back to the *Fujian*.

Wang then looked past the Z-18s to two more aircraft, also preparing to take off from the aircraft carrier's giant deck. Changhe Z-10s. Attack helicopters.

They had waited long enough. It was time to collect their payment from Kincaid. Even if they had to blast it out of that canyon.

One by one, the helicopters lifted from the deck and began to rise into the air. Gradually pivoting and turning toward the lights of Puerto Peñasco. From there it was a mere fifty miles to the US border and then nothing but open, empty desert and a direct path to Arizona's Tonto National Forest.

111

Rachel could barely keep up, with Reiff moving up the stairs fast enough for her to think he was taking two at a time. Pulling her behind him, stumbling up the stairs while trying to keep a hand on a cold, unseen handrail for support.

Thankfully, each new level allowed her a moment of respite, to regain her balance while Reiff stopped and listened through the door, before quickly continuing on.

It felt like she was "falling upward," pulled almost entirely by Reiff's momentum, when she heard a door being flung open a few levels below them.

Reiff either didn't hear it or didn't care. He merely continued at a dizzying pace until finally stopping at the top level and turning to help stabilize her.

"Is this it?" she panted.

"Yeah." He moved her away from the door and tested the handle. It was unlocked. He eased it open with his free hand and peered through the crack.

Hearing movement below, he double checked her hand on his belt and opened the door wide, slipping through and pulling her with him. Once inside, he stayed along the wall and followed it until reaching a corner.

It was the main level where Reiff had been rolled in less than two days before. Completely dark except for something in the middle of the room, where hundreds of tiny dots of light appeared, like a cluster of faint and unmoving fireflies. Providing just enough ambient light to make out a few pieces of furniture below them.

Rachel realized what it was, the giant chandelier. Her eyes followed the dots of light upward and determined there must have been a natural skylight somewhere in the ceiling, where rays of the moon were likely reflecting off the chandelier's hundreds of individual crystals.

Reiff paid little attention to it. Instead, he worked to orient himself and determine the direction of the front entrance. Reinforced, double doors that were now the only thing between them and the outside.

He continued forward in the darkness, cautiously along the meandering wall with gun drawn, when the giant room abruptly lit up in a red hue.

They both stopped. "Someone got the emergency lighting working."

"DeSilva."

The emergency lighting was muted but more than bright enough to reveal the double doors in the distance. Where Rachel spotted them and instinctively rushed forward but was stopped immediately by Reiff.

"Wait."

"What? There's nobody here!"

"There was someone else in the stairwell with Wicks."

Rachel paused, scanning the giant room around them. "I don't hear him."

"And you wouldn't, if he's not moving."

Reiff continued forward more cautiously. Moving in brief spurts between sections of wall and large pieces of furniture that might serve as cover if necessary. He and Rachel were now visible and much more vulnerable.

Behind him, Rachel continued searching in all directions. "There's no one here."

Reiff didn't respond. He remained still, staring quietly at the entrance. Studying the doors, and what appeared to be a square plate on the wall next to them.

She squinted. "What are you looking at?"

"That plate looks like a release."

"For the door?"

He nodded. The doors themselves appeared seamless, with large designer handles but nothing else he could see that looked like a lock or release.

"What are we waiting for?"

"If they're electronic, the doors may be disabled with the power off." Surprisingly, after a moment of contemplation, he shrugged and took a deep breath. "Wait here."

He checked the open area one last time and broke into a run. Weaving past a large set of high-backed chairs around a naturally cut wooden table and then on to the entrance wall, where he stopped at the doors and immediately pressed the plate.

Nothing happened. He tried again. Still nothing. He examined the plate more closely and cursed. *It's a damn scanner.* He then inspected the doors, looking for a manual latch but found nothing except their giant oversized V-shaped handles. He ran his fingers around the inside edges of each handle but still came up empty. And nothing on the walls either.

There has to be a manual release somewhere.

Gunfire suddenly erupted and bullets glanced off the doors in front of him in a barrage of sparks.

Reiff ducked and turned, racing back to the first thing he could find. Diving and knocking over one of the high-backed chairs and immediately grabbing the table to prop it up in front of him.

It was little more than a stopgap as Reiff angled the small table and searched for better cover, simultaneously waving Rachel back from her position.

More shots. Destroying pieces of chairs and sending splinters of wood and fabric into the air all around him. Hitting the table multiple times, causing Reiff to struggle to maintain his grip and keep it from spinning away from him. They were coming from one of the room's far corners, forty feet away, maybe less. And a handgun, probably a .45.

He returned fire, still searching for an escape when a bullet punched a large hole through the wooden table just inches from his left hand.

Reiff fired off another two rounds and scrambled to his feet, rushing for the nearest wall and reaching it a split second before chunks of marble exploded behind him.

He had eleven rounds left in his gun and another full magazine in his back pocket. Enough to keep his attacker pinned, but what he didn't have was the *time*. He was protected from the shooter behind a slowly disintegrating wall, but from the opposite direction, he and Rachel were wide open. Easy targets to anyone emerging from the stairway or elevator.

He squeezed off a couple more rounds and briefly glimpsed past the wall's edge, spotting the shadowed silhouette in the room's red glare. The man was hiding behind a door in the far corner, and partially obscured behind a giant statue of some Aztec-looking headpiece directly between them.

Reiff shot again from behind the corner and then lowered himself to the floor. He stole another momentary glance and saw a narrow path past the base of the statue to the outer edge of the door, where the tip of the man's boot extended beyond by a few inches. And between them, nothing but open marble floor.

It reminded Reiff of why police never hide behind the hood of their patrol car in a gun fight, at least not in real life. The hood was a flat surface and any bullet striking the hood would skip off it like a rock skipping off a pond.

The hard marble floor was Reiff's hood.

He waited for his moment, a brief lull when he could fire back. Enough to briefly take aim . . . at the floor between him and his attacker's door.

The brief pause came and Reiff immediately peeked out past the corner, already at ground level, then aimed his gun and squeezed.

The scream came instantly. With an impact that caused the man to fall out from the door in pain, inadvertently exposing more of his body.

Reiff's next shot shattered the man's knee.

There was another yell followed immediately by a third shot from Reiff into the man's thigh.

The lights suddenly came on. Bathing the entire level in bright white light and illuminating the chandelier overhead like a giant sun.

Reiff shielded his eyes while they adjusted, before squinting and spotting the struggling man in the corner. With a glance at the double doors, Reiff jumped to his feet and quickly closed the distance between him and his shooter, his gun aimed and ready to fire again.

He reached the man to find him bleeding badly and struggling to get a makeshift tourniquet around his upper thigh. He stopped and looked up when Reiff appeared. The man was young, not one Reiff had seen before, but just as grizzled. Now scrambling to find his gun but it was too late.

"Don't," advised Reiff. He kept his weapon aimed and pulled the man up by his hair.

Reiff then began back toward the door. Pulling the man squirming and stumbling on his knees twenty feet over polished marble until reaching the scanner on the wall. With his free hand, Reiff made a fist and struck the man as hard as he could, almost knocking him out. He then grabbed the mercenary's right hand and lifted it up, twisting and about to slam it against the scanner, when the large mechanical doors suddenly began to open.

112

Reiff dropped the man and retreated. "Get back," he shouted to Rachel.

The doors had barely parted before another of Wicks's men rushed through. Running and caught by surprise at seeing Reiff immediately inside the door.

Reiff grabbed the man's weapon in midstride, twisting it up and over the man's head, dropping him onto his back with a heavy thud. Reiff stomped on his chest and wrestled the rifle free, raising it to his own shoulder and opening fire at the next man through the door, whose body shuddered and contorted from the impacts.

The second man lurched forward, reaching for Reiff, and fell onto him like a heavy bag, taking them both to the ground in a jumble of limbs.

Reiff struggled to get free and heard shots fired from outside. A third man, seeing what happened to his comrades, did not make the mistake of rushing through the ever-widening heavy doors. Instead, he remained outside and opened fire at the parts of Reiff that were exposed.

But the struggle on the floor was too frantic. The man couldn't get a clear shot. He continued moving back behind one of the doors as it widened waiting for another chance.

When Reiff was finally free and searching for his weapon, the man quickly aimed again.

"*Stop!*"

The man at the door froze and Reiff peered up to find Kincaid and the others standing behind him, perhaps twenty feet away with Wicks in front next to Kincaid, gripping Rachel by the throat with one hand and his gun in the other.

"Stop," repeated Kincaid, "just stop." The old man advanced and peered down at Reiff, who appeared to be bleeding lightly from a wound on his shoulder. "It's over. It was a valiant effort, but it's over."

Reiff watched Kincaid circle him as he slowly stood up. "I don't hear any fat lady singing."

Kincaid grinned. "I see you're walking again."

"What can I tell you, I'm an overachiever."

Kincaid smirked. "I'll say." He then looked past him at Wicks's other three men outside and motioned them in.

The third man began forward, making it only a few steps when he abruptly jerked sideways and slumped to the ground, followed by the sound of a distant gunshot.

It was Waterman.

Another shot zipped through the open door and struck Wicks directly in his chest.

With his eyes and mouth wide open, Wicks remained motionless before slowly sinking to the ground as the report from the second shot sounded.

113

Everyone around Kincaid remained like stone.

Kincaid was speechless, looking as though he was having trouble breathing. Glancing helplessly down at Wicks's lifeless body.

The only person to move . . . was Murray. Calmly reaching down to retrieve Wicks's gun, spurring a reaction from Reiff only to have Rachel jump in front of him. "Don't! He's innocent!" She turned around to face him. "He's the astronaut."

Reiff paused, studying the stranger, who, to everyone's surprise, raised Wicks's gun and pointed it not at Reiff, but at Kincaid. While the sound of approaching helicopters could be heard in the background.

114

Kincaid's face contorted again. "What are you doing?"

"You should have asked me," said Murray in a strange, eerie tone. "You should have asked."

"A-asked what?"

"You should have asked why."

Kincaid didn't answer, leaving Rachel blinking and staring at Murray. "Why what?"

The lieutenant's eyes moved to her, but the gun remained on Kincaid. "Why we were trying to get to Proxima so badly."

Rachel glanced at the others, confused.

"It wasn't as much about arriving," said Murray, "as it was about leaving."

"What do you mean?"

The man's eyes returned to his target. "You are Douglas Kincaid. Are you not?"

The old man nodded nervously.

Murray displayed a strange smile. "I recognized you," he said. "Your face is older, much older, but I recognized you the moment we met."

"Recognized him?" said Rachel.

"You should have asked," repeated Murray, "what the world I left was like. That *was* your intent, wasn't it?"

There was no response from Kincaid, and Murray's eyes slowly drifted to the others next to him. One after another. "That's what all of you wanted to know."

The other members now wore the same frightened expressions as Kincaid.

And then it all happened, suddenly, in a blur. Murray pulled the trigger, quickly and repeatedly, shooting Kincaid, then Cannon, then Sandhu, Lagner, and finally Anna Lu, dropping them all where they stood. Leaving the gun hanging in the air, still gripped tightly in his hand, while a faint wisp of smoke emerged from the gun's barrel.

Rachel jumped back in shock, covering her ears and falling to the floor. Scrambling toward John who rushed to cover her. But Murray remained still. Never turning the gun toward them. Instead, he peered down with an odd look of detachment . . . and curiosity, at the members of The Nine lying at his feet.

The sound of helicopters grew louder in the background.

Reiff helped Rachel to her feet and pushed her behind him. "I don't know who's coming," he said to Murray, "but I think they're coming for that ship of yours."

The astronaut accepted the answer and nodded. "I didn't want to believe it," he said, finally turning to Reiff. "That I had somehow woken up in the past. As impossible as it sounds. But the one thing that truly convinced me . . . was seeing Kincaid in the flesh."

"You said you recognized him."

Murray looked back down at the old man's bleeding body. "The future is not a happy place," he said. "It's a world of totalitarian control and widescale suffering. Ruled by a small group of people wielding unimaginable control over the masses. Nine tyrants, that many claimed had found the secret to immortality. To everlasting life and everlasting power. Not to mention limitless wealth.

"They promised this immortality to the leaders of countries who swore allegiance to them, slowly and methodically taking control of everything. Supported by scores of sheep and raging fanatics, until the concept of freedom was nothing more than a memory." Murray raised his head. "And the man who led it all, was Douglas Kincaid."

Reiff and Rachel looked shocked.

"Our ship's engine malfunctioned," he continued. "Somehow, some way. As did my suspension pod, leaving me stuck in the ice . . . all this time. Awoken by the man who would use our same technology to enslave the world. What are the odds of that?"

Reiff shrugged. "Pretty high."

"And how high do the odds need to be . . . before something begins to feel like fate?" asked Murray. "Like destiny." After a pause he looked back down. "I see now that it was my fate to kill Kincaid." He then stared at Reiff with an odd look, almost as if finally noticing him for the first time. "What is your name?"

"John Reiff."

"You are the lab rat?"

"Among other things."

A grin spread across Murray's face. "They did not like you very much."

There was a ding behind them and they all turned to see the elevator doors open and DeSilva step out, then abruptly stop upon seeing the carnage.

Murray raised the gun and aimed when Rachel shouted, "No!"

"He's another one," seethed Murray, aiming at a stunned DeSilva.

Rachel rushed forward and put a hand on Murray's arm. "He is. But we can use him."

"For what?"

Rachel turned and looked at Reiff. "If anyone knows where all their resources are, he would."

Murray contemplated for several long seconds before raising his voice and commanding DeSilva to come forward, which he did.

"Where are the others?"

DeSilva was shaking. "W-what others?"

"Where are the Hustons?"

"Downstairs," he said, "frozen."

Murray was surprised. "Already?"

"Yes."

"Where?"

"On level five."

The astronaut nodded with a look of satisfaction. "And Sorontine?"

DeSilva swallowed. "He hasn't arrived yet."

"Who's Sorontine?" Rachel asked.

"The last member of The Nine." Murray turned to Reiff. "Promise me something. Promise me you will find Sorontine and kill him."

"Well, if it helps the future of mankind."

The helicopters were close now, prompting them all to turn and peer out through the open doors. Where they saw a set of headlights also fast approaching.

Murray lowered the gun and began walking toward the elevator.

"Where are you going?"

He turned and looked back. "I'm not Murray. My name is Wallace. Lieutenant Murray was the mission's commander. *I'm* the engineer." He turned and continued walking.

Rachel turned to Reiff. "What's he going to do? Is he going to destroy the ship or something?"

"I have no idea."

The headlights became bright as the truck reached the main entrance and skidded to a stop. The passenger door flew open, and Waterman jumped out of the cab, running toward them still clutching his rifle.

Once through the entrance, he came to a stop and looked around, pausing on Wicks's body on the floor. "Not a bad shot, eh?"

"What took you so long?"

Waterman stared back in surprise. "Seriously? Do you know how long we had to wait out there?"

"Trust me," said Reiff, "it was no picnic in here either."

"Listen, I don't mean to rain on your little triumph here, but we have incoming choppers. And I just got word they're not ours. I suggest we hightail it out of here." He glanced at Reiff's bleeding shoulder. "You okay?"

"I've had worse." Reiff reached down for the rifle and with a wince, ushered Rachel forward before turning back to DeSilva, several feet away and still motionless. "Get your ass into that truck before I shoot it off."

115

The elevator doors opened, and Wallace stepped out noting all the systems and machinery before him. His eyes searched and immediately located the large cryonic silos along the left side of the room. Ten in all, with only two apparently in use.

He briskly approached and stopped in front of them. They were tall, white, and cylindrical, with a small glass window at the bottom revealing a section of what looked like thick Mylar body bags inside. And on the front of each silo, a computerized control panel, carefully maintaining the perfect conditions within.

Wallace raised his gun and briefly released its magazine before sliding it back up into the handle. He took a few steps back and raised the weapon, firing a single bullet into each of the Hustons' control panels. He then lowered and fired a round through both windows, punching giant holes in each pane.

Less than a minute later, the elevator returned him to level six, where Wallace stepped out and continued toward his ship and its still brightly lit interior. As he made his way inside, he took one last look at the outer room's rocky ceiling and walls; the natural cavern Kincaid claimed had existed for eons.

Inside, Wallace quickly returned to the ship's main computer console. This time, placing his hand on a different section of wall than when the others had been watching.

The message on the ship's computer screen immediately changed, and the computer's artificial intelligence voice echoed around him.

Authentication confirmed. Hello, Mr. Wallace.

"Hello," replied Wallace. "I need information, quickly."

What information do you need?

"How many times was our warp drive activated?"

There was a brief pause before the resulting text appeared, accompanied again by the AI's voice. To date, the ship's warp drive has been activated once.

As Wallace suspected. "For how long?"

Initial warp drive activation was six hours and fifteen minutes.

Wallace calculated in his head. Three hundred seventy-five minutes.

It was called fast roping and was used in areas difficult for helicopters to safely touch down. There was enough room outside the compound's main entrance for one Changhe Z-18 chopper, but not all four. And they elected to fast rope all their soldiers to the ground rather than landing in turn.

Simultaneously dropping two men at a time from each craft, the Chinese had all Special Operations Forces members on the ground in less than two minutes. Armed and immediately rushing the compound's open double doors.

Kincaid said that carbon testing of the site where Wallace's ship was found pegged the craft's arrival around the year 1200. Approximately 932 years before the commencement of Wallace's mission.

That calculated to roughly two and a half years backward for every minute the ship's warp drive was engaged. If the calculation was linear, then the ship would require no less than 341 minutes to return the ship back to the same time frame.

"Run a complete diagnostic on the warp drive and all related components," instructed Wallace.

Beginning analysis.

Wallace didn't need the ship's main propulsion system. He only needed the warp drive. If Kincaid was correct about the cavern, the physical location of the ship would not have to be moved at all. Only chronologically.

And if Wallace overshot his target year of 1200, he still had five working suspension capsules to fast forward himself, if necessary. He also had more than enough technology aboard the ship to find a way across the Atlantic. More than a fighting chance of finding his Helena.

Diagnostic tests complete. Warp drive operational.

Wallace knew there were countless dangers involved in what he was about to do. Any number of variables that could kill him. For example, if the cavern was not as old as Kincaid claimed, Wallace and his ship would instantly become *part* of the rock. Or if the warp drive destabilized the giant cave and caused a collapse. Or if the drive did not malfunction in the same way it had before, propelling him forward in time as it originally should have. The risks were endless, but there was no life for him here. Helena and the others were already long dead. Therefore, there was nothing to lose. The decision was simple. And the future could only be better with The Nine dead.

"Prepare to activate warp drive."

Warp drive preparing for activation, confirmed the computer. *Powering up magnetic field.*

The Chinese soldiers fanned out over the main floor like a wave, passing over the numerous dead bodies at the entrance and merging at the rear of the first floor, near the elevator and stairs. The team's commander held up a fist for his men to hold and opened the door to the stairwell. He could hear a loud whining noise below.

He continued forward with his squad. Dozens of boots clambering down the metal steps like a herd of buffalo until reaching level two.

The whining sound was still far below them and growing louder, prompting the commander to begin breaking up the team in smaller five-man groups to clear each level simultaneously.

They continued downward, level by level, where each new team, with rifles pressed tightly into their shoulders, burst through the next set of doors and continued inside. Leaving the rest to descend again. Level after level, quickly and methodically.

Magnetic field creation complete. Hydrogen core initializing.

Wallace set the timing for warp engagement. There was a good chance that his calculation was not linear, that he would either under or overshoot by a wide margin. But he didn't care. Their trip to Proxima Centauri was fraught with its own dangers. Dangers that each of the astronauts had readily accepted and were prepared to trade their lives for. This was no different. In fact, *this* attempt came with an odd and somewhat peaceful thought. If he died, either by becoming solid rock, or crushed by a cave-in, or any other number of ways, chances are he would never know it. Most would come instantaneously, faster than his mind could acknowledge. Which meant he would only know if he survived. In other words, he would likely never know if it failed. He would only know if it succeeded, even partially. And that meant he would only succeed.

It all had a strange and comforting logic to it, as Wallace moved back to the previous section of ship. He chose one of the chairs, wet and cold, and dug out its lap belt. And calmly fastened it around his lower waist. Not exactly what the belts had been designed for, but it didn't matter.

Warp activation commencing. In ten . . . nine . . . eight . . .

Wallace heard a scuffling outside, followed by sudden shouting. In a language that sounded like Chinese. He leaned forward and looked between sections, glimpsing out through the oval opening cut by Kincaid and his men, at a small swarm of darkly dressed commandos flooding into the cavern.

Outside the ship, the whining had become almost deafening before the sound disappeared all at once. Followed by a bright flash and a giant blue electrical sphere spreading out and encompassing the length of the ship.

It then occurred to Wallace that this would be his first opportunity to see the warp drive in action from within. The last time, he had already been frozen for several days.

He continued peering out through the hole at the dozens of men now yelling and running toward the ship.

And then they were gone.

116

The morning sky was covered in a light scattering of orange and pink clouds, against an azure background like a painting that never ended, with a brightly glowing sun in the process of breaching the desert horizon below it; truly an image to behold.

Leaning back against Rieff, Rachel was overwhelmed. "That's about as beautiful as it gets."

He nodded behind her. "It's what freedom looks like."

"Yes, it is." She turned to face him and glanced at his bandaged shoulder. To her relief, the patch of blood on his was no larger. After a moment, something occurred to her, and she looked at him. "Why did you do it?"

"What?"

"Why did you give yourself up to Kincaid?"

Reiff looked back up at the sky. "To either get you out . . ."

"Or?"

"Or make sure you didn't die alone."

She stared at him, stunned, while her heart abruptly melted. She had no words for that. None at all. And instead, simply leaned forward and kissed him deeply.

"Devin's right. You're quite the fighter."

Reiff almost chuckled. "I had a little help." When Rachel tilted her head, he explained. "My visions seemed to include pieces of things that were going to happen. Or at least I think so, but I have no idea how that's possible."

"I do," said Rachel. She grinned, almost as if to herself. "I saw things like that in some of the mice."

"What do you mean?"

She continued grinning and just shook her head. "It's a long story. In the meantime, we need to get you to a hospital, and that brain of yours figured out."

Reiff laughed. "Don't hold your breath."

Behind them, Waterman's voice sounded. "Oh, geez, is this how it's going to be?"

Rachel drew back and peered longingly at Reiff. "Yes," she said, "this is how it's going to be."

"My God, you guys are acting like you saved the world or something."

Rachel continued smiling.

Waterman turned back toward the truck, where Coleman and Yamada were putting the tools away. "Tire's fixed. Time to get moving."

Reiff looked at his friend. "Would it have killed you to put better tires on it?"

"Hey, it's not my truck!"

Rachel stood up from the large flat rock and pulled an exhausted John to his feet. "How are you feeling?"

"Better, actually. Much better."

She looked past him, back over the distant hills. "What do you think happened back there?"

"I don't know," replied Reiff. "To be honest, I don't really care."

"There you go!" said Waterman and slapped his friend on the shoulder. "Now let's get out of here. Nick's making some breakfast for us at his place."

Rieff nodded and, with an arm around Rachel, followed his friend toward the truck. "Wonder if he has any fruit."

ABOUT THE AUTHOR

MICHAEL C. GRUMLEY is the bestselling author of the Breakthrough, Revival, and Monument series. He lives in Northern California with his two young daughters, where he's an avid reader, runner, and most of all father, and dotes on his girls every chance he gets.

michaelgrumley.com
Facebook: Michael C. Grumley, Writer